"Do you know who took her?"

This time, Detective Montalvo made no effort to hide her surprise. "Who *took* her?"

"Do you have any leads? Any suspects? And don't tell me you can't share that information with me, because I'm not leaving here until you tell me what you know."

"Mr. Davis—"

"Please don't put me off, Detective. I need to know what you've found out so far."

All at once her expression shifted and something very close to pity filled her eyes. "Mr. Davis, I'm afraid you may be functioning under a misunderstanding. We have no proof that Angelina has been abducted."

Just like that, the brittle fear that had kept Jackson on tenterhooks all morning began to crumble. "But—"

"We don't know anything definite," she said, "but it's far more likely that Angelina left home on her own."

Dear Reader,

What an incredible experience it has been working on the WOMEN IN BLUE continuity series—stories about six women who met while at the Houston Police Academy, and whose lives remain entwined afterward. This book stands alone, but I hope you'll enjoy reading the other five, too.

The Children's Cop is first and foremost a love story between Lucy Montalvo and Jackson Davis, two people whose paths would probably never have crossed if not for Angel, Jackson's niece. But sometimes those meetings are the best!

Lucy is a detective with the juvenile division of Missing Persons at the Houston Police Department, Jackson a horse breeder from the other side of Texas. As I worked on this story I asked myself repeatedly if it's really possible to find love when the world is falling apart around you. I think I found the answer to that question, and I hope you enjoy getting there as much as I did.

It's been a wonderful experience working with Kay David, Linda Style, Anna Adams, Roz Denny Fox and K.N. Casper on the WOMEN IN BLUE series. Of course I've admired their work in the past, just as all of you do, but seeing them in action has only made my admiration for each of them grow.

I hope you'll enjoy *The Children's Cop*, and the other books in the WOMEN IN BLUE series.

All the best,

Sherry Lewis

I love hearing from readers! You can write to me P.O. Box 540010, North Salt Lake, UT 84054 or via my Web site, www.sherrylewisbooks.com.

The Children's Cop
Sherry Lewis

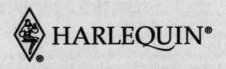

HARLEQUIN®

TORONTO • NEW YORK • LONDON
AMSTERDAM • PARIS • SYDNEY • HAMBURG
STOCKHOLM • ATHÉNS • TOKYO • MILAN • MADRID
PRAGUE • WARSAW • BUDAPEST • AUCKLAND

ISBN 0-373-71237-5

THE CHILDREN'S COP

Copyright © 2004 by Sherry Lewis.

All rights reserved. Except for use in any review, the reproduction or utilization of this work in whole or in part in any form by any electronic, mechanical or other means, now known or hereafter invented, including xerography, photocopying and recording, or in any information storage or retrieval system, is forbidden without the written permission of the publisher, Harlequin Enterprises Limited, 225 Duncan Mill Road, Don Mills, Ontario, Canada M3B 3K9.

All characters in this book have no existence outside the imagination of the author and have no relation whatsoever to anyone bearing the same name or names. They are not even distantly inspired by any individual known or unknown to the author, and all incidents are pure invention.

This edition published by arrangement with Harlequin Books S.A.

® and TM are trademarks of the publisher. Trademarks indicated with ® are registered in the United States Patent and Trademark Office, the Canadian Trade Marks Office and in other countries.

www.eHarlequin.com

Printed in U.S.A.

For Marcus McBride
A true-life hero

Books by Sherry Lewis

HARLEQUIN SUPERROMANCE

Don't miss any of our special offers. Write to us at the
following address for information on our newest releases.

Harlequin Reader Service
U.S.: 3010 Walden Ave., P.O. Box 1325, Buffalo, NY 14269
Canadian: P.O. Box 609, Fort Erie, Ont. L2A 5X3

CHAPTER ONE

LEAVES RUSTLED IN THE WIND and moonlight spilled across the lawn as Lucy Montalvo locked her car and started up the sidewalk toward her Houston condo. Every muscle in her body was on fire, and the dull headache that had been teasing her all afternoon had spread across her forehead and settled behind one eye.

A few porch lamps burned away the late-night shadows, and the soft blue flicker of a TV lit a couple of nearby windows, but most of the complex was dark. Usually, Lucy battled a slight loneliness when she came home after her neighbors were asleep, but tonight was different.

She walked slowly, trying to find solace in the near silence, the autumn breeze that stirred the heavy humid air and the faint glimmer of starlight overhead. The temperature had dropped a little from its midday high, but the humidity had been unbearable all day and ninety degrees of Texas heat still lingered close to the ground.

Lucy had no idea how late it was. She'd lost track of time holding Maria Avila's hand, offering comfort. She'd spent the past few hours trying to wipe away the memory of little Tomas Avila's body, discovered by a couple of construction workers earlier that afternoon. But it was a scene she knew she'd never forget. She was just grateful that she'd been able to keep his grieving mother from the sight.

Her conversation with Mrs. Avila had left Lucy feeling slow and lethargic. She was more than ready for a day off, but she wasn't going to let anything get in the way of bringing Tomas's killer to justice.

Much as Lucy loved her career, the constant search for missing children sometimes got to her. Six years after graduating from the police academy and hiring on with the Houston Police Department, she still hadn't learned how to lock her heart away. Even her training as a patrol officer and the years she'd spent in the Domestic Violence Unit hadn't hardened her.

A few months ago, Lucy could have released some of tonight's tension and despair over margaritas with the six-pack, a group of friends she'd made during her training in the academy. For the grueling six months the course lasted, Risa Taylor, Crista Santiago, Abby Carlton and Mei Ling had been as close to Lucy as sisters. Together with Catherine Tanner, their favorite instructor, they'd formed a bond they'd all believed would never break. Even after completing their training, they'd remained close friends, getting together at least once a month for lunch, more often when their schedules allowed.

The six-pack would have understood both the grim reality of finding Tomas Avila too late, and the pain of having to carry that news to his mother. Abby and Risa would have known the right things to say. Catherine, now chief of police, would have offered her unique brand of wisdom, and Mei and Crista would have done their best to chase away the gloom.

A few months earlier, Risa had been suspected of shooting her partner. Though Risa had been cleared eventually, the friendships had been a casualty. Now the other members of the six-pack were the last people Lucy could turn to in a crisis.

Battling a huge yawn, Lucy climbed the steps to her front door and slipped the key into the lock. She rotated her shoulders to release some of the tightness there. Melancholy and exhaustion almost got the best of her, but the allure of a hot shower kept her moving.

"Lucy?"

The unexpected sound of a woman's voice in the shadows behind her brought her around on the balls of her feet. "Yes?"

A figure moved out of the shadows, and Lucy recognized Gwen Small from the unit next door. Gwen had to be at least fifty, but she dressed like someone far younger. Tonight, wearing pink shorts, a white tank top and sequined flip-flops, she plodded across the lawn as quickly as her short legs could carry her, obviously eager for conversation.

Trying to hide her irritation at the interruption, Lucy moved to the railing so she wouldn't have to raise her voice. "Hi, Gwen. Is something wrong?"

"I'm afraid so. I've been watching for you." Gwen smoothed a hand across her flyaway blond hair and came to rest at the bottom of the steps. "Nathan thought I should warn you before you go inside."

The Smalls were good people, but both had far too much time on their hands and Nathan took his job as president of the homeowners' association way too seriously. Compared to what Lucy had just been through, grass clippings left on the sidewalk and visitor-parking violations didn't even rate mild concern.

Trying to ignore the ache in her head, she tugged the handle of her workout bag higher on her shoulder and smoothed the annoyance out of her voice. "Warn me about what?"

"Nathan and I found water on our kitchen floor this morning. He tried to figure out what was wrong by himself, but he couldn't, so we had to call a plumber. Apparently, there's something wrong with the pipes in your unit."

This is why Gwen had waited up on her? "Okay," she said, and hoped it would be enough to placate her eager neighbor. "I'll look into it."

"I don't think you understand." Gwen climbed the first step and leaned against the railing. "The damage is so severe, the plumber thinks your pipes have been leaking for quite a while. I'm afraid you won't be able to stay in your unit until it's fixed."

Lucy struggled to follow. "*What* damage?"

"Below the floors somewhere." Gwen motioned vaguely toward Lucy's darkened windows. "He says the supports have been weakened, so it's not safe to even walk around in there."

"But that's impossible! I was there just this morning and everything was fine."

"Well, that's the point. If it's structural damage, you wouldn't see it, would you?" Gwen fished a business card from her pocket and passed it over. "That's from the plumber. He comes highly recommended, of course. We try to get the best."

Lucy glanced at the card, but she couldn't see well enough in the dark to make out anything it said. This had to be some kind of joke. She'd bought the condo only a year ago. It simply couldn't be falling apart beneath her feet. But Gwen and Nathan weren't the kind of neighbors who played practical jokes, and even in the dim glow of her porch light, Lucy could see that Gwen's expression was unhappy.

And that made her spirits slip even lower. "How does the plumber know the water is coming from my place?"

"We had to let him in, of course. That's another reason

I've been watching for you. We had to turn off the water to stop the leaking, and there's a bit of a mess, I'm afraid." Gwen squeaked out a high-pitched laugh. "I guess more than a *bit*. He's torn up the kitchen floor in front of the sink, and the bathroom is completely unusable."

A protest rose to Lucy's lips, but she *had* given them a key for emergencies, and obviously this qualified as one.

"You're welcome to stay with us," Gwen continued. "We were a bit flooded this morning, but we don't have any structural damage to our place. We're lucky it's contained to your unit." She brushed something from the front of her blouse. "Nathan didn't feel right about giving the go-ahead to start working, but the plumber did say that he could have everything fixed and get you back home in two or three weeks."

"Two or three *weeks?*" Lucy's heart plummeted and the pounding in her head grew even stronger. "You're kidding, right?"

"I wish I were," Gwen said with an apologetic smile, "but apparently there's a lot of work to do. Nathan can explain it all better than I can, and I'm sure you'll want to talk to the plumber yourself in the morning."

"You're right about that." Still struggling against disbelief, Lucy wheeled back to the door and turned the key. The musty odors of mold and rotten wood rushed out to meet her, and her spirits took another nosedive. Even she couldn't deny that something was dreadfully wrong.

As she turned on the light in the kitchen, she could almost see her plans for an early-morning meeting with Homicide flying out the window. Even with Gwen's warning, she wasn't prepared for the deep hole gouged into the floor, or for the smell. This problem might not rate up there with the tragedy she'd just faced, but it was too big to ignore.

"If I were you," Gwen said from just inside the front door, "I'd grab a few things now. If this is as bad as they say, there's no telling when you'll be able to get back inside."

Numb, Lucy could only nod.

Gwen gave her an understanding smile. "I'll head home and get the guest room ready."

That brought Lucy out of her trance. She shook her head quickly. "Thanks, but I'll give my parents a call. They just live over in Pearland."

"Are you sure? It's awfully late."

Lucy managed a weak smile. "They're always after me to visit more, and I don't want to put you and Nathan to any trouble."

"Well, all right," Gwen said uncertainly. "But you know you're welcome."

Lucy tore her gaze away from the trail of muddy footprints on her new off-white carpet and tried to shake off her daze. "Thanks, Gwen. I appreciate it, but if I don't call Mom and Dad, they'll never let me hear the end of it." She rubbed her forehead and closed her eyes against the pain. "This is just such a shock. I'm still trying to take it all in."

"Well, of course you are." Gwen put a hand on Lucy's shoulder and gave a gentle squeeze. "I'll be glad to help you pull a few things together."

"No. Thanks." Lucy opened her eyes again. Gwen was a good neighbor, but Lucy had never been comfortable with having people nose through her belongings. Risa had once told her she had a thing about privacy because she was an only child. Whether or not that was true, Lucy did like to protect her space.

Putting a touch of warmth into her smile, she walked Gwen to the door and urged her outside. "I really appreciate you and Nathan taking care of this. I'll get in touch with the plumber in the morning, and I'll make sure you have my cell phone number and the number at my parents' house in case you need to reach me."

"You'll be careful? I don't want you getting hurt."

"I'll only stay a minute," Lucy promised.

Though she still looked unconvinced, Gwen gave in and toddled down the steps onto the lawn, and Lucy watched as she crossed the lawn and disappeared through her front door. Only then did she turn back to her own condo. So much for a hot shower and a good night's sleep. It had already been one of the longest days of her life. Obviously it wasn't over yet.

TWO HOURS LATER, LUCY parked in front of her parents' two-story brick house and shut off the ignition of her Eclipse with a sigh. The ibuprofen she'd swallowed with the last of her bottled water on the drive over was finally kicking in, and she was beginning to think she might be able to sleep, after all.

Though it was nearly two o'clock in the morning and her parents were notorious early risers, porch lights blazed a cheerful welcome and Lucy could see her mother's shadow moving in the upstairs window of Lucy's childhood bedroom.

Rolling her eyes in fond exasperation, Lucy climbed out of the car and reached into the back seat for her bag. She'd made her mother promise to leave the bed alone until she arrived, but she wasn't surprised to see that her mom had ignored her. She just wasn't sure whether Ellen was making the bed out of concern, or because she didn't trust Lucy to do it right. Lucy's mediocre homemaking skills had long been a joke in the family, so it was a good thing her parents were both quick to point out her other talents.

Stifling a yawn, she let herself in through the front door and locked it behind her. The house smelled as it always did, of flowers and home cooking. She gave an appreciative sniff, and the shoe-leather sandwich she'd wolfed down at the station rolled over in her stomach.

Leaving her bag near the door, she detoured into her parents' spacious kitchen and found her dad sitting at the table in front of a bowl of dessert, his attention riveted on a book. At fifty-eight, her father was a vital man with boundless energy, and he still had only a slight paunch above his belt in spite of his love of midnight snacks. In the past few years, strands of gray had started appearing in his hair, and tonight she noticed that the hair at his temples was more silver than brown.

He wore his glasses low on his nose, his hands shielding his eyes from the glare of the overhead light. He was so focused on the pages in front of him, he didn't even hear her come in.

It was at Doug Montalvo's knee that Lucy had learned her unbending work ethic. From her mother, she'd inherited a desire to make the world a better place. Both parents excelled in their own pursuits, and Lucy had grown up determined to make them proud of her.

With a grin, she hurried toward him and pressed a kiss to his receding hairline. "Hey, Dad." She picked up his abandoned spoon and lifted a piece of her mother's apple brown Betty for a better look. "What's the matter? No good?"

Doug's head shot up, but it took a moment for him to focus on her and process what she said. Lucy loved watching his recognition dawn and his expression change as he went from stern concentration to obvious delight at seeing her.

"Hey hey! What's this?" Scowling playfully, he motioned for her to put down the spoon. "Has the world sunk so low that a man can't turn his back for a second without somebody pilfering his food?"

"I'm not pilfering, and I'd be willing to bet your back's been turned for longer than a second. I think forgotten food should be fair game."

"It's not forgotten. I'm just taking my time, that's all. Savoring." He closed his book, moved it out of the way and patted the chair beside his. "You look tired. Sit down and tell me what you've been up to."

"Besides discovering that my house is falling apart under my feet?" She dropped into the chair and propped her legs on the closest empty one. Now that she was here, the exhaustion and memories came rushing back. "It's been a very long day."

"Anything you can talk about?"

There was no question that her father would never betray a confidence, but Lucy had strict personal rules, on top of the usual departmental ones, against discussing her cases—especially with people who weren't on the force. Besides, she didn't know how to explain the emotions she'd been struggling with all night. "Thanks," she said, sliding down in her chair and leaning her head back. "Wish I could, but…you know."

Wearing a smile of approval, her father gave her hand a squeeze. "Have you seen your mother?"

"Just her shadow in the window," Lucy admitted. "I wish she wouldn't go to so much trouble. I told her I'd make the bed."

Her dad laughed. "You know your mother. She's been hauling things into that room for more than an hour already, getting it set up just so."

"I brought everything I'll need."

"And when has that ever stopped her?"

"Never," Lucy said around another yawn. "Mom's going to do what she wants, and I'm too tired to argue with her. I was going to go straight up, but that dessert smelled too good to resist."

"You haven't eaten?"

"A piece of horse meat on white bread a few hours ago," she said with a half smile. "Don't tell Mom, though. I don't want her thinking she has to cook supper."

"I'm sure we could rustle up some leftovers. There are always some in the fridge."

A third yawn brought tears to her eyes, so Lucy shook her head. "I'd love some, but I'd probably just fall asleep in my plate. All I really want is a soft bed and a dry floor."

Her father stood and pulled her to her feet. "Well, you came to the right place. We just happen to have both. How long does the contractor think it will take to make the repairs on your condo?"

"According to Gwen, it will be two or three weeks." She slid an arm around her dad's waist and walked with him into the foyer. "Does that sound reasonable to you?"

"I'm not an expert on home repairs," Doug said with a thoughtful frown, "but it does seem like a long time. What about the cost? Any idea what he's going to charge you?"

"I won't know that until I can talk to him."

"And how are you fixed for money?"

"I'll be fine. I have a little set aside."

"Good for you. Financial stability, that's the key." Her dad guided her toward the stairs and gave her a gentle push onto the bottom step. "I know you're busy, and I probably have more spare time than you do. I could make a few calls on Monday if you want me to."

"Thanks, Dad, but I can take care of it. I just wondered what you thought."

"Well, then, I think you have a place to stay as long as you need one. Now, go say hello to your mother. I'll bring your bag up in a few minutes."

Lucy climbed the steps toward her old bedroom, but her legs felt as if someone had strapped weights to them. Tomorrow was only a few short hours away, but maybe, with luck, she'd be able to forget the look on Mrs. Avila's face long enough to catch some sleep. She wanted to be clearheaded when she met with the homicide detectives in the morning, and ready to work when they began the search for Tomas's killer again.

AN INCESSANT AND ANNOYING buzzing pulled Lucy from a troubling dream far too early the next morning. Moaning in protest, she threw one arm over her eyes and rolled onto her side just as the buzzing finally let up.

The muscles she'd overworked in the gym the day before had grown stiff in the air-conditioning that had poured into her childhood bedroom all night. But even in the cold air, her skin felt sticky from the muggy September heat.

When the buzzing began again, she groaned aloud, pushed upright and began a search for the source of the irritation. She fumbled with the alarm clock beside the bed, accidentally turning on the radio. Only then did her head clear enough to realize that the noise was coming from the cell phone she'd left on the nightstand.

Swearing under her breath, she grabbed the phone and punched a button to answer. "Whoever you are, you'd better have a damn good reason for calling."

"Good morning, sunshine."

Even half asleep she recognized Orry Keenan's voice, and some of her irritation faded. Orry was a good cop and a good friend—one of her favorites in Missing Persons.

He'd been with her through much of the horror the previous evening, and she knew he was trying to help by not letting her become maudlin. But he was skating on thin ice.

"Don't 'sunshine' me," she warned. "I'm not in the mood." She caught sight of her reflection in a full-length mirror on the back of the bedroom door and winced. As a teenager, she'd hated that mirror. Now, at a week past her thirtieth birthday, she liked it even less.

"What's the matter?" Orry asked. "Did I wake you?"

"It's seven-thirty on a Sunday morning. What do you think?"

"I think you've gotten lazy in your old age. You should be at the gym by now, or at least on the track."

"Not today." Turning away from her reflection, she rolled back onto the bed and dragged the pillow with her. "Why are you calling me so early, anyway?"

"I just wanted to hear your cheerful voice. I can't start a day without it."

"Funny, but you're calling the wrong person." She tried to find the comfortable position she'd been in before the phone rang, but somehow it had disappeared. "What's the real reason?"

Orry's voice sobered. "I just wanted to make sure you're okay. Mrs. Avila was pretty rough on you."

Lucy didn't want to think about last night, and she didn't want anyone—even Orry—to think she couldn't handle a little adversity. "It's no big deal," she insisted. "Mrs. Avila was understandably upset. Anyone would have been under the circumstances."

"That's a bit of an understatement, don't you think?"

"She was devastated," Lucy said, rolling onto her side. "I had to tell her that her son is dead. What do you expect her to do, thank me?" She threw one arm over her head and wished for a hole to crawl into, away from the memories, away from the world, away even from Orry's concerns. "Now, can I go back to sleep?"

"'Fraid not, sunshine. We have a problem and Nick thought you might like to know about it."

"What problem?"

"Nick wants you on a new case that was just phoned in."

Lucy's eyes flew open again and she sat bolt upright. "He can't do that. I'm meeting with Homicide about the Avila case in a couple of hours."

"Not anymore you're not."

"But he can't do this."

"He has no choice, Luce. Phil's out for his mother's funeral and Marcus is still on his honeymoon. You're the only one in the unit without an active case."

"The Avila case is still active," she argued. "Not to mention the scores of others sitting on my desk waiting for me to get back to them."

"Yeah, but those cases are old, and Avila is Homicide now. If those guys need something from you, they can call."

Fully awake now, she paced the length of her bedroom, dodging the pile of clothes she'd left on her floor. "This isn't right, Orry. Nobody knows this case like I do."

"So you'll give Homicide what you've got. Happens all the time, Luce. You know that."

"But I—" Afraid of sounding whiny, she broke off and swallowed what she'd been about to say.

Too late. Orry must have guessed what was coming. "You what, Lucy? You're emotionally involved in the Avila case? You're taking it personally?"

She stopped walking and sank onto the foot of her bed. "Of course not. But finding Tomas was my responsibility, and I failed him."

"You did everything you could," Orry said, his voice uncharacteristically gentle. "It's a sad fact of life that we don't win 'em all. And you know how Nick gets when he suspects one of us is too close to a case. You're lucky he let you stay on that one as long as he did."

"For all the good it did."

"The only way to be of help to the families and the kids is to remain objective. You know that."

"That might be true," Lucy said, "but it doesn't make me feel better."

"It's not supposed to. Your feelings aren't part of the equation. So pull it together and get your tail in here. What should I tell Nick? Fifteen minutes?"

"Give me a break," she said, sighing with resignation. "I'm not even home."

"Well congratulations! It's about damn time you hooked up with somebody. Anybody I know?"

"It's not like that."

"So you say. But even a night of hot romance won't save you this morning. So rise and shine, and kiss your boyfriend goodbye. Just don't tell him that you're going to share the details with your poor married friends later. He might not appreciate it."

That was supposed to drag a laugh out of her, but she still couldn't manage one. She drew up her knees and pressed her forehead against them. She'd become a police officer to help people. To make a difference in the world. She'd been drawn to work with children for reasons she couldn't completely understand. Maybe because she was an only child and that sense of isolation she'd felt around friends with siblings had never quite left her.

Whatever it was, the need to help kids was as much a part of her as the color of her eyes, the shade of her skin.

And no matter how much she ached for Tomas Avila, no matter how desperately she wanted to catch the person who'd ended his life, she couldn't flaunt the rules and regulations of the system she'd sworn to uphold. If Nick wanted her on the new case, she'd take it. But she wouldn't forget about Tomas. Not even Nick could make her do that.

"All right," she said. "Tell me what you've got."

"We just got the call. Possible missing kid. Female. Fourteen years old."

"*Possibly* missing? Nick's pulling me off Avila and he's not even sure we have a case?"

"The old man who lives next door to her called in the report. Patrol officers have talked to him already. He says the mother took off a few days ago and the girl disappeared some time last night."

Lucy let out a tired laugh and tried again to get her mind to focus. "The sun's barely up. How does he know she's not home in bed?"

"He claims she usually comes over to his place on Sunday mornings. She didn't show up when she was supposed to."

"Maybe she's gone somewhere with her mother, or maybe she's staying with a friend."

"Neighbor claims she wouldn't leave without telling him. Apparently she's alone a lot, but he insists she's steady and reliable in spite of her home life."

Lucy stood, stretched, and reached for the jeans she'd left in a pool on the floor. "So where am I going? Do you have a name and address?"

"Missing girl is Angelina Beckett," Orry said. "Close as we can figure, she disappeared sometime after eleven last night. The mother is Patrice, same last name."

"What about the father?"

"Parents are either divorced or never married. Father never comes around, anyway. Neighbor says the father's family is from up near Nacogdoches, but he's never met any of them."

Lucy had no use for absentee parents, and no patience with them, either. She pulled a clean white T-shirt from her bag, tugged socks onto her feet and looked around for her shoes. "I suppose nobody's tried to contact him."

"It's your case, Luce. Guess you'll get to do that. The neighbor you want to see is Henry Livingston." Orry rattled off an address in Channelview, a suburb of Houston near the shipping channel. Lucy made notes on a scrap of paper and tucked it into her pocket.

While they talked, she ran a brush through her hair and pulled it back with a clip. Lowering her voice to just above a whisper, she headed into the bathroom to splash her face with cold water. "Any reason to think the neighbor isn't telling the truth?"

"Not from this end. You'll have to see what you think when you get there. Officers Yamaguchi and Hanson responded to the call." He rattled off a phone number for them and asked, "What's your ETA? I'm sure Nick will want to know."

Ignoring the dark circles under her eyes, she tiptoed back to her bedroom, stole one last glance at her childhood bed with its beckoning sheets and snagged her favorite jacket from the back of a chair. "Estimated time of arrival one hour if traffic is light and road construction isn't an issue."

She'd have to leave a note for her mother, but she knew her parents would understand. She was lucky. Some of her colleagues had to do battle every time they walked out the door—with parents, with spouses, with significant others.

Some people just couldn't understand what drove police officers out of their comfortable beds at a moment's notice. Lucy barely understood it herself. The job was hard and often thankless, but the need to make a difference in her community was as much a part of her as the air she breathed.

There were times when she longed to settle down and have a family of her own, but she'd seen so many marriages ruined by the job, she wasn't willing to take the chance. Some spouses could take the hours, the uncertainty, and the danger. Some couldn't.

Lucy had never even gotten that far with a relationship, and the way things looked, she never would. It would take a stronger, smarter, more secure man than any she'd met so far to welcome a woman with a badge into his life. And someone close to a saint to keep her there.

CHAPTER TWO

JACKSON DAVIS WAS KNEE-DEEP in muck when his cell phone let out a bleat and startled the horses in the paddock in front of him. Swearing softly, he checked his watch and rolled an exasperated glance heavenward. "I haven't even been working for an hour yet," he muttered, "and already Wiley's found a reason to call. This has to be some kind of record."

His friend, Rush Fisher, planted his shovel in the mire and ran a sleeve across his forehead. Two years older than Jackson's thirty-two, Rush had been his closest friend since they were boys. Now that they were adults, he was still one of the two people on the earth Jackson trusted. In short, Rush was the brother Jackson should have had.

"Cut him some slack," Rush urged. "He's going crazy sitting at home while you're out here having fun."

Jackson shook a glob of manure from his boot and made a face. "Only Wiley would think of *this* as fun." He pulled the phone from his pocket just as the ringing died away and, with a grateful smile, shoved it back. "I give him three minutes."

"I say five." Rush grabbed the water bottle he'd left on a nearby fence post, drank and passed the bottle to Jackson. "It's early yet. He's just getting started."

Before Jackson could even get the bottle to his mouth,

the ringing began again. If Wiley's impatience hadn't been so damned irritating, it might even have been funny. Refusing to answer quickly, he drank, recapped the bottle and passed it back before pulling out the phone for the second time.

He loved the old man. Wiley had been the only rock in the stormy sea of Jackson's childhood. But there were times when the pressures of keeping the ranch running and caring for an aging grandparent got to him. Despite his best efforts and Rush's help, too many things were slipping between his fingers. Wiley was still mentally sharp. He caught—and pointed out—every mistake Jackson made, and somehow believed the fault-finding was constructive.

Struggling to remain patient, Jackson punched a button and cradled the tiny phone between chin and shoulder. "Can this wait, Wiley? I'm up to my neck in horse slop."

"I know where you are, boy, but we got ourselves a problem. You need to drop everything and come on back to the house."

Jackson peeled off one dirt-crusted glove so he could get a better grip on the phone. A trickle of perspiration snaked down his cheek and he wiped it away with the back of his sleeve. "I've been trying to get to this mess for three days. Every time I head over here, you come up with something that needs doing first. But I'm here now, and I'm not leaving until the job is done."

"This can't wait."

Nothing ever could, that was part of the problem. Jackson held back an irritated sigh and leaned one elbow on the fence railing. "Wiley, we've been over this a hundred times—"

"Listen to me, dagnabit. I just got off the phone with a fella from down Houston way. A neighbor of Patrice's.

Somehow he found us and called to let us know that Angel's missing."

Hearing his niece's name spoken almost casually after all these years hit Jackson as if someone had whacked him in the chest with a fence post. It took a few seconds to convince himself he'd heard right, and another for Wiley's words to really sink in. One expensive leather glove slipped into the muck at his feet, but he didn't even bother to pick it up. A hundred questions raced through his mind, but he focused on the most important. "What do you mean, missing?"

"I mean missing. This old boy who called says he's been living next door to our girl for a couple of years. Seems he keeps an eye on her because that mother of hers is never home."

Jackson's heart turned over, but he couldn't say he was surprised. His brother's ex-girlfriend would never win awards for her parenting skills. "How does he know Angel's gone?"

"I've got the particulars written down, but I don't want to discuss it on the phone. Get back here and I'll tell you everything."

Jackson's mind raced, trying to absorb the news. "Wait! What does Patrice have to say about all this? And why in the hell didn't *she* call?"

"Well, son, it's like I said. Patrice has been gone for a few days—on a bender somewhere, no doubt. She doesn't even know that Angel's gone yet." Wiley's voice quavered, but he cleared his throat firmly and went on. "Now, are you coming back to the house, or are you going to waste precious time standing around in horseshit?"

"I'll be there in two minutes." In a daze, Jackson shut the phone and looked up at Rush. "I need to get back to the house. Angelina's gone."

Rush looked almost as stunned as Jackson felt. He'd been through that long-ago nightmare with them, and he knew more than anyone how deeply losing Angelina had affected Jackson.

From the moment of her birth, Jackson had felt a special bond with the baby girl. He'd played with her every chance he got, and he'd carted her around with him whenever Patrice would let him. He'd found peace in her eyes and the unconditional love he'd always longed for in her presence. She had been, quite simply, a miracle. And when Holden took off and Patrice shut him out of Angel's life, he'd been devastated.

Questions played across Rush's face, but he was a good enough friend to not expect an answer. "Get yourself out of here," he said with a nod at the truck. "That little girl's gonna need you."

Grateful for his friend's understanding, Jackson headed across the field. Just hearing about Angel again had knocked the wind out of him. Knowing that she was missing made it almost impossible to breathe.

When he reached the truck, he kicked mud from his boots, climbed behind the wheel and set off as fast as he dared. It had been fifteen years since all hell had broken loose in the family, fourteen since Angelina's birth and thirteen since she and her mother disappeared, but he remembered every painful second as if the events had happened just yesterday.

Wiley had poured money, heart and soul into trying to find Patrice and Angel for the first couple of years, but money was no match for the determination of a distraught young mother. In thirteen years, they hadn't seen or heard from Angel once. Every effort they'd made to find her had met with failure. Every letter and package they'd sent had been returned. Wiley had long ago stopped talking about her, but Jackson had never given up hoping that he'd see her again one day. Gritting his teeth so hard they hurt, he bounced across the rutted field, kicking up dust and wishing he could pull more speed out of the truck.

After far too long, Jackson pulled into the circular drive in front of the ranch house and pounded up the steps. He found Wiley in his favorite chair near the fireplace, one of his ever-present mugs of coffee at his side. Wiley lifted his gaze and Jackson's heart dropped. Other than the day his grandmother died, Jackson couldn't remember ever seeing his grandfather cry. The proof of it now froze him to the floor.

"We have to find her, son."

"We will." It was a rash promise, but he couldn't help himself. Even at eighteen, he would have thrown himself in front of a speeding truck for his niece. He wouldn't do any less now.

"I don't care what it costs."

Jackson forced himself to move, but his legs felt as if they belonged to someone else, and a dull, rhythmic thumping sounded in his ears. The ranch had been teetering on the verge of bankruptcy for the past few years. Pouring money into another fruitless search might ruin them both. But left on his own, he'd have sold the ranch, if necessary, to find Angelina.

"Maybe she's just gone to the store," he said, sinking into a chair and trying to gain some perspective. "There are probably a hundred explanations for why she's not where she's supposed to be."

"That's what I thought, too. But this neighbor-friend insists she wouldn't leave without telling him. Says she always lets him know where she's going to be and when she'll be home."

"That's still not a reason to panic. Let's get the facts first." Just as they always did when Holden screwed up, when he called from the police station or begged for money.

Shoving Holden out of his head, Jackson tried to focus on today's problem. "Who is this neighbor?"

"Fella by the name of Henry Livingston." Wiley lifted a piece of paper containing the notes he'd made. "I have his address and phone number right here."

"That's good. When did this Henry hear from her last?"

"Last night about eleven. He got up this morning and waited for her to help him with breakfast before services. I guess that's their Sunday ritual." Wiley's voice caught, and Jackson knew he must be envying Henry the relationship he'd been denied. Hell, Jackson felt the same way. Angel should have been eating breakfast at Crescent Valley, not with some stranger in Houston.

"She never showed up," Wiley said when he could speak again. "That's when he decided to check on her, and that's when he found out that she was gone."

An image of Angel as she had been the last time he saw her flashed through Jackson's mind. Only a year old, tiny and perfect, unspeakably beautiful, and so helpless. As he remembered the dark hair and eyes she'd inherited from her mother, the dimple near the corner of her mouth, his stomach twisted painfully and fear pulsed through his veins.

"You've gotta go find her," Wiley said, his voice tight. "Do whatever it takes to bring her home again."

"We don't have a whole lot of money, Grandpa. We're still struggling to pay off what we owe from Holden's last visit."

"Blast the money. None of this means a damned thing unless that girl of ours is safe."

Relieved, Jackson nodded and stood. "Then I'm going to Houston, and I won't come back until I find her."

Wiley turned his head and wiped his eyes with the back of his hand. Even when they'd been sitting in the hospital getting the word about Wiley's failing health, Jackson hadn't seen his grandfather as an old man. Now Wiley looked worn and weathered, beaten down by life. Could he get through another storm?

"What if it's too late?" Wiley asked, his voice just above a whisper.

The idea made him so sick, Jackson couldn't stand still. Just as they had the first time Holden took off without warning, possibilities raced through his mind—none of them good. Had Angel run away? Or had something even worse happened?

"It's *not* too late," he said firmly. "I'll find her. And when I do, I'll bring her back here where she belongs. We're not going to lose her again."

Jackson just hoped that he could live up to the promise.

FIFTY-EIGHT MINUTES AFTER she left home, Lucy pulled off the interstate in Channelview. She'd had time to think as she drove. Plenty of time to formulate a plan to keep her on the Avila case. She wasn't sure how she'd accomplish it, but somehow she had to convince Nick to change his mind. It shouldn't be hard, especially if she could pull together enough evidence to convince him that Angelina Beckett wasn't in danger.

Turning away from the shipping district, she wound through industrial areas and working-class neighborhoods toward the address Orry had given her. She found it in an older neighborhood, probably built around the end of World War II. House after house looked exactly alike, one painted white, another blue, one with green shutters on the windows, another with shutters sagging from broken hinges.

Though a few of the houses and yards were well tended, the majority showed signs of apathy and neglect. Peeling paint, sagging screens, yards choked with weeds and driveways filled with cars, many of which probably wouldn't even start.

After several minutes, she pulled to the curb behind a van that had seen better days and tried to focus. Even if she didn't plan to stay on this case to the end, she needed to make sure she didn't miss anything. She wanted to turn in the best report possible so the next guy didn't have to retrace her steps.

She found Henry Livingston waiting for her on his front porch. When he stepped out into the sunlight, she sized him up. He was about six feet, somewhere around sixty, with bronzed skin and a shaft of gray hair, tied back with a leather thong, hanging down the middle of his back. He wore faded jeans and sandals, a chambray shirt over a paint-stained T-shirt. He looked like an old hippie. Maybe that explained why a fourteen-year-old girl considered him a friend.

Grabbing her badge from the seat beside her, she climbed out of the car to meet him. "Mr. Livingston?"

"Make it Hank. Are you the police?"

"Detective Lucy Montalvo, Missing Persons." She showed him her badge before clipping it to her waistband. "You reported a missing girl?"

"Angel." He nodded toward the house next door, a worried look on his face. "I try to keep an eye on her since her mother's gone so much."

In sharp contrast to Hank's trim house and neatly tended yard, the property next door had definitely seen better days. Curtains with missing hooks sagged in the windows, dark strips of paint showed through a chipped and peeling coat of yellow and the flowers someone had stuck into the flower beds drooped from lack of water. It looked like Angelina wasn't the only thing being neglected.

"Do you know where her mother is?"

Hank shook his head. "Patrice? I never know where she is. She's a free spirit, I guess, but she's gone too much if you ask me."

That was a story Lucy heard far too often, and it always grated like fingernails on a chalkboard, but she managed to keep her expression neutral. "Is there any chance Angel's with her?"

"I doubt it. Patrice doesn't like taking Angel when she goes out. It cramps her style." He squinted into the bright morning sunlight and wrinkles formed in the weathered skin around his eyes. "It's not that I think Patrice should stay home all the time. Nothing wrong with going out. But not all the time when you've got a kid…"

"Sounds like Angel's lucky you're around. Have you ever reported the situation to Family Services?"

He rolled his eyes at her. "I'm not a fan of big government. Bureaucrats don't always make things better."

"The system works when people give it a chance," she said almost automatically. "Do you know if anyone else has reported the situation?"

"No one else pays much attention. You know how it is."

Unfortunately she did, but it wasn't her job to speculate. At least not while she was supposed to be gathering facts. "Do you have a phone number for Patrice? A cell phone? Or do you know where she works?"

Hank shook his head. "She was working at a truck stop until a few months ago, but she lost that job and I don't know if she's even bothered to look for another. If she has, Angel hasn't mentioned it."

"Are they friendly with anyone else in the neighborhood?"

"Patrice keeps to herself mostly. She's not real friendly with anyone. Angel is more outgoing, but there aren't many young people around here."

Beads of sweat formed on Lucy's nose and forehead, and she longed for a patch of shade or a blast of air-conditioning. "Are you sure she's not inside sleeping? Maybe she's just not answering the door."

Hank dangled a silver key on his finger. "She gave me this when her mother first started spending so much time away. It made her feel better knowing she could get inside if she locked herself out."

"You used the key this morning?"

"Wouldn't you?"

Lucy sent him a noncommittal smile. "What did you find when you went inside?"

"An empty house. You want to see?"

She shook her head quickly. She wasn't about to ignore regulations and walk into a house without backup. "Not just now. Maybe later. I'll check the outside and see if there's any sign of forced entry and we'll go from there. What about Angel's friends? Is there any chance she's with one of them?"

Hank slipped the key back into his pocket. "She'd have told me. We have a deal. If she goes out, she tells me. Gives me a place to start looking if she doesn't come back."

"There's always a first time for everything," Lucy said. "Teenage girls sometimes do strange things, especially if they feel pressured by their friends."

"Not Angelina."

He seemed so certain, she decided to drop that line of questioning for the moment. "Do you know any of her friends? It might help if I could talk with some of them."

"I know first names, but that's all. Never really thought I'd need more than that."

So much for that direction. "What about her family?"

"I tracked down a grandfather and an uncle on a ranch outside Nacogdoches. Just got off the phone with the uncle a few minutes ago. He's on his way here." Hank's mouth curved into an apologetic smile. "I don't know Patrice's family. They've never come around that I know of. I don't mind admitting that I'm worried. Angel and her mom had an argument before Patrice left this time. That's not unusual, I'm afraid. They can really go at it when they want to, but this argument was worse than most."

Now they were getting somewhere. "Do you know what they argued about?"

"Angel didn't tell me much," he said with a shake of his head. "I heard voices, but I couldn't tell what they were saying, and Angel would only tell me that she hates her mother. When she didn't show up for breakfast, I knew something was wrong."

"She comes over for breakfast every morning?"

"Only on weekends." Hank smiled almost sheepishly. "She's young enough to think I'm an old man, and I let her think I need help. It gets her up and doing instead of sleeping the day away."

Lucy bit back a smile of her own. "I'm sure she enjoys coming over or she wouldn't do it. Do you happen to know what school she goes to?"

"Alice Johnson Junior High. It's just a few blocks over off Ashland."

"And do you happen to have a picture of her? It would help."

Hank perked up at that. "I have one right inside. You want me to get it?"

"Please."

He disappeared into the house and returned a few seconds later carrying a small photograph in a plain silver frame. "It's last year's school picture so she's grown up a little, but she still looks about the same."

This would be the hardest part, Lucy told herself. It always was. Even meeting the distraught parents wasn't as difficult as looking into the trusting eyes of a child who'd disappeared. She squared her shoulders and lowered her gaze to the photograph in her hand. A beautiful young girl with shoulder-length brown hair and clear dark eyes smiled shyly up at her. She didn't look like the kind of child who would run away, but what child did?

Unwanted concern tugged at Lucy's heart, and she looked away before little Tomas Avila's face could replace Angel's. "Do you mind if I keep this until I can get copies?"

Hank waved off the question. "Bring her home, and you can keep the picture."

"I'll do my best," she assured him. They both knew her best might not be good enough, but neither of them acknowledged it aloud. Lucy could barely acknowledge it to herself. Every case was different, she reminded herself. Each one brought a new opportunity to produce a happy ending. A runaway of fourteen was a far cry from an abducted eight-year-old, but Lucy desperately needed a happy ending. She just prayed that she could find one this time.

WITH HIS HEART IN HIS throat, Jackson took the steps to the police station two at a time. He'd been running at full speed from the moment he'd made the decision to drive to Houston, but it felt as if he'd been moving in slow motion for most of the day.

It had taken too long to convince Wiley to let Rush and

his wife stay at the ranch in his absence. Even longer to locate his mother on her honeymoon, give her the news and make arrangements to stay in her condo while he was in town. He'd spent the better part of an hour going over the ranch's schedule and making sure Rush knew what to keep an eye on, but his mind had wandered the whole time and he still wasn't sure he'd covered everything.

After finally hitting the road, he'd been on his cell phone almost constantly. In the blink of an eye, the phone had gone from being a damned nuisance to his most prized possession. He'd talked to Henry Livingston no less than four times and tried repeatedly to find anyone in the police department who could fill him in on their investigation. He'd managed to pin down Detective Montalvo at last, and she'd agreed to meet with him at noon. He just hoped she'd have something positive to report.

Pushing through the station's glass doors, he paused for a heartbeat in the air-conditioned lobby to get his bearings, and the shock of cold dry air sent a shiver up his spine. All around him, conversations between uniformed officers and people in civilian clothes hummed, punctuated occasionally by the muted ringing of a nearby telephone. A laugh echoed through the corridor and Jackson battled a flash of irritation that anyone could laugh while his niece was missing.

When he noticed a bank of elevators, he set off toward it and caught a car just before the doors closed. But the elevator climbed so slowly and stopped so often, he nearly jumped out of his skin before he reached the eighteenth floor. When the doors finally opened, he strode down a crowded corridor, searching for the room number he'd been given.

He went halfway around the building before he found a

busy office filled with desks and ringing telephones. Four or five plainclothes police officers moved about the room, talking over one another, scribbling notes and answering calls.

It wasn't Jackson's first time in a police station—not by a long shot. Thanks to his old man and his little brother, he was more familiar with police stations and jails than any decent person ought to be. But today a sense of unreality filled him, and he wondered for a split second if he'd only dreamed the phone calls that had brought him here.

"Hey!" A voice reached him over the din and jerked him back to reality. "Can I help you with something?"

He found the harried-looking cop who'd shouted at him and nodded. "I'm looking for Detective Montalvo. Is she around?"

Without answering, the cop punched a few numbers into the phone on his desk. "Luce? Somebody here to see you." Replacing the receiver, he nodded toward an empty desk. "Wait there. She'll be with you in a second."

Jackson didn't have a choice, but the energy in the room, combined with his own agitation, made it impossible to sit still. He paced from one end of the desk to the other until a door at the opposite end of the long office opened and a brunette roughly his own age strode toward him. Her dark eyes took his measure, and he could almost see her filing away her first impression in a mental database.

She was younger than he'd expected, and surprisingly pretty for a cop. Jackson didn't care about anything but her ability on the job, but it would have taken a smarter man than he was to read her unsmiling face. Though he towered over her by at least six inches, she gave the impression of looking him squarely with eyes that were carefully neutral. "Jackson Davis?"

"That's right."

"Detective Lucy Montalvo." She shook his hand briefly and fished a notebook from her pocket. "Thanks for coming. I'd like to ask you a few questions, if you don't mind."

He frowned in confusion. "I thought I was going to ask the questions."

"I'll be happy to tell you anything I can." Her tone was as flat as her expression. "Would you come with me?"

Doing his best to rope in his impatience, Jackson followed her to a small room furnished with one small table and a few hard plastic chairs. It wasn't his first visit to an interrogation room, either, and he wondered what Detective Montalvo would file away about him in her mental bank by the time they were through. He was used to cops drawing conclusions about him thanks to Holden, too, but that didn't mean he liked it.

She sat in one of the chairs and pointed to another, waiting to speak until he'd made himself reasonably comfortable. "How long have you been in Houston, Mr. Davis?"

He glanced at his watch instinctively, but he didn't need to. He'd been watching the minutes click past in his truck for well over three hours. "I crossed the city limits exactly fifty-three minutes ago. What are you doing to find my niece?"

"Everything we can. You live where?"

"On the Crescent Valley Ranch outside Nacogdoches, but I assume you already know that."

She acknowledged that with a dip of her head. "Have you heard from Angelina lately?"

Lately? Try "ever." He shook his head. "No, I haven't."

"What about your sister-in-law?"

"Patrice was never my sister-in-law, and I haven't heard from her, either. I have no idea where my niece is, Detective. I was hoping you would be able to tell me."

She made a note in her book and lifted those disconcerting dark eyes to his. "Not yet, I'm afraid. When was the last time you talked to Angelina?"

"You want an exact date?"

"If you have one."

"August 23, thirteen years ago."

For the first time, a flash of emotion showed in her eyes, but it disappeared again almost immediately. "Thirteen years?"

"On her first birthday."

She rolled the pen between her fingers and leaned back in her chair. "Why so long?"

"Because I didn't know where to find her. Patrice disappeared with her shortly after that."

"But you're here today."

"And more surprised than you are, I assure you." He drummed the fingers of one hand on the table. "I'm here because my grandfather, Wiley, got a call from a man named Henry Livingston this morning, telling us that Angelina was missing. I don't know how he knew about us. I can only assume that Patrice or Angel told him where to find us."

"I see."

"Then you're a step ahead of me." He shifted in his seat, eager to get things moving. "I don't understand a damned thing, but I'm here and I'll do whatever needs doing to bring Angelina home again."

"Of course."

Her tone cut through the last, slim hold he had on his irritation. "Look, I know it sounds weird, Detective. I'm sure you think I'm making a lot of noise that doesn't mean much. After all, I've let thirteen years go by without seeing her, right?"

The detective's eyes registered shock for only an instant before they shuttered again. "I never said that."

"You didn't have to." Trying to regain control, Jackson stood and paced to the edge of the tiny room. When he trusted himself to speak again, he turned back to face her. "Angelina is my only niece. If I'd had my choice, I'd have seen her every day for the past thirteen years, but I didn't have the chance. I love her, Detective. It doesn't matter how much time has passed since I saw her."

"Of course," she said again, but this time she seemed slightly less sure of herself, or at least a little less suspicious of him.

He returned to the table and looked into her eyes. "Now it's my turn. Have you turned up any leads yet? Do you know who took her?"

This time, she made no effort to hide her surprise. "Who took her?"

"Do you have any leads? Any suspects? And don't tell me you can't share that information with me because I'm not leaving here until you tell me what you know."

"Mr. Davis—"

"Please don't put me off, Detective. I need to know what you've found so far."

All at once her expression shifted and something very close to pity filled her eyes. "Mr. Davis, I'm afraid you may be functioning under a misunderstanding. We have no proof that Angelina has been abducted."

Just like that, the brittle fear that had kept him on tenterhooks all morning began to crumble. "But—"

"We don't know anything definite," she said, "but it's far more likely that Angelina left home on her own."

"But I thought—"

"I'm sorry. If I'd realized, I would have set your mind at ease sooner."

Suddenly unable to speak, he nodded and looked away.

He tried to focus on the clock, the table, the marbled pattern on the floor—anything but the almost-painful rush of relief that had him off balance. He'd reluctantly considered this possibility, but hearing the detective confirm it suddenly made it almost real.

He wasn't naive enough to believe that a runaway wasn't in any danger. Holden had started out exactly this way, and Jackson could have papered a room with proof of the trouble he'd been in. It would be even worse for a young woman on her own. Chasing Holden all over creation in the early years had opened Jackson's eyes to the seamy side of society, and robbed him of what little faith he'd had left in people. Fourteen was too young for any child to be on her own, especially a girl in a world filled with predators.

But for just a minute, he let himself relax. Like it or not, he was back in familiar territory. But how could he tell Wiley that they were starting the cycle all over again? That alone might be enough to kill him.

CHAPTER THREE

KICKING HERSELF FOR NOT realizing sooner what Jackson was thinking, Lucy waited while he digested the news. She hated causing pain—especially when it was unnecessary. She'd been thinking about the upcoming press conference on the Avila case and wondering how she'd make it through without cracking. Too wrapped up in her own concerns, Lucy hadn't been paying enough attention to the job at hand.

She couldn't let that happen again.

Jackson took a few minutes to pull himself together, and Lucy tried to keep herself in the moment by watching him. He was a good-looking guy. Tall. Solidly built. He had that windswept look a person could only get from spending time outdoors. Dark blond hair curled lazily to his collar. Muscles strained in his arms and legs with even the slightest movement. He was in terrific shape, no doubt about that. And it was natural. He probably didn't even know what a cross-trainer was.

After a long moment, he looked up at her from a pair of deep-set eyes—green or hazel, she couldn't be sure which.

"All right. So now what?"

Feeling a little guilty at having been caught studying him so intently, she smiled. "Now we start again. Would you like something to drink? We have a vending machine on the other side of the building—"

"I'm fine," he said, brushing aside her offer. "Let's just get to work."

"All right. I take it you're not particularly fond of Angelina's mother." It was an understatement. There was no way to miss the harsh glare in his eyes whenever he spoke of her, and it came again now, right on cue.

"Patrice and I have never been exactly friendly. I had a few opinions about her relationship with my brother and I didn't exactly keep them to myself. She didn't care for what I had to say."

"Do you have any idea where to find her?"

"Absolutely none."

"Do you mind telling me what your opinions of her relationship with your brother were?"

His brows knit into a frown. "Is that really necessary? It was a long time ago."

"I realize that, but at this point in our search, I have no idea what may be important and what may not."

Jackson shifted in his chair. "Holden was a kid when he got involved with Patrice. Angelina was born when they were just sixteen. They were both young, but I thought Patrice was trying to trap him. You hear about girls doing that, and her family wasn't as well off as ours. I was convinced she was trying to get her hands on Wiley's money. It turned out I was wrong."

"She wasn't interested in money?"

"Oh, she was interested enough when she and Holden were together. Just not as interested as I thought." One corner of his mouth lifted slightly. "Grandpa was fully prepared to help her financially after Holden disappeared, but Patrice sent everything back, even the checks, and she disappeared herself only a few weeks later."

"And that surprised you?"

His lips curved again, but the smile didn't reach his eyes. "Which? Patrice sending the money back, or taking off for parts unknown?"

"Both."

Crossing an ankle on his knee, Jackson shrugged. "Patrice surprised me more than a little. I never believed that she loved my brother. They were too different. Holden was a people person. Patrice was more of a loner. It did surprise me when she took off, but maybe it shouldn't have. She was famous for taking off whenever she and Holden had a fight. Wiley sent me out to chase her down more than once."

He paused as if he expected Lucy to say something, but she waited him out. She had the feeling she'd learn more by letting him talk than she would by feeding him questions, and since the press conference wasn't for another hour, she had time to spare.

"I always thought she was manipulating all of us when she ran off," he admitted after a few seconds. "Trying to make Holden react in a certain way. Trying to get him to feel something for her. I guess it worked. She got to Wiley, all right, but she just never did understand how emotionally bankrupt Holden was. When she left town, I thought it was just more of the same. Wiley and I tried to track her. Even hired a private detective, but we couldn't find her— or Angelina, who really mattered to us."

"Why did you go to all that trouble? She was with her mother."

"Why?" He blurted a disbelieving laugh. "Because Patrice had Angel and she hadn't even finished high school. She had no skills and no way to support the baby. Wiley thought they'd both be better off with family at the ranch."

"And what about Patrice's family?"

"She was living with an aunt who didn't seem too worried about anything, including the fact that her teenage niece was sexually active and then pregnant."

"But your grandfather was concerned?"

"To put it mildly." His gaze faltered, but his voice remained strong. "Disappointing people is what my brother does best. Along with breaking promises and spending money that doesn't belong to him. Angel was born with two strikes against her, Detective. Wiley could have made a difference."

Lucy looked away from the heartache on his face, and she wondered how he'd feel if he knew how badly she'd botched her last case. Would he trust her to find his niece, or would he ask for someone more competent to take her place?

She couldn't think about that. "Can you tell me when you saw your brother last?"

Jackson's gaze flew to hers. "You think Holden made contact with her?"

"We can't afford to overlook any possibility," she said. "Can you remember the last time you saw him?"

"I haven't seen or heard from him in five years."

"Do *you* think he might have come after Angelina?"

"Holden?" He blurted another disbelieving laugh that echoed through the small room, but he sobered again almost instantly. "It's possible, I suppose. I wouldn't put anything past him. But I have a tough time imagining him suddenly becoming paternal after all this time. He never was interested in being a father, especially after he found out the job came with responsibilities. He hasn't exactly been a model citizen, so I can't imagine he's changed."

"Is it possible that Patrice and Angel have gone to stay with the aunt you mentioned?"

"Mattie passed away a few years ago."

"Does Patrice have any other family?"

He nodded. "Wiley and I traced her parents to Cleveland, and she has an older sister living in California. I've managed to keep track of them, even if I've never been able to find Patrice."

"Then we should check with them. Do you have names and addresses?"

"I do, and I'll be happy to give them to you."

Lucy allowed herself a satisfied smile. "And your parents? Where can I find them?"

Jackson's posture became rigid, his expression somber. "My father is dead," he said without inflection. "My mother has a condo here in Houston, but she's in Greece at the moment with her new husband."

"She lives here in Houston?" Couldn't he have mentioned that earlier? "Does she ever see Angelina?"

"Never. Even if we'd known where to find them, Patrice would never have allowed it."

"You're sure about that?"

"As sure as I can be. I talked to my mother this morning. She would have told me if she'd had contact with Angel."

"You're probably right, but I'll want information on your mother's whereabouts in case I need to contact her." The request drew his brows together again, and she found herself wanting to wipe that look from his face. "We're trying to cover all of our bases, but it's still possible that Angel is just with friends. Girls that age have been known to take advantage of too much freedom."

"Considering my brother's history, that's not exactly a comforting thought."

"It's a lot better than the alternative," Lucy reminded him. "I'm going to need a way to contact your mother, just in case. And a way to reach you, as well."

Jackson nodded slowly. "I have my mother's itinerary in the truck. I can call you with it after I get settled if that's okay." He jotted something on the back of a business card and shoved it across the table. "That's the address where I'll be staying, along with the phone number there and my cell phone."

Lucy slipped the information into her pocket. "How long do you plan to stay in Houston?"

"As long as it takes."

"That could be awhile, you know. If Angel is with friends, we'll have a relatively easy job of finding her, but if she's run away it might not be so easy. Fourteen-year-olds are pretty resourceful."

"I'm not leaving until I know she's safe."

Lucy believed he meant it. She sent him a thin smile. "Well, then, we'll just have to work as quickly as we can. I'm sure you'll want to get home to the ranch and your grandfather."

He dipped his head in agreement, then leaned back in his seat and dragged his gaze across her so slowly she felt a little uncomfortable. "Tell me something, Detective. Are you even considering the possibility that Angel *didn't* walk out the door on her own?"

She felt herself flinch, but prayed he wouldn't notice. "Of course."

"And?"

"I don't think that's likely, but if that's the case, we'll do whatever is necessary to bring her home again." What a weak assurance. Hadn't she told Maria Avila the same thing?

"So you're not writing her off as a runaway?"

Oddly disconcerted by his unwavering gaze, Lucy shut her notebook and stood. "I can assure you, Mr. Davis, I haven't 'written her off' at all."

She was a little surprised by his intensity since he'd been out of Angelina's life for so many years. He probably wouldn't even recognize his own niece if he passed her on the street.

That realization brought her up short. He *wouldn't* know Angel if he ran into her, and that must weigh on him horribly. Sliding a hand into her pocket, Lucy removed a copy of the photo Hank had given her and handed it to him. "It just occurred to me that you might want this."

If she'd had any doubts about his commitment to Angelina, they disappeared as he took the picture from her. Holding it almost reverently, he blinked several times as he tried to focus on Angel's face. Lucy suspected he couldn't see a thing. Finally, he gave in and wiped tears away with the back of his hand, then lifted his gaze and managed a choked, "Thank you."

It wasn't easy to maintain her professional demeanor in the face of such strong emotion. Lucy's throat tightened and her vision blurred, but her reaction only frustrated her. She waited in silence, giving him a moment to pull himself together, taking the time for herself, as well.

"I don't know if Hank mentioned it," she said when the lump in her throat faded again, "but apparently Angelina had an argument with her mother before she disappeared. That's one of the reasons we think she ran away. There's also a small chance she didn't, but we have no reason to suspect foul play. I know how frustrating this is for you, but please try to understand that there are procedures to follow, and without evidence of a crime, there's not a lot I can do."

He nodded and traced the outline of Angelina's face with one finger.

Lucy bit the inside of her cheek, hoping physical pain would help ground her emotionally. When the pager on her belt beeped, she seized the excuse to turn away. It was a sad commentary on her emotional state that she considered a return phone call from her plumber as a gift from heaven, but the call simply couldn't have come at a better time.

Working up a smile that she hoped carried a touch of regret, she put an end to the interview. "Thank you, Mr. Davis. I need to make a call, but I have your address and phone number. I'll be in touch."

Jackson shot to his feet. "That's it?"

"Yes…for now."

He made it to the door at the same time she did, and once again she was aware of his height and his raw strength. "What is it?"

She paused with her hand on the doorknob. "Excuse me?"

"The message. Is it something about Angel?"

"No. I'm sorry. It's…" The telltale heat of a blush crept into her cheeks and she shoved the pager into her pocket. She thought of a dozen different explanations she could have offered, but every one of them would have been a lie, and she had the uncomfortable feeling that she'd have a hard time lying to this man—even for a good cause.

"It's my plumber," she finally admitted. "Now, if you'll excuse me—"

He must have been as surprised as she was because he didn't try to stop her when she opened the door. But as she walked away, punching numbers on her cell phone to keep him from following her, Lucy had the sinking feeling that keeping her emotions in check around Jackson Davis wasn't going to be easy.

HOPING TO AVOID REPORTERS, Lucy kept her head down and moved quickly toward her parking spot as the press conference came to an end. The Avila case was officially a homicide now. Out of Lucy's hands. After promising not to rest until Tomas's abductor was brought to justice, now she was expected to just walk away.

How could she explain that to Maria Avila? She wasn't certain she understood it herself and she sure wasn't ready to just quietly accept it. Though she hadn't found a moment to approach Nick with her request, she hadn't given up on the idea of working with the homicide team. For the public, however, she had to play the role she'd been assigned.

Swatting a mosquito that landed on her arm, she slipped around the edge of the crowd. Usually they dealt with the press at police headquarters, but today, in an attempt to accommodate the grieving family, they'd come back to the church that had served as command center during the search. She could hear Nick and his superior, Captain Dunning, dodging questions from persistent reporters as they moved away from the microphones, but nobody, thank God, seemed to notice her.

A noise on her right drew her attention to Maria Avila, who sobbed into her hands and leaned heavily on the arms of her grim-faced brother. Mrs. Avila looked so small. So forlorn.

Lucy's heart twisted painfully, and the tears that had been so close to the surface all day stung her eyes. The urge to go to her came over Lucy, but she ignored it. There was nothing she could do to help. Nothing she could say.

Averting her gaze, she slipped into the shadows of a tree. Someday, Maria would realize that they'd done everything humanly possible to save her son. Someday. Maybe then Lucy could tell her how deeply losing Tomas had affected her, how much she wished they could have saved him. Maybe then Mrs. Avila would believe her.

When she finally reached her parking spot and saw a

muddy pickup truck parked just inches from her car, she growled in frustration. This definitely was not her day. She'd never be able to open the door far enough to get inside.

Pressing Unlock on her keyless entry, she headed for the passenger-side door. A gust of wind brought with it the keening sound of Maria Avila's grief, and Lucy felt a piercing urgency to distance herself from it before it worked even further into her psyche and made it harder to do her job.

"Hey! Lucy!"

The shout turned her around as Gavin Mossburg, a reporter from the *Chronicle,* strode toward her. With his short-cropped brown hair and pale eyes protected by a pair of wire-rimmed glasses, Gavin had a studious look that seemed perfectly suited to his profession. She'd met him the first year she'd worked Domestic Violence, and though he wasn't her type—she suspected the feeling was mutual—they had indulged in a mild flirtation for the past three years. Neither ever took it seriously, and neither had ever let down their professional guard.

"Rough case," Gavin said when he drew close enough.

"Every one that ends badly is rough," Lucy said, resting one arm on the roof of her car. The Eclipse had been sitting too long in the sun and the metal burned her skin. Pulling away sharply, she swore under her breath and gingerly touched the sore spot. "What's up, Gavin? Why aren't you over there trying to pry answers out of Nick?"

"I can talk to Nick anytime. I'd rather talk to you."

Lucy lowered her hand and frowned up at him. "Why?"

"You were there last night?"

"You know I was. My name is in the press release."

"You want to talk about it?"

Not even if her life depended on it. "There's nothing to talk about," she said stiffly. "Anything I know, you've already heard." The department had procedures for dealing with the press, and the Elizabeth Smart case had left every cop in the nation aware of the media's power. Lucy wasn't about to create tension for the department with reporters, but neither did she want to give away her continued interest in the case before she had a chance to talk to Nick.

"I'm sorry for the Avilas' loss," she said, carefully putting a lid on her own emotions. "We did everything humanly possible to find Tomas and bring him home safely."

"The Avilas don't seem to agree."

"They're understandably upset. Anyone would be in their shoes. But I'm sure that when the shock and horror wear off a little, and they have time to reflect on the investigation, they'll be able to see that there was nothing more we could have done."

Gavin nodded, let his gaze travel toward the family cluster, and then looked back at her with a tight smile. "So what about this new case you've got?"

"Which new case?"

"Angelina Beckett. I got a call from her uncle about an hour ago. He wants us to cover the story, but I'm hearing rumors that the girl is just a runaway."

"*Just* a runaway?" Ignoring the guilty twinge that his assessment so closely mirrored her own, Lucy pocketed her keys and leaned against the inside of the car door. "That's kind of a cynical attitude, isn't it?"

"Come on, Luce. You know what I mean. You got an abduction, I'll do a story, but we don't have room in the paper to cover every teenage kid who gets mad at their parents and takes a walk. So what's with the Beckett kid?"

"I don't know yet. I'm looking into it."

"She disappeared this morning?"

"As far as we know."

"No sign of forced entry?"

"None."

"I guess that means you won't be issuing an Amber Alert?"

He sounded almost disappointed, and on a professional level he probably was. No human with a conscience wanted to hear about a child being taken out of her own home, but there was no question that an abduction would make an exciting news story.

"If the evidence shows that she walked out the door on her own, then of course we won't. You know the drill, Gavin. To issue an alert, we need proof that she's been abducted and reason to believe her life is in imminent danger. We also need enough information about the abductor to help the public find them. I don't have any of those things right now." She ran another glance across the thinning crowd, noticed that the Avilas had moved away, and breathed a sigh of relief. "Have you talked to anybody about her disappearance?"

"Not yet, but I might check with a few neighbors if I get time. The uncle was pretty adamant."

Yes, she could imagine Jackson would be. "I've talked with a few of them, but nobody seems to know much about her except that she's alone a lot."

Gavin smiled halfheartedly. "Well, that's not unusual."

He had a point. The world had changed since Lucy was a kid. Too many middle- and lower-class working parents were left with little choice when it came to child care. Children of seven, eight and nine, and in some cases even younger, were being left at home alone or in charge of younger siblings. Five-year-old latchkey kids came home to empty houses after kindergarten. Though Lucy's personal sensors went off at the thought of leaving a fourteen-year-old alone so much, Angel had a good life compared to some of the kids she'd encountered.

The familiar knot began forming in her chest, but she pushed it away. She'd walked too close to the line with Tomas Avila; she couldn't let herself become emotionally wrapped up in the Beckett case. "If you hear anything," she said, "you'll let me know, right?"

Gavin grinned. "Sure. I probably won't spend much time on it unless I have a slow day, but sure. You scratch my back, I'll scratch yours."

That was a deal she intended to take advantage of once she was back at work finding Tomas Avila's killer. She managed a nonchalant grin, hoping it matched his. "You bet. I'll personally make sure you get an invitation to every press conference we hold."

The smile slipped from Gavin's face and an expression of mock annoyance replaced it. "Funny, Montalvo."

Managing a laugh, she pulled out her keys and slid into the car. "What can I say? You're my favorite reporter on the beat."

Suddenly serious, Gavin leaned into the open door. "Look, I know the Avila case was rough on you. It got to all of us."

The abrupt change of subject gouged painfully at Lucy's self-control. "No child deserves what happened to Tomas," she said, hating that her voice came out high and thick with emotion.

Gavin locked eyes with her before she could look away. "How are you handling it?"

"I'm fine." Maybe if she said it often enough, she would begin to believe it. "Are you asking everyone involved in the case that question, or just the 'girls'?"

His eyes narrowed slightly. "Lighten up, Lucy. I thought we were friends."

"Sure we are."

"Then don't be so sensitive, okay?"

Damn him! She didn't need kindness right now. Or understanding. She needed... Aw, hell, she didn't know what she needed. One thing she *didn't* need was to lose control over her already shaky emotions.

She cranked the key and shifted into Reverse, feeling a flicker of guilt over the hurt and confusion on Gavin's face. "I'm not sensitive," she growled. "I'm just busy."

"Right." Without taking his eyes from her, Gavin stepped away from the car, but even then he didn't back off. "If you need to talk, you know where to find me."

"Yeah. Thanks." She leaned across the seat and pulled the door shut. "I'll let you know."

But they both knew she wouldn't. There was only one thing that would make her feel better—finding the person responsible for Tomas Avila's death. And she wouldn't do that by talking.

AT A FEW MINUTES BEFORE seven o'clock that evening, Lucy carried sodas and sandwiches from the corner deli through the darkened bull pen into the glass-walled office that belonged to her commanding officer.

It had taken a while to shift gears after the press conference, but she'd finally been able to get her focus back on her current case. She'd spent the afternoon talking to Angelina Beckett's neighbors, trying to find someone who knew where the girl had gone. No one admitted noticing anything suspicious. No one admitted noticing anything that wasn't suspicious, either. In fact, nobody had paid much attention at all to the quiet young girl with the wide dark eyes.

Nick looked up as she entered his office, grinned at the

sight of food and motioned her toward a chair. All muscle and bulk, with a neck the size of a tree trunk, Nick was in his midforties, but he took pride in his ability to keep pace with men half his age. He accepted a sandwich and chips and leaned up in his chair to dig in.

Lucy sat across the desk from him and kicked off her shoes. "I want to talk to you about Angelina Beckett."

Nick nodded, cracked open his Coke, and drank. "Fine. What have you found?"

"Not a whole lot. The neighbor who reported her missing insists that she wouldn't go off on her own, but there's no sign of a forced entry at the house, nothing to make me believe she was taken against her will."

"Any word from her mother?"

"No sign of her. Of course, there's a possibility that Angelina could be with her...." Remembering her conversation with Jackson, she hesitated. "But I don't think she is. I guess she may have gone with friends, but nobody knows who her friends are or where to find them. My guess is that we're looking at a typical runaway."

Nick cocked one eyebrow. "Have you talked to anyone at her school?"

"It's Sunday."

"What about family? Any chance she's with them?"

"I was able to track down the grandparents on her mother's side. They haven't heard from her, but they'll call if they do. She has an aunt in California. No contact there, either. Paternal grandfather is dead. Grandmother is out of the country, and her father dropped out of her life years ago. But she does have an uncle and a great-grandfather who seem concerned."

Nick looked interested at that. "Have you talked to them?"

"The uncle is here in Houston. He came in to help search

for her. He and the grandfather run a horse-breeding out-
fit near Nacogdoches." Jackson's wind-blown blond image
filled her mind for half a second, but she shook it off. She
had to admit to a certain amount of curiosity about him,
but only because she felt sorry for him. Obviously, he
cared about Angelina and wanted to find her, but he was
definitely at a disadvantage.

Nick tore open his bag of chips and poured some onto
his sandwich wrapper. "Why do I get the feeling that you're
leading up to something?"

With a frown, Lucy unwrapped her own sandwich. It
was an opening. She might as well take it. "This is a simple case," she said. "Anyone can handle it. I'd like to get
back to work on the Avila case instead."

Nick munched slowly, taking forever on one mouthful
of chips. "We've turned everything over to Homicide," he
said after a long time. "There's nothing for you to do."

"Nobody knows that case like I do. I could work with
them. Liaise between the two departments…"

Nick stirred potato chip crumbs with one finger. "I don't
think so, Lucy."

"At least hear me out," she protested.

Nick shook his head and mashed some of the crumbs.
Lifting the finger, he stared at it for an annoyingly long
time. "I need you on the Beckett case. It's as simple as
that."

"Come on, Nick. Let's be honest. This case is a waste
of my time and my energy. It's a mistake to make too much
of it."

That eyebrow winged upward again and his neck
seemed to swell. "And I think we'd be wrong to make too
little of it. Talk to her school tomorrow. See if she's there.
If not, maybe they can tell us who she hangs out with."

"Someone else can do that."

Nick leaned back in his seat and regarded her intently. "Why don't you talk to me about Tomas Avila?"

Lucy felt the blood drain from her face. "There's nothing to talk about."

"He's the first one you've lost, isn't he?"

She felt that traitorous burn behind her eyes. Horrified, she tried to will the tears away. "It was a tough case."

"You need some downtime?"

"No!" She caught herself and tried again to shut down her emotions, but they remained close to the surface, just waiting to get the best of her. "I can handle my job, Nick."

"You wouldn't be the first person to shut down after a tough case."

"I haven't shut down. I just don't think the Beckett case is the best use of my time and talents."

Nick tapped his fingers together beneath his chin. "You want my honest opinion?"

"Probably not."

"Too bad. I'll give it to you, anyway." He shoved the sandwich out of his way and leaned both arms on the desktop. "I watched you with the Avila case, and I think you allowed yourself to become personally involved. I think losing Tomas was a direct hit, and I don't think you're in any condition to work it now that it's a homicide."

Feeling as if she'd been hit, Lucy sat back hard in her chair. "But that's ridiculous—"

"Is it? You want me to call Darren in here so you can hear what he thinks?"

Darren Brady had talked to her a couple of times about her growing emotional involvement during the search for Tomas, but she'd never suspected that he'd taken his concerns to Nick. Her breath came in short gasps and her thoughts buzzed in disconnected circles. "But I—"

"This is all new to you," Nick said, his voice unbearably kind. "Losing a kid is enough to push anybody over the edge, and the first one is especially tough. What I want you to do is make an appointment to meet with Cecily Fontaine some time in the next couple of weeks. Let's see what she thinks before we give you anything too taxing. In the meantime, you can keep one foot in the water by working the Beckett case."

"But I—" she began again, but this time she cut herself off. Equal measures of anger, shock and horror rolled through her, each so strong they robbed her of coherent speech. The idea of being sent to the department psychiatrist was so abhorrent to her, she could hardly think. "Nick," she managed to say at last, "this isn't right."

"You don't think so?"

"No. I'm fine. There's nothing wrong with me." She stood, horrified to find that her knees almost didn't hold her upright. "I know I've been distracted today, but that's because of the problems with my plumbing."

"Great. If that's the case, Cecily will give you the all clear after just a few sessions."

Lucy had lost count of the number of times tears had threatened that day, and here they came again. Furious with herself, she strained against them, locking down every emotion she could identify.

She imagined telling her parents that she'd been sent to a psychiatrist and felt the twist of her stomach that always came when she thought about disappointing them. She imagined the reactions of her co-workers, the teasing she'd endure, the trust she'd have to rebuild, and she wondered if she'd ever be able to fix this.

"I'm fine," she insisted again, but she could hear the hated catch in her voice, and she knew Nick heard it, too. She fought to sound normal, whatever that was. "Maybe I have had a rough day, and maybe I need a couple of days to get over the shock. But I don't think that's any reason to see a therapist."

"It's standard procedure, Lucy. Don't sweat it."

Easy for him to say. He hadn't clawed his way up the ranks in a profession dominated by the opposite gender. He hadn't spent a lifetime worrying about living up to his parents' expectations. The spiny knot in her stomach took another twist.

She forced a laugh, but it came out sounding choked and unnatural. "It's not that I'm sweating it," she said. "It's just such a waste of time."

"I don't think so." Nick stood to face her, his expression suddenly somber. "If it's too much, Lucy, I'll put you on administrative leave while you're working through this. Would that be better?"

"No!" She caught the desperation in her response and tempered it with a thin laugh. "No. That's not necessary, Nick. I'll go visit Angelina Beckett's school tomorrow."

"You're sure?"

He had no idea just how sure she was. "Absolutely."

"And you'll make an appointment with Cecily?"

Agreeing to that was a little harder, but she nodded and kept her smile in place. "First chance I get."

"All right, then. We'll keep going this way for the time being." Nick crumpled his sandwich wrapper and tossed it into the garbage can in the corner. "I want you to keep the uncle close. Maria Avila is complaining that we shut her out of the investigation, and she's convinced that she could have made a difference if we'd let her in."

A steady drumming set up in the back of Lucy's head, and a strange sort of dread crept through her veins when she thought of spending time with Jackson Davis. "You want me to use this guy to smooth ruffled feathers?"

"Something like that. Just don't make it obvious that's what you're doing. Let him think you need his help."

Lucy bleated a stunned laugh. "Are you serious?"

"It's called public relations, Lucy."

"I know, but—"

"It's only for a couple of days," Nick assured her. "Find proof that Angelina Beckett ran away and we can take the spotlight off. Spend some time with Cecily and get yourself cleared for regular duty. Things will be back to normal before you know it."

Normal. With her fingertips numb and her brain not far behind, Lucy wondered if she'd even recognize normal again if she fell over it.

Nick glanced at her, his expression stern. "Anything else?"

It was all she could do to shake her head.

"All right, then. I'll see you in the morning."

She fought to keep her head up and the tears at bay as she walked through the darkened bull pen and into the deserted corridor. But once she knew Nick couldn't see her anymore, she sagged against the wall and buried her face in her hands.

For one brief moment, she wondered if Cecily Fontaine really could help her, but she shoved that possibility aside almost as quickly as it arose. Somehow, she had to convince Nick that she was emotionally stable and ready to work, and she needed to do it without professional help.

CHAPTER FOUR

MONDAY MORNING, JACKSON began making more phone calls. Someone out there had to care about Angel's disappearance. He just had to find the right person.

In spite of Detective Montalvo's certainty that Angel had run away, Jackson wasn't convinced. He'd spent all of the previous afternoon and most of the evening trying to get somebody interested in his story, but all he had to show for his efforts were a splitting headache and indigestion from the leftover pizza he'd wolfed down some time in the middle of the night.

Pouring his third cup of coffee, he closed his eyes and took several deep breaths as he tried to calm his agitation. Anger was his one legacy from his father, the one thing he had in common with his brother, the thing he hated most about himself.

He hadn't expected to find Angel the minute he set foot in Houston, but he *had* expected to hear that the police had a few clues. He'd foolishly—perhaps naively—expected the media to be interested in finding a missing teenager. It just went to show how little he knew about the way things worked.

When he finally felt the return of some control, he sipped again and set his cup aside. Guilt he was used to, but it had been years since he'd had to worry about his temper. The stress of Angelina's disappearance and the added strain of having to think about his family had brought it on.

He knew it. Didn't like it.

Jackson didn't think about his father often—almost never by choice—but Alexander Davis always seemed to show up with a vengeance when trouble came around.

After a few more minutes his pulse slowed and the tension in his jaw relaxed. He glanced at his watch and realized that Wiley would be up by now, waiting for an update. Anxious to keep his grandfather as calm as possible during this ordeal, he picked up the phone and punched in the number for the ranch. He'd called a couple of times already, once just after he arrived in Houston and again after he'd settled in at his mother's house, but if he waited much longer, Wiley would be on him like a duck on a June bug.

Wiley answered on the second ring. The worry in his voice made him sound every one of his eighty-three years "You sure took your time," he snapped when he heard Jackson's voice. "I've been up for hours already."

"Sorry. The battery on my cell phone died overnight, and I've been on the house phone all morning. I was hoping to have some good news when I called."

"And do you?"

"Not exactly." Jackson lay back on the couch and covered his eyes with one arm. "Things are going as well as can be expected, I guess. The police are doing what they can to bring her home."

"I've been watching the TV regular," Wiley said, his tone faintly accusing, "and I haven't heard a blasted thing yet. Doesn't sound to me like the police are doing much of anything."

"That's because they're not convinced she's in trouble. They think she ran away."

Wiley sucked in a sharp breath and Jackson pulled his arm away from his eyes. It killed him to think Angel might be following in her father's footsteps, and he knew Wiley felt the same way.

"So maybe she ran away," Wiley said at last. "I guess we know a thing or two about that. What are you doing to help?"

"Everything I can. I met with the detective in charge of the case yesterday and I was on the phone all evening with newspapers, television and radio stations. I've got a meeting with the detective again this morning and then I plan to spend the day talking to neighbors and going through the neighborhood house by house."

"On your own?"

"If I have to."

Wiley let out a noisy groan, a sure sign that he was either getting up or sitting down in his chair. "So how is Pat-Reese? Have you seen her yet?"

Jackson grinned at the way his grandfather pronounced the name, but his humor was short-lived. "I haven't seen her. As far as I know, she still hasn't come home."

"Still cattin' around, is she?"

"Sounds like it."

"We shoulda pushed harder, son. We shoulda hired another detective or gotten us a lawyer and taken her to court. We never shoulda never left Angel with her."

"We had no choice. We didn't know where to find her. And we can't undo the past, anyway." Jackson reached for his cup, decided he'd had enough caffeine and wished for an antacid instead. "I talked with Hank Livingston on the phone. He seems pretty sharp. I'm planning to stop by his place as soon as I've finished talking with the police."

"Good idea. Keep in touch with him. What's he have to say about Pat-Reese?"

"About what you'd expect."

"And how'd he find us? Did he tell you that?"

That was the one bright spot in an otherwise dark day. "Apparently, Angel told him about the ranch. How she knew about it is still a mystery. I can't imagine Patrice telling her, but somehow she knew. When she didn't show up yesterday, Hank remembered that conversation and called directory assistance."

"Well thank the good Lord for that. What do the police say about Pat-Reese?"

Jackson dragged his gaze from the ceiling to the window and watched the neighbors backing out of the driveway as they started their day. "You know how they are. They're being careful not to say much of anything."

"They know we're not talking about Mother of the Year?"

"They know." Remembering his conversation with Detective Montalvo stirred his own impatience. Though she'd seemed attentive enough, he couldn't shake the feeling that something had been on her mind. "I wish I could say more, but there's just not much to tell yet. How's everything at the ranch?"

"Fine. You ought to know it would be."

"I'm not worried," Jackson said quickly. "But I did leave in a hurry."

"I ran this place on my own for forty years," Wiley grumbled. "I think I can do it for a few days."

"I didn't mean that," Jackson said carefully. "It's just that I was pretty distracted when I left. I'm not sure I gave Rush all the information he needs."

"You got information in that head of yours that Rush and I can't find in the files?"

"No, but—"

"Then quit worrying. We'll be fine. By the way, I sent Rush and Annette back home."

That brought Jackson bolt upright in a hurry. "You did *what?*"

"Sent 'em home. I told you I didn't need anybody looking after me, and I meant it."

"But you can't—"

"Can't what? Can't spend a few nights in my own home without a keeper? Is that what you think?"

"Rush and Annette weren't there to act as your keepers," Jackson said evenly. "They were there in case you need something."

"If I need something, I'll call 'em. I'm a grown man, not a baby. I know how to use the telephone."

Losing the battle with frustration, Jackson stood and walked to the window. "I know, but what if you can't get to the phone?"

"Oh, for God's sake, boy! I'm fine. Rush and Annette don't live that far away."

"I realize that." And in most cases, the half-hour drive between their house and the ranch felt like nothing. But if the stress were to get to Wiley, half an hour might be too long. "Look, Grandpa—"

"No, *you* look. I know exactly what you're going to say. I can hear it in your voice. But you quit worrying about me and focus on finding that little girl of ours. If something happens to me, it happens. I've lived my life and I'm ready to go when the Good Lord wants me. But I won't go out with a baby-sitter in the spare bedroom, and that's all there is to it."

Another groan probably meant that Wiley was getting to his feet again. "Call me when you know something," he snarled. "And next time, don't coddle me and tell me everything's fine when we both know it ain't. Give me the truth, y'hear? I didn't raise you to lie."

With that, the conversation ended and the dial tone sounded in Jackson's ear. He tossed the handset onto the cushion and dropped onto the couch beside it. He'd never been able to pull the wool over Wiley's eyes. He'd been a fool to even try.

But what else was he supposed to do? Wiley was the only family he had. Maybe he wasn't afraid to depart this world, but Jackson wasn't ready to let him. And he sure wasn't going to hasten the process. No matter what Wiley said.

JUST AS THE SUN CRESTED the horizon, Lucy rounded the bend onto her parents' street and jogged toward their house at the end of the block. The sky was awash with sunlight nearly ready to break, and already the temperature had climbed to an uncomfortable high. Heavy humidity made it hard to breathe deeply, but three miles on the road had stretched her tight muscles into working order. She found great satisfaction in the slow burn that came with exercise, but she wished she could find some peace of mind to go along with it.

She'd slept fitfully all night. If she'd been at home, she'd have numbed her mind with some late-night television. But she hadn't wanted to wake her parents. They'd have wanted to know why she couldn't sleep, and she wasn't ready to answer that question yet.

Now, with two hours until the meeting she'd arranged with Jackson, she had just enough time for a quick shower before heading through rush-hour traffic to the station. Even if she ran into construction delays, she should be early for the morning briefing—a move she hoped would earn a mark in the plus column of Nick's running tally.

Dashing a trickle of perspiration from her temple, she checked the quiet neighborhood street for traffic, then crossed the pavement and began her cooldown routine in front of her parents' house. Her mother was probably making breakfast, she thought as she waited for her heartbeat to slow. Bacon. Eggs. Coffee. Her mouth began to water. Cinnamon rolls, too.

She'd lived on her own for the past five years and cooking, like housework, had never been a strong point. Most of her meals consisted of takeout and visits to the drive-through, so the aroma of homemade anything made her almost weak in the knees. She would learn to cook one of these days, she vowed as she mopped her face with her towel. When her schedule became less hectic. When she stopped putting in ten- and twelve-hour days.

When she retired.

Checking her watch again, she hurried across the lawn, but as she opened the door her step faltered. Her mother's breakfasts weren't the kind of meals she could eat on the fly and the last thing she wanted this morning was a lengthy conversation with her parents. They both had some kind of parental radar that zoned in whenever Lucy had something on her mind. She'd always harbored a secret wish for brothers and sisters, but never more than when she found herself under her parents' magnifying glass.

Feeling guilty, Lucy closed the front door soundlessly behind her and tiptoed up the first couple of steps.

"Lucy? Is that you?" Her mother appeared in the doorway and beamed a smile far too bright for Lucy's foul mood. "Come to breakfast, honey. It's almost ready."

Offering excuses would only draw attention to her so, with a silent sigh of resignation, Lucy tossed her towel over the banister and headed downstairs again. In the kitchen, she found her mother standing over the stove, slowly stirring something.

Just two years younger than her husband, Ellen Montalvo was every bit as vibrant as he was. She kept her hair carefully colored its natural ash-blond and cut in a classic chin-length style. While Lucy's beauty routine consisted of Ivory soap and mascara on special occasions, makeup was an absolute necessity to Ellen. In thirty years Lucy had seen her mother without her face on only a handful of times.

She looked up as Lucy strolled into the breakfast nook and motioned her toward the table where a small vase of late roses, matched perfectly to the intricate pattern on the dishes, sat on a pressed linen cloth. A far cry from the typical centerpiece of unsorted junk mail that usually sat on Lucy's table.

Mopping her face with her sleeve, Lucy tried to stop the inevitable list of comparisons between herself and her mother. Though Lucy only stood five-five, she'd always felt big and clumsy next to Ellen. The differences were more glaring than usual this morning—Ellen in her peach silk blouse, beige pants and sandals; Lucy in her frayed jogging suit with holes in the knees, a stain on the butt, and shoes that looked as if she'd been jogging through mud.

Readjusting the rubber band that held back her hair, Lucy gave her watch a cursory glance. "Everything smells great, Mom. What can I do to help?"

Ellen smiled over her shoulder. "Nothing, sweetheart. I have it under control. You can turn on the news if you'd like. *Daybreak* should be on."

Lucy aimed the remote at the portable TV and snagged a piece of toast from the unguarded plate beside it. "Is there coffee?"

"Of course. Help yourself." Ellen put her spoon on a

trivet and turned toward her next task. "What time do you need to be at work?"

"In about an hour, but I still need to shower."

"Then we'll eat fast." Ellen pulled jam and marmalade from the refrigerator and began spooning some of each into a crystal serving dish. "What time will you be home this evening?"

"Tonight?" Lucy shrugged out of her warm-up jacket, crossed to the coffeemaker and poured a cup. "I'll probably be late again. I have a full day scheduled, and I want to stop by my place to pick up a few more things after my shift is over."

Ellen recapped the marmalade jar and pulled spoons from a drawer. "Don't be silly. I have some errands to run this morning. I'll be happy to go over there while you're at work. Just leave me a list of what you want."

And have her mother see her disorganized sock-and-underwear drawers, or the mound of laundry on the floor of her bedroom? Not on her life. Lucy hid her dismay behind her mug. "I appreciate the offer, but it'll be easier if I just do it. I don't know what time I'll get here, though, so don't hold dinner for me."

Her mother's smile faded. "Oh, but you promised to be here for dinner tonight. We've invited the Spanglers."

Lucy scowled in confusion. "I promised? When did that happen?"

"Last night when you came in. I told you all about it. They're bringing their daughter. The one who went through such an ugly divorce? You know how long they've been wanting to introduce the two of you."

Lucy thought back over their conversation, but she couldn't remember her mother saying anything about dinner guests. "I'm sorry, Mom. I don't—"

"Oh, now, don't tease me, sweetheart. I know darn well you remember. Janelle is the daughter whose husband took off with another woman and got her pregnant, remember? Poor girl has been in a funk ever since."

Cradling her mug in both hands, Lucy leaned into the corner of the cabinets. Had she really been so lost in thought that she'd missed an entire conversation? "I'm sure you did tell me," she conceded, "but with this new case and the trouble at home, I really can't commit to anything."

Disappointment pinched her mother's expression. "Can't you get away for just one evening? We won't eat until eight."

"I don't think so. Life always gets unpredictable when I'm in the middle of a case."

Ellen added another piece of bacon to a plate on the counter. "You're always in the middle of a case. Surely they give you time for a life of your own."

Lucy turned away, hoping she looked casual and unconcerned. "That's how the job is, Mom."

"Yes, but working all the time—"

"Is fine with me." Lucy realized that she'd sounded abrupt and tried to water it down with a smile. "I love my job."

"Well of course you do." Ellen carried the bacon and a pitcher of orange juice to the table. "And you know Daddy and I are as proud of you as we can be. That's why Marlene and Scott want to bring Janelle to meet you. They want her to see that she doesn't have to spend the rest of her life working in dead-end jobs, making little more than minimum wage. And she's become so dependent on her therapist, Marlene is getting worried."

And they expected Lucy to serve as some kind of role model? Their timing couldn't have been worse. "I don't know why anyone would want to compare us," Lucy argued. "Our situations are entirely different. Who knows? If I went through a messy divorce, I might be in worse shape than Janelle is."

Ellen rolled her eyes and gave a little laugh as if to say *Don't be silly.* "Frankly, I think they made a big mistake in letting her get started in all that. I don't know what good they think it's going to do."

"It might help her a lot."

"Oh, really, honey. You hear all the time about how those people plant ideas in their patients' heads. It's best to just take care of things the good, old-fashioned way. At home. That's where problems belong."

Feeling a little sick, Lucy pushed aside her cup and stood. "I'm sorry. I know it's important to you, but I can't be here."

"But sweetheart—"

From somewhere deep inside came the urge to confide in her mother, but Lucy shoved it away. "Maybe another time," she said, doing her best not to look like someone who wanted desperately to escape. "I'd better get into the shower or I'll be late."

"But you haven't eaten—"

"I know. I'm sorry." She felt horrible, but what else could she do? Admit the truth? Tell her mother that she was apparently cracking under the pressure? That she wasn't sure she could even do her job? That was something she wouldn't admit unless she absolutely had to. The disappointment in her mother's eyes over one missed breakfast was hard enough to bear.

BY EIGHT-THIRTY, LUCY WAS pacing restlessly along the sidewalk in front of the café where she'd arranged to meet Jackson. She kept one eye on the passing cars, another on pedestrians, alert for young women who matched Angel's description. She didn't expect to find the girl that easily, but with the threat of suspension already hanging over her head, she couldn't afford to be careless.

A gull landed on the sidewalk a few feet ahead of her and snagged a dried piece of hamburger bun. With wings hunched, it hopped away just as three other gulls came in for a landing. Before they could steal the crumb, a red truck roared into the parking lot, scattering the gulls and setting off raucous cries of protest.

Lucy smiled, pleased that the bird had been able to keep its prize, but when she recognized Jackson behind the wheel her smile faded. With his eyes hidden by mirrored sunglasses and a deep scowl forming creases around his mouth, he looked wild and a little dangerous.

She laughed off that assessment and ignored the flicker of interest as he jumped from the truck. He strode toward her—long, lean, and supremely confident—as if the world had been made just for him. But, of course, her interest was purely professional.

He didn't even wait to reach her before he started talking. "Okay, I'm here. I'm assuming you're going to explain why."

"Absolutely. Let's go inside for a minute."

He raked a disapproving look across her face. "You can't tell me right here?"

"I just thought it would be more comfortable if we sat. Maybe had some coffee…"

"I'm not here to be comfortable, Detective. I'm here to find my niece. You asked to see me. I'm assuming you have news?"

"Not exactly."

"Then why waste time?"

Lucy refused to let him intimidate her. "I have no intention of wasting time, Mr. Davis, and I think you'll be glad you took a few minutes to talk to me." When he still didn't show any signs of budging, she added, "Humor me."

He ran a hand along the back of his neck. "Look, Detective, pleasant as breakfast with you might be under other circumstances, I really don't want to linger while my niece is missing."

Lucy ignored the backhanded compliment. Keeping her expression neutral, she started walking toward the restaurant and hoped he'd follow. "I don't plan to linger, but I do have a proposition for you." She reached the door and turned back to face him. "Ten minutes, that's all I ask. I'll even buy."

He hesitated for a moment, then shrugged and started toward her. He was a large man, and she knew he was probably used to getting his own way, but the gentleness she saw in his eyes each time he talked about Angelina convinced her that he had a softer side, as well.

Out of nowhere, she found herself wondering how he'd look if he smiled. Judging from the laugh lines around his eyes, that was probably something he did regularly when life was running smoothly, but it was something she'd probably never see.

She turned back to the door and caught a glimpse of her reflection in the glass. She'd left the house in a hurry, and now loose hair fell into her eyes and a splotch of something white adorned one lapel of her jacket. Her mother would have a fit if she could see Lucy looking like this. And though Lucy usually didn't waste time and energy on her appearance, she was uncomfortably conscious of it now.

Resisting the urge to brush at the stain and call attention to it, she reached for the door handle. She had the fleeting impression that Jackson reached for it a split second after her. It was over as quickly as it happened, but it had been a while since any man had thought of opening a door for her, and the gesture touched her.

Not good, she told herself firmly. He was involved in a case. No matter how good-looking he was, no matter how intense his eyes, no matter how intriguing the expressions on his face, she had to keep her interest in him strictly professional. Especially now.

Determined to stop taking inventory of his charms, she set off for a table before the door could close and ordered coffee from a passing waitress before Jackson could get into his seat. Just seeing him a little off-step as he dodged the harried waitress made her feel a little more in control, and that put a smile on her lips. "I know you don't want to waste time," she said as he slid into the seat across from her, "and I understand that you're worried, but we have no reason to believe that Angel is in danger. So let's not panic. Searching for a missing person can be slow, tedious work, but we still need a plan to make sure we don't miss anything."

Jackson tugged off his sunglasses and set them on the table. "We?"

She wasn't about to admit that Nick had ordered her to include him, so she lifted her chin and met his gaze squarely. "I'm assuming you want to be part of the search effort?"

"Sure I do, but why the change of heart?"

"It's not a change of heart, Mr. Davis. It's the only way I can come up with to approach this case and make the best use of the limited time and resources we have."

Jackson eyed her warily. "And that is…?"

"I think we should work on this together. I want to visit Angel's school this morning, see if she showed up for class, maybe talk to some of her friends. While I do that, you can try to track Patrice down. You've spoken with their neighbor Hank, right?" At his nod, she went on. "He says that Patrice was working at a truck stop a few months ago. I want you to find out if he remembers the name of the place, or anything else about it. Even narrowing down the section of the city it's in would help. If he still doesn't remember, maybe one of their other neighbors will. We need to make absolutely certain Angel isn't with her before we go much farther."

"You want *me* to look for Patrice?" He laughed without humor. "Weren't you listening when I explained about our…relationship yesterday?"

"Of course, but I'm counting that you're not the kind of person to let the past get in the way."

"Patrice has been hiding from Wiley and me for the past thirteen years," Jackson said, his voice taut. "She's not going to just wait around for me to catch up with her now."

"You have a point," Lucy conceded, "but I doubt the school will give you the same kind of information they'll give me. I know it's a gamble, but I think it's a risk we need to take."

Jackson still looked skeptical. He stirred cream into his coffee and slanted a glance her way. "On a scale of one to ten, how convinced are you that Angel left home on her own?"

Questions like that always made Lucy uneasy. It was so hard to tell how a person would react. Would her answer sound optimistic or pessimistic? Would it make him more determined or fill him with despair?

"From one to ten, I'm at about seven," she admitted.

"Is that supposed to make me feel better?"

"I'm just trying to be honest, but yes. I think it should give you some hope. It's much better than believing she was taken against her will, isn't it?"

He mopped his face with one hand and stared out the window for a long time while the muscles in his jaw and neck jumped. "You're right. I don't want to give you the wrong impression. It's just that I honestly don't know how I feel." He turned slowly to look at her, and the torment in his eyes tugged at her heartstrings. "One minute I'm angry at the world and everyone in it, the next I feel as if I've been gut-punched and I'm not even sure where I am."

"That's understandable." Lucy stirred sugar into her cup and pulled her notebook and pen from her pocket so she could keep track of their plans. "Have you talked with anyone else?"

"Only every television station, radio station and newspaper in the yellow pages. Nobody's interested in looking for a kid who might have simply run away."

She thought about mentioning her conversation with Gavin, but decided not to get his hopes up. "Did you have time for anything else?"

He shook his head slowly. "I called my grandfather and gave him the news. When it got too late to make calls, I stared at the ceiling. That's about it." He picked up his cup and stared at it as if he didn't know what it was for. "Weren't there *any* clues about Angel's plans in her room? A journal? A note? Anything?"

"I haven't gone through her room yet. Without Patrice to give us permission, I need more than just a 'maybe' to warrant going inside. But if we can find evidence that she didn't leave home on her own, that will make a difference."

His eyes narrowed. "You haven't gone through her room? You haven't even looked inside the house?"

"I've checked the exterior, but without some sign of a forced entry, I can't just let myself in and start searching.

There's still a strong possibility that Angel has gone some-where with her mother."

"She didn't."

"If you can prove that, we'll cross it off our list." A wait-ress passed carrying a tray filled with bacon, eggs, toast and hash browns, and Lucy's stomach reminded her that she'd ducked out of her mother's house before breakfast. Slid-ing another look at Jackson's drawn expression, she asked, "When was the last time you ate?"

"I don't know. I'm not really thinking about food."

"Well I haven't had breakfast, and I think it's pretty ob-vious that we both need something." She handed him a menu and opened another on the table in front of her. When he didn't even look at his, she forced another smile. "Come on. Pick something. You won't do Angel a bit of good if you make yourself sick, and if you're going to help me, I need you clearheaded and physically strong. Besides, I said I'd buy, and who knows when you'll get another offer like this?"

He didn't actually smile, but his lips did twitch slightly. "I have to admit, it would be a first for me. I don't remem-ber the last time a cop bought me breakfast."

A cop, not a woman. It was probably just the strange emotional state she was in that made her even notice, but the uncomfortable pricking of her self-esteem and the worry in his eyes made it hard to stay behind the walls she knew she had to keep in place.

It wasn't smart. She knew that. But without the six-pack and her parents to confide in, Lucy felt horribly alone and more frightened than she wanted to admit. More than anything, she needed a friend, and though Jackson didn't qualify, he was here, he was alone, and he was as fright-ened and confused as she was.

"Tell you what," she said. "Why don't we forget, just for ten minutes, that I'm a cop working on a case. I'll just be Lucy and you can be Jackson, and it will just be one person buying breakfast for another. Surely, *that* can't be a first."

He did almost smile at that. "I have had breakfast bought for me a time or two. Lucy."

"Okay, then…Jackson. What would you like?"

He turned his attention to the menu for a few seconds. "Steak and eggs. Over easy on the eggs, medium on the steak. Hash browns—crisp. More coffee."

His choice was so predictable for a Texas rancher, she couldn't hold back a smile, and when he lifted his gaze to hers again she thought that some of the shadows there had lightened. She knew it wasn't a permanent change. The haunted look would come back again as soon as they hit the streets, and so would hers. But she liked thinking that she could relieve some of the pressure, even for a moment. She just wasn't sure which of them needed it most.

CHAPTER FIVE

AFTER THEY PLACED THEIR orders and the waitress refilled their cups, Jackson leaned back in his seat and cradled his mug in both hands. His tension didn't vanish, but he did look a little less ready to snap. "Thank you," he said. "I probably needed this."

"I know the pressure can get to you," Lucy said, "but trust me when I say that we won't accomplish anything if we don't take a break from it now and then." She fished an ice cube from her water glass and slid it into her coffee. "While we're waiting, why don't you tell me a little about yourself and your family? The good stuff."

He laughed softly. "The good stuff, huh? Okay. That would be Wiley, I guess." He scratched lazily just below one ear, sorting things out in his mind.

She waited in silence, letting him make the shift at his own pace.

"Wiley's the salt of the earth," he said after a while. "The kind of guy who walks tall and shoots straight. You never have to wonder where you stand with him." A light she hadn't seen before burned in his eyes and love brought his face to life for the first time since they met. "It's hard to believe my brother and my dad come from the same stock."

"He must be very special to you."

Jackson nodded. "My father was a typical drunk. He

managed to ruin every holiday, birthday and special occasion we ever had—not to mention more than his share of regular days. Holden started running his life into the gutter when he was fourteen, and my mom has her own share of problems, so when I was young, being around Wiley… well, it was like being on another planet."

His story made her own complaints seem puny by comparison. "Sounds like you're lucky to have him."

"That's for sure." His eyes shadowed again. "I don't know what I'll do when he's not around. I try not to think about it, but he's already eighty-three and he isn't going to be here forever. The doctors have told him he has to slow down and that's making him a little crotchety, but underneath it all, he's still just who he is."

Again that vulnerable expression softened his face and Lucy felt herself drawn to him in ways she shouldn't have been. But he clearly needed to unload, and he didn't seem to have anyone else who could listen to him. Keeping him grounded and centered was in her best interest, and Angelina's. "How long has your mother lived in Houston?"

His posture changed subtly, but she couldn't read his expression. "About ten years, I guess. Mom put up with Dad long enough to get Holden and me mostly raised. Fought their whole married life to get Dad out of the bottle, but he was never interested so she finally gave up." He paused while the waitress delivered toast and jam, and even seemed to relax a little.

"That must have been hard on the two of you," Lucy said.

"We got through it."

Yes, but at what cost? Lucy spread butter on her toast and dug through the jam dispenser for a packet of grape jelly. "What did your mom do after the divorce?"

"I guess you could say that she rose out of the ashes.

She went to work, got promoted, moved away. She just re-married a few weeks ago, and that's why she's out of the country."

"Do you like her new husband?"

Again the waitress interrupted, and Jackson fell silent while she slid two plates of steak and eggs in front of them. When they were alone again, he sprinkled hot sauce across his eggs and shrugged. "He's all right, I guess. I haven't spent much time around him, but Mom seems happy so I'm willing to give him a chance." He recapped the bottle and looked up at her. "What about yours?"

"Mine?"

"Your family."

She never shared her personal life with people involved in a case, but after opening the door on Jackson's private life with the offer of friendship, she didn't have the heart to slam it shut now. "I'm an only child," she said as she cut into her steak. "Dad works with an accounting firm and Mom is Houston's answer to Martha Stewart—before her legal trou-ble. She can fold a napkin twenty-four different ways with one hand and arrange flowers with the other." Grinning, she reached for the steak sauce. "I take after my dad."

"No flower arranging for you?"

"Or napkin folding. But Mom is completely supportive of my career choice." She smiled sadly and admitted, "They're both proud of me, but sometimes that can be a little embarrassing."

Jackson shrugged. "There are worse things."

"I know. I'm not complaining, really. It's just that they expect so much from me, and I'm not always sure I can deliver. Sometimes I think it would be easier if they just wanted me to have a normal life. Husband, kids…dog."

"You don't want that?"

"I do. Some day. I just don't think it's ever going to happen."

He looked up sharply. "Why not?"

How had their conversation gotten here? Her cheeks burned with embarrassment, but she tried not to let him see how uncomfortable she was. "It's just not in the cards, I guess."

"Why not? You're hardly a troll. Surely there are a few men in Houston with eyes."

She laughed in spite of her growing discomfort. "You're quite the silver-tongued devil, aren't you? Are you always this charming with the women you meet?"

His eyes actually twinkled. "Sorry. Guess I'm a little out of practice. The only women I meet in a typical month are mares in heat. Not," he said, holding up a hand to ward off her protest, "that I'm comparing you to them."

Lucy had a sudden, unexpected image of taking him home to meet her parents. They'd like him. She knew that instinctively. "Not a troll. Not a mare in heat, either. I'm flattered."

His smile faded, but the light in his eyes remained. "You should be. It's the nicest thing I've said to a woman in a long time."

"Oh, please. I find that hard to believe. You're not exactly a troll, either."

"Well, I thank you for that." He cut into his egg and dipped one corner of toast into the yolk. "So what do you do when you're not looking for missing children?"

She thought about her answer for a moment, but there was really no way to respond to that. Three months ago, she could have told him about her monthly luncheons with the six-pack. Now she had nothing, and she hated thinking that the lack of balance in her life might have contributed to the situation she found herself in now.

"My job keeps me pretty busy," she said with a shrug.

"No real time for hobbies. And you? Apparently you're not married."

"Not yet. Too busy." He wiped his mouth with his napkin and reached for the hot sauce again. "First with school, then trying to hold the family together, and now the ranch. Life hasn't left me with a lot of time to think about much else."

"But you like what you do?"

He nodded, but his gaze faltered. "I like it fine. It's good, honest work."

"But…?"

"But…" He took a heavy breath and let it out slowly. "But it's not what I dreamed of doing as a kid." One corner of his mouth lifted. "I don't usually admit that to people, and I'd kill the first person who said a thing about it to Wiley, but staying on the ranch wasn't in my plans back then. I had dreams of moving to the city, working with the environment and cleaning up some of the messes out there. You know…making the world a better place. I was all set to make it happen, too. Even had a scholarship."

"So why didn't you follow through?"

"My dad died, Holden got worse, the ranch was in trouble, and Wiley needed me."

"And so you stayed on the ranch."

"Yep."

"And you've never regretted it?"

"Not enough to do anything about it."

But that darkness passed behind his eyes again, and Lucy knew that he'd given up his dreams to make an old man happy. The realization made her heart squeeze painfully. She cleared her throat and changed the subject, but she couldn't pretend that the moment had never happened. And she had the sinking feeling that spending time with Jackson Davis was going to be dangerous…in more ways than one.

HALF AN HOUR LATER, Jackson pulled into the subdivision where Patrice and Angelina had been living for the past few years. Much as he hated to admit it, taking a few minutes for breakfast had been a good idea. Though neither of them had forgotten about Angelina while they ate, the meal had helped him find his feet again. Physically, he felt strong and clearheaded, and that couldn't hurt. But emotionally—

Well, that was a different story.

Several times during breakfast he'd caught himself wondering what Lucy was like when she wasn't on duty. She was a very attractive woman. Attractive and interesting enough to make him wish he didn't have to rush straight back to the ranch once Angel was home safe and sound.

It had been a long time since he'd thought about dating. Even longer since he'd done much of it, thanks to Holden. But rushing back home was probably the best thing he could do. It was definitely the smart thing. Nothing had changed in the past hour. He still didn't have time for life beyond the ranch. And his head was all mixed up, anyway. Even he couldn't quite wrap his mind around what he was feeling half the time.

Like now.

On one hand, he was hungry for details about Angel's life and desperate to find out about her friends and associates. He wanted to find proof that she was safe. But a cold fist of dread had settled in his stomach as he drove back through the neighborhood, and uncertainty over what he might hear sat as heavily on his shoulders as his desperation.

What if Angel wasn't the reliable, responsible child Jackson wanted her to be? What if, instead, she'd inherited the wild streak that had ended his father's life prematurely and landed Holden in jail more times than he could count?

All these years, he'd carried an image of her in his

mind—the perfect child, the beautiful niece who'd once adored him, who'd giggled whenever he walked into the room and reached for him eagerly when she saw him. But what if she wasn't that child? How would he feel about her if she'd grown hard and cold, if her bright smile had been replaced by the cynical scowl that had so long been part of Holden's expression?

Trying not to think about that, he pulled into the driveway of the depressingly small house and shut off the engine. All around him neighbors filtered into their yards, pretending to be occupied with something worthwhile but watching him closely. Children, obviously frightened by the news about Angel, shied away from his truck. The younger they were, the closer they stayed to their parents.

If this was a scene in a movie, there would have been loud rap music blaring from an unseen stereo. This morning, with one of its own missing, the neighborhood's silence was almost deafening.

He slid out from behind the wheel and took in the weed-choked driveway leading to Patrice's house. Paint chipped and peeled from the siding and curtains sagged unevenly at the front window, but the driveway sat empty, which probably meant that Patrice still wasn't around.

He curled his nose at the aromas in the air—a strong mixture of industry and the sea, as different from the clear air on the ranch as anything he'd ever experienced. Overhead, gulls circled lazily, then dipped and dove for treasures on the ground.

The thought of Angel living here curdled like sour milk in his stomach. It would have taken nothing more than a flick of the wrist, one quick signature on a check, to provide her with more. Even with the financial trouble at the ranch, they had enough to make Angel's life better, and if it hadn't been for Patrice, Angel would have had all the things she needed. Instead, she was lost and alone, possibly even in the hands of some deviant. God willing, she was still alive. She'd better be or Patrice would have hell to pay.

He knocked on the front door and reminded himself for the umpteenth time in an hour to let the past stay in the past. Rocking onto the balls of his feet, he strained to hear through the door. Was someone moving around in there, or was that just his imagination?

Growing impatient, he knocked a second time and a third, but if Patrice was inside, she was ignoring him. Since they'd gone at each other like a couple of barnyard dogs the last time they spoke, he wouldn't be surprised to find out she was lurking behind the sagging curtain in the front window, watching and waiting for him to leave.

He banged the door with his fist and hollered, "Patrice? Are you in there? It's me, Jackson. Open up, dammit. We need to talk."

Another gust of wind carried the strong scent of salt water onto the front porch and brought with it the sound of footsteps from somewhere behind him. He wheeled around, half expecting to find Patrice standing behind him. Instead, he found himself staring at a middle-aged woman with short-cropped hair and a broad, unattractive face. She stared at him through narrowed eyes, but she looked more curious than suspicious. "Can I help you?"

"I'm looking for the people who live here."

"What do you want with them?"

Jackson stepped down from the porch and put himself on her level. "They're family."

The woman raked an assessing gaze from his head to his boots. "Family, huh?"

"That's right. I'm Angelina's uncle."

"The little girl?" At his nod, the woman folded her arms tightly on her chest. "So the family's showing up. I guess that makes it true, then? The little girl is gone?"

"It appears that way. We don't know what's happened for sure, but I'm trying to find out. Do you have any idea where she is?"

The woman gave her head another shake. "No, but that's nothing new. She's in and out all the time. I'm not sure what makes Hank think this time is any different."

Jackson looked at the sad-looking window behind him. "Do you have any idea where she goes when she leaves?"

"With friends, I guess. Where does any teenager go?"

Jackson didn't bother answering. It was a rhetorical question, anyway. "What about Patrice? Do you have any idea where I might find her?"

"The mother?" The woman gave a brief shake of her head. "I haven't seen her for a couple of days but, then, I'm not in the habit of keeping tabs on my neighbors. This time of day, she's probably at work."

"Do you have any idea where that is?"

The woman's eyes narrowed in suspicion and she pulled back slightly to get a better look at him. "I thought you said you were family."

He wondered which would get him the most information, the truth or a white lie. "I am," he admitted carefully. "But I haven't seen them for a while." She was still regarding him skeptically, so he offered a bit more. "The truth is, I haven't seen Angel in quite a while. When Hank got worried about her, he tracked me down and I came to see if I could find her, but I'm starting from scratch."

"Why don't you go to the police?"

"I have. They think Angelina has run away, or maybe she's gone somewhere with her mother, but we won't know that until I can find Patrice. If you know anything about where she works, where she hangs out, her favorite stores or restaurants, or who her friends are, it would be really helpful."

The woman studied him for another long moment, then seemed to decide that he was telling the truth. "Geraldine Sawyer. I live across the street, two houses down."

Jackson stored her name away in a mental file and jerked his head toward the front door. "So are you and Patrice friends?"

"Friends? With that one?" Letting out a snort of laughter, Geraldine shook her head. "She keeps to herself a lot. Doesn't really have time for the rest of us."

"So you don't know when she'll be back?"

"Could be later tonight, could be tomorrow or two days from now. It's hard to say."

An all-too-familiar discouragement settled on Jackson's shoulders like a blanket. "She doesn't keep a regular schedule?"

Geraldine narrowed her eyes and looked him over as if he was a sorry dog dragging home from a hunt. "Are you sure you're family?"

"You want to see some identification?"

Her lips curved in a smile, but she held out a hand and waggled her fingers impatiently. "Come to think of it, that might not be a bad idea."

He pulled his wallet from his pocket and extracted a business card and his driver's license. "I'm not sure what this will tell you. Patrice and my brother were never married, so we don't share a name, but maybe it will convince you that I'm not hiding anything."

She studied his driver's license for a while, then handed it back. "I guess maybe it does."

"So do you know anything that can help me?" he asked as he slipped his wallet back into his pocket.

"Not really. I know Patrice just to nod to, mainly. Like I said, she's not exactly the neighborly type. She has this attitude…like she's better than everyone else. She's not one to sit on the porch visiting with her neighbors, if you know what I mean. Hardly ever talks to anybody else."

"Do you know what kind of car she drives?"

"An old Escort, I think. White."

"But probably not licensed in her name, or one quick search would have found it. You don't happen to know the license number, do you?"

"No. Sorry."

"How about where she works? Hank said something about a truck stop…."

"Well, that could be. Seems like she did wear a uniform for a while—you know, one of those smock things. Blue and yellow, if I remember right. The kind they wear at the Truck Haven."

Jackson's heart leapt. "Are you sure?"

"Well, not positive, but that's what it seems like in my memory." A gull's cry shattered the silence and she looked into the sky. "I wish I could tell you for sure, but I just don't remember."

"That helps. Thank you. What about Angel? What do you know about her?"

Geraldine pursed her lips thoughtfully. "She's a kid, but she seems all right. Keeps to herself a lot, just like her mother." Geraldine leaned in closer and lowered her voice.

"If you want my honest opinion, I think she's an unhappy little thing. She's alone so much, I guess you can't really blame her for running away."

"And you think she ran away?"

Geraldine shrugged casually. "I wouldn't be surprised, let's just say that."

"If things are that bad, why didn't somebody do something?"

"I've got a family of my own. The last thing I need is that one coming after me because I had a hand in taking her kid away."

"You think she'd do that?"

"She's a mother. Even bad ones can turn on you like a bear if they feel threatened."

Jackson looked over the neighborhood and took a moment to pull his thoughts together. "Do you know if Patrice has *any* friends in the area?" he asked when he trusted himself to speak again.

"None that I know of."

"You've never seen anyone at her house? Never noticed a car in the driveway that might help us find her?"

Geraldine shook her head again. "Like I said, she mostly keeps to herself. But things aren't always this bad. Sometimes she's around and sometimes she isn't."

"What about men? Does she date much?"

"Not that I've noticed."

At least she wasn't subjecting Angelina to an endless parade of men. That made him feel a little better. "Is there anything you can think of that might help me locate her?"

"Not really. Like I said, she's not exactly neighborly." The sound of raised voices reached them, and Geraldine glanced over her shoulder. "Look, I'm sorry," she said with an apologetic smile, "but my daughter's kids are living with me, and they're at each other again. I'd better get back there so they don't kill each other." She took a couple of steps away and turned back. "But you know where to find me if you have any questions, right? The white house over there with the red van in the driveway."

Nodding, he watched her race away to prevent whatever trouble was brewing at her house. He just wished the trouble in his was so easy to fix.

THE SUN HAD RISEN HIGH in the sky and the humidity had soared to over ninety percent by the time Lucy stepped into the sprawling redbrick school building. Just walking from her car to the school's front doors had left her sticky with sweat and regretting the jacket she'd chosen to wear this morning.

She let the door swing shut behind her and immediately that peculiar school smell of sweat, industrial cleaner and mass-produced lunch enveloped her. Memories of her own childhood came with it, and a sudden tight feeling in the pit of her stomach, as if she might actually be expected to take another pre-algebra test or turn in a term paper.

Laughing at herself, she located the office on the far side of the foyer and set off toward it. She paused at the door while a couple of girls scooted past her, heads together, laughing like conspirators. They were close to Angel's age—young, just growing into their bodies, full of life and standing on the threshold of the future. A future that Tomas Avila would never know. A future Angelina deserved.

Their enthusiasm for life brought a smile to Lucy's lips, their innocence tugged at her heart. Looking away, she stepped into the office and approached a long counter that

separated a small wait area from the cluster of desks behind it.

A blond woman of about forty smiled up at her. "Can I
help you?"

Lucy produced her ID and introduced herself. "I'm trying to locate one of your students. Her name is Angelina
Beckett. Would you mind checking to see if she's in class
this morning?"

The friendly smile slid from her face. "Is she in some
kind of trouble?"

"No. Nothing like that. I just need to talk with her if
she's here."

"I suppose I could…" She glanced around and smiled
uncertainly. "Actually, I'm new here and I'm not sure what
the protocol is under these circumstances. Do you mind if
I have you talk with someone else?"

"I'd be happy to do that."

"Great. Wait here. I'll see if Mr. Smith is free."

While Lucy cooled her heels, the secretary hurried
down a short hallway and stepped into an office at the far
end. She reappeared a minute later and motioned Lucy
into a postage-stamp office with just enough room for a
desk, credenza and two chairs. Inside, a middle-aged man
with a receding hairline and a kind smile stood and ex-
tended a hand. "Alan Smith, vice principal. What can I do
for you?"

Lucy shook his hand and produced her identification
once more. "I'm Detective Lucy Montalvo, Houston Police Department. I'm trying to locate one of your students—Angelina Beckett."

"Ah, yes. Angel." His smile softened with recognition,
and he sank into the chair behind his desk. "She's a fine
student. But the police… Is there some kind of trouble?"

"I hope not. We've had a report that Angel might be missing, but I'd like to determine whether or not she's in class this morning before we jump to conclusions."

His smile evaporated and he sat back hard in his chair. "Missing? But how…? Who…?"

"We don't know anything yet, Mr. Smith. If you could check her schedule and contact her teacher, that would be a big help."

He came out of his trance and rolled toward his computer terminal. "Of course. That's easy enough." He clicked through a couple of screens, then glanced back at her. "She's supposed to be in English right now. Mrs. Hawthorne's class." Scooting back toward his desk, he flipped on the intercom system and pulled a microphone toward him. Disembodied voices floated in the air for an instant before he called "Mrs. Hawthorne?"

The voices fell silent for a moment, then, "Yes?"

"I'm sorry to bother you, but could you please send Angelina Beckett to the office for a few minutes?"

With her eyes locked on the far wall, Lucy prayed silently for the right response. *Please,* she begged, *let Angel be there.* But even before the teacher's tinny-sounding voice reached her, she had a feeling that she knew what the answer would be.

"I'm sorry, Mr. Smith. Angel isn't in class today."

His gaze shot to hers and she saw the worry and concern in them that she knew must surely be showing in her own. "I see. Sorry for the interruption."

Sighing heavily, he turned off the intercom and turned to face her fully. "We have a problem, don't we."

Lucy nodded. "I'm afraid we may. There's still a chance she's with her mother, but we can't locate her, either. There's no need to panic yet, but I would like to talk with

Angel's teachers and some of her friends. Maybe one of them can tell us something helpful."

Mr. Smith nodded eagerly. "Of course. For that we'll need permission from parents, but I'm sure some will agree."

"Thank you. Do you know Angelina well, Mr. Smith?"

His kind eyes locked on hers. "Fairly well. At least I like to think so. I like to think I know all of my students."

"Have you noticed anything different about her lately? Has she been moody? Distracted? Has she changed friends or lost interest in school?"

Mr. Smith gave that some thought, then shook his head. "Not particularly. She's a friendly girl. Bright and cheerful, and she's well liked by the other kids. She's a good student, too, which doesn't always follow on the heels of popularity, and she's extremely focused for a girl her age."

"Do you have any reason to believe Angelina would run away?"

"I don't know much about her home life. She doesn't talk about it a lot, and her mother hasn't been able to attend any parent-teacher conferences since Angel started here. But if you're asking if she seemed dissatisfied with her life, I'd have to say no. No more than the average kid, anyway."

Lucy desperately wanted to feel relieved at hearing that, but it only opened the door on possibilities she didn't want to seriously consider.

"Do you know who her friends are?"

"Some of them. I'll be glad to give you names." He turned away again and pulled his computer keyboard closer. "I'll print Angelina's schedule. That will give you teacher names and classroom numbers, but the school year has just started, and her teachers probably don't know her very well."

"Good point. Could you give me last year's schedule, too?"

"Absolutely."

"Thank you. I'm sure that will be a big help. Can you tell me about her friends? What kind of kids are they?"

He shrugged. "A mix. Mostly good kids from regular families. Some from single-parent homes. Mostly blue collar. There's not a lot of money in this school, but that puts most of the kids on equal footing."

"Do Angel and her friends get into trouble?"

"Not really. Oh, they might occasionally skip a class. Grades not as high as they could be. The usual teenage trouble, but nothing hard core like drugs or gang activity. They're good kids, really."

Again, that odd mix of emotions rolled through Lucy. Jackson would be glad to know she was in with a good crowd, but that only drove the chances that she was in danger higher.

"What about boys? Is she involved with any?"

"Not that I've noticed. She likes them well enough, but she's not as involved as some of the girls her age." Mr. Smith retrieved the schedules from the printer and slid them across the desk toward her. "I can let you use one of the offices in the counseling center to talk with people if that will help. Just let me know who you'd like to see and I'll make sure they're available."

She couldn't have asked for more. Cooperation, answers, information. But there was only one thing that could have made her feel better, and that was if Angel walked through the door right that minute.

Like it or not, she was going to have to accept that it wasn't going to happen.

CHAPTER SIX

LUCY'S STOMACH WAS GROWLING again by the time she left the high school that afternoon. Though she'd been at it for hours, she'd made little progress on the list of friends and teachers Mr. Smith had given her. Unless Jackson had something concrete to report, she'd have to come back tomorrow and do it all again.

She wasn't looking forward to meeting Jackson later, telling him she'd come up empty. He was so determined to find Angelina. So convinced that she'd left a trail. So absolutely unfaltering in his determination not to fail another member of his family, she wasn't sure he'd accept the truth.

Glancing at her watch, she slid behind the wheel of her car, rolled down the windows and turned the air conditioner on high in an effort to blow out some of the hot air that had been locked inside for hours. While she was waiting for the steering wheel to cool down enough to touch it, the cell phone in her pocket let out a chirp. She answered without looking at the caller ID, and immediately regretted it.

"Lucy?" A woman's low voice came through the connection, and Lucy had a sick feeling she knew who it was. "Cecily Fontaine here. I hope you don't mind, but Nick Vega gave me your number. He said you'd be calling."

Lucy could have sworn that the temperature had just climbed by at least ten degrees. She sank back in her seat and rolled her eyes at the roof of her car. "That's right, but we only spoke about this last night. I haven't had time—"

"I hope you don't think I'm trying to pressure you. It's just that I had an unexpected cancellation this afternoon. I thought maybe you'd like to take advantage of the opening."

"Today?"

"Incredible, huh?"

"Unheard of," Lucy agreed. She tried not to let Cecily's friendly manner and lilting laugh annoy her. She resented the head games, and was in no mood to play along. "I wasn't expecting you to have free time for several days."

"Neither was I," Cecily admitted. "It's quite a stroke of luck."

That certainly wasn't how Lucy would describe it. Nor did she think it was a coincidence. She'd have bet a month's pay Nick had put Cecily up to calling.

"So what do you say?" Cecily asked. "Shall I put you down for five o'clock?"

"Five?" Lucy squinted at her watch and realized with a sinking heart that she could actually make it if she tried. "Shouldn't you be out of the office by that time of day?"

"I rarely get away that early, I'm afraid." Cecily's tone changed subtly. "You might as well come. Avoiding our meeting won't make it go away."

So much for the friendly banter. "I'm not trying to avoid our meeting," Lucy assured her. "But I'm in the middle of a case. I can't drop everything to run downtown just because you have a free hour."

"I see. I was under the impression you wanted this matter handled quickly. Did I get the wrong information?"

"No, but since you're evaluating me to see what kind of cop I make, I'm assuming I should continue to treat my cases as if they're important." Lucy heard the challenge in her voice, but couldn't seem to do anything about it. Just like the tears that she'd been unable to control yesterday, the anger she felt today seemed to come from someplace she couldn't access.

"Well it was worth a try, wasn't it? I guess I'll have to catch up on paperwork instead. But while I have you on the phone, shall we set an appointment for a time that's convenient for you?"

Feeling railroaded, Lucy rolled up the windows to trap the cool air inside. In spite of her assurance to the contrary, she would cheerfully have avoided a meeting if she thought she could get away with it. But the writing was on the wall, and Nick apparently wasn't taking any chances.

"I don't have my calendar with me," she said. "Can I call you when I get back to my desk?"

"*Will* you call?"

"Do I have a choice?"

"Of course."

"Not if I want to keep my job. Trust me, I'll call."

"Great. When do you think that will be?"

The woman was a predator, circling relentlessly, trying to pin her down. A bell rang and kids began to pour out of the doors, and Lucy felt the sudden, intense need to get away from the noise and confusion. "I'll call tomorrow."

"All right, then. I'll look forward to hearing from you. And Lucy?"

"Yes?"

"There's no shame in coming to see me, you know. It's more common than you might think."

"Not to me."

"You're not alone in feeling that way, either. I just want to assure you that our sessions will remain completely confidential. No one has to know you've been to see me unless you want them to."

"Except Nick." And anyone else up the chain of command.

Cecily paused for a split second. "Are you worried about that?"

"Wouldn't you be?" Even as the words left her mouth, Lucy wished she could call them back. She just couldn't seem to control her resentment. She didn't understand how this kind of pressure was supposed to help her. How was she to recover from the tragedy if people wouldn't leave her alone?

"You're worried that meeting with me may affect your future with the force?"

Lucy shifted into Reverse. "In a nutshell. I don't think that a history of psychiatric care is going to work in my favor."

"This isn't exactly a history."

"It will be in my file. What would you call it?"

"An incident."

Semantics. But Lucy could play that game, too. "Well, then, I don't think an *incident* of psychiatric help is going to work in my favor."

"A little consultation after a case goes wrong isn't a bad thing."

The smoothness of her voice rankled. The unflappable answers grated on Lucy's nerves. "Really? You can guarantee that nobody in the next twenty years is going to look at that *incident* on my record and wonder? That nobody's going to doubt my ability to deal with a crisis? That nobody will think I'm unstable? Worry about me in a pinch? Pass me over when it comes time to work on a tough case? Because if you can guarantee that, then maybe I'll stop worrying about it."

"Are those your only concerns?"

"Those are the main ones." She refused to admit her family's prejudice against psychiatric care. Cecily would have a heyday with that, and Lucy didn't want to hear all the arguments she knew the psychiatrist would offer.

"As I said, it's more common than you might think. There are officers on active duty all through the force who've come in for consultations."

"I feel so much safer now," Lucy quipped. Swarms of children moved past the car, some laughing, some arguing mildly. One boy stopped in front of her windshield to throw something to a friend. His resemblance to Tomas made Lucy's hands grow clammy. "I'll call tomorrow," she said again. "You can count on it."

She disconnected before Cecily could prolong the conversation, but she wondered what was happening to her. She'd never run from an argument in her life—but lately it seemed that's all she did.

MOONLIGHT SHADOWS DANCED on the walls as Lucy lay in bed that night, wide awake, staring at the ceiling, thinking about the future and wondering what it held. All afternoon and evening, the question had played through her mind, a never-ending tape casting doubt upon her past, making her question the future.

What kind of cop needed a head doctor? No matter how normal Cecily claimed it was, Lucy knew she'd never feel safe working with a fellow officer who broke down under stress. And what would Jackson think if he knew? How could she expect him to trust her? She didn't even trust herself.

Maybe she wasn't cut out for the job.

Just thinking that struck terror in her heart. She'd never wanted to do anything else. Never even considered another line of work. If she walked away from the department tomorrow, what would she do instead? Fold napkins? Learn accounting? Procreate?

She rolled from one side to the other, trying to find a comfortable position in the single bed that suddenly felt too confining. With a sigh, she got up and crossed to the window. Pulling back the curtain, she looked out over the quiet street. Could she be happy living a life like her mother's? Could she settle down, have children, join the PTA and host family dinners every Sunday?

Jackson had walked away from his dreams. He'd substituted Wiley's dreams for his own, and he'd survived. But Lucy had no idea how he'd done it. She felt lost. Completely adrift in a sea she didn't recognize.

She stood that way for a while, watching trees swaying in the breeze and wondering where she'd be six months from now. When she couldn't bear thinking about it any longer, she tiptoed from her bedroom, down the stairs and into the family room at the back of the house.

Praying that she wouldn't wake her parents, she turned on one dim light just long enough to find the remote control. After flicking on the set and turning down the sound, she extinguished the lamp again and curled into her father's easy chair.

Familiar things wrapped themselves around her—the spicy scent of her dad's aftershave, the well-worn nap of the fabric, the shape of the seat beneath her. Her mother had redecorated the family room half a dozen times in recent years but, in spite of her arguments, this chair remained.

Yawning, Lucy aimlessly flicked through channels, finally settling on a rerun of *Blackbeard's Ghost,* one of her favorite movies from childhood. But even that couldn't hold her attention for long.

For some reason, watching the growing attraction between the characters played by Suzanne Pleshette and Dean Jones made her think about Jackson again. But she didn't want to think about him.

Oh, sure, she found him attractive. Who wouldn't? Those eyes. That smile. Those shoulders. She couldn't even deny that the soft drawl of his voice did a little something to her when she heard it on the phone, but she wasn't interested in *that* way.

Or was she?

Kicking her legs over the arm of the chair, she closed her eyes and tried to analyze her feelings. If only she hadn't ruined everything with the six-pack. She'd give anything to talk to one of them right now. Abby, maybe. Though Risa had been Lucy's closest friend, Abby had been the undisputed nurturer of the group. The one most likely to understand whatever Lucy was going through. Or maybe she was just the one least likely to be surprised by this abrupt and inexplicable shift.

She reached for the remote again, but when the light came on overhead, she let out a soft squeal of surprise and the remote dropped to the floor beside her.

Blinking in the sudden glare of light, she finally focused on her dad standing in the open doorway. His hair stood up in soft spikes, and wrinkled pajamas hanging slightly off kilter convinced her that he'd been asleep not long ago.

"I guess your mother was right," he said. "You *are* down here."

Lucy swung her legs to the floor and scooped up the remote so she could turn off the television. "I'm sorry. I was trying to be quiet."

"You can't be quiet enough to get past your mother." He

came into the room, slippers scuffing softly on the carpet. "What are you doing down here in the middle of the night?"

Lucy shrugged and vacated his chair so he could sit. "I was having trouble sleeping but I was too tired to read. I swear I didn't make a sound when I went past your room."

With a laugh, her dad sank into his chair and raked his fingers through his hair. "I'm sure you didn't, sweetheart. Your mother comes equipped with radar. I think all mothers do." He put a hand over one of hers and added, "You'll have the same thing once you start your own family."

"*If* I start a family." Lucy clutched his hand and stared at the familiar lines and the shape of his knuckles. They were so like her grandfather's, it never failed to amaze her, and she realized, not for the first time, that if she never married and had children, everything that had been passed down for generations would disappear. No more slightly square fingers. No more middle fingernails that sloped toward the thumb. How sad it suddenly seemed to her.

She lifted her gaze and found her father watching her. His face was so dear, his love for her so obvious, that lump of emotion she'd been fighting since Saturday night filled her throat again.

"Will you be terribly disappointed in me if I don't get married and give you grandchildren?"

"Disappointed?" Doug laughed as if he'd never heard anything so preposterous. "Honey, I could never be disappointed in you."

"Never?" She ran a thumb across the scar he'd acquired trying to tow her first car home one night during her senior year of high school. "Are you sure about that?"

Her dad's smile slipped a little. "Are you worried?"

"I don't know if I'd say 'worried,'" she hedged, "but

sometimes I wonder if I can live up to what you and Mom expect from me."

"Mom and I don't expect all that much. We only want you to be happy."

"I know, but…" She wondered how to explain what was bothering her and how he'd react if she told him the truth. "I don't know— It's just that sometimes I wonder how proud of me you'd be if I decided to leave the police department, or if I made some other big change in my life."

Her dad pulled back slightly to get a better look at her. "Are you contemplating a change?"

"No. I don't think so." She sent him a weak smile and added, "I don't know, Dad. It's been a rough week and I feel like I'm running in circles all the time. I'm not sure what I'm thinking of doing."

"Well, honey, I wish I could give you a clear-cut answer, but in my experience, answers like the one you're looking for are hard to come by. There's only one person who can find it, anyway. Are you unhappy with your job?"

She shook her head and looked down at her own fingertips. "Not really."

"But you're thinking about leaving? May I ask why?"

Suddenly overcome with the need to talk it through, she drew her hand away from his and stood. "I lost a child this week. We did everything to find him, but we were too late."

"The little boy on the news?"

Lucy nodded miserably. "I can't stop thinking about it— about how his body looked in the field where they found him. About the look on his mother's face when I gave her the news. About all the things I should have done differently. I close my eyes, and I see him, or I see his mother. I hear her crying. I see his face in the pictures they gave us when he first disappeared, and I'm not sure I can do this again."

"You know it's not your fault, don't you?"

She turned back to face him. "I want to believe that, but I don't. I swore to protect and serve. I promised to make this world a better place, but I don't feel as if I'm doing that. I'm not even sure I know how."

"All because one case ended badly?"

"Badly?" She let out a harsh laugh and wrapped her arms around herself. "An eight-year-old boy is dead. I think that's a little worse than 'badly,' don't you?"

"It's a horrible tragedy," her dad agreed. "But you're not to blame for what happened."

"I should have found him."

"I know you wanted to find him," her dad said gently, "but you did what you knew how to do at the time. If you'd known something different, you'd have done different."

"It's this horrible feeling of being out of control I hate. You'd think I'd be used to it by now. You'd think that in six years, I'd understand that I'm never going to be in control. Never. No matter how hard I try, someone else is always going to have the upper hand."

"So you want to give up?"

She slanted a glance at him. "That makes me sound weak, doesn't it?"

He crossed the room to her and pulled her into his arms.

"No, sweetheart, it makes you sound human. There's a reason most of us don't become police officers."

"Because you're all smarter than I am?"

He laughed softly and kissed her cheek. "No, because we all know our limitations. We're afraid, but that doesn't mean we don't need people like you who have courage enough to do the job. In fact, it means we need you more than ever."

But did she have what it took? Or had she been deluding herself until now?

The possibility chilled her. "I don't know, Daddy. Maybe I'm not cut out for it, after all. Maybe I'd be better off with a husband and a carload of kids, cheering at soccer games and planning school fund-raisers."

Her dad laughed and chucked her under the chin. "Now, that's just a load of nonsense. You're letting your imagination run away with you, and you're letting one bad experience throw you. But that's not how you were raised, and that's not who you are. Maybe you don't realize that right now, but I know it, and so does your mother."

Ruffling her hair affectionately, he nudged her toward the door. "Things will look better in the morning. Just you wait and see. And if not tomorrow, then the next day. But you're not a quitter, Lucy. My girl is made of sterner stuff than that."

She followed him into the darkened corridor, but only because she couldn't think of a good reason to stay. She wanted desperately to believe what he said, but he had more faith in her than she had in herself. She wasn't at all sure he was right.

THE NEXT DAY, JACKSON insisted on going with Lucy to the school. He'd spent most of the previous afternoon trying to find out about Patrice's job at the Truck Haven, but he'd made the mistake of being honest with the Human Resources Director at the company's headquarters. Even a missing family member hadn't been enough to pull information from the tight-lipped woman.

He wasn't sure what difference he could make here, either. Maybe none at all. But he needed to feel part of the investigation, and Lucy had been surprisingly receptive to the suggestion.

There was something different about her this morning,

but he couldn't put his finger on what it was. She seemed quieter. A little less confident, maybe. Or perhaps she was just tired. He thought about asking, but she didn't seem to be interested in idle chatter, and whatever it was seemed to fade as teachers came and went.

None of the faculty members knew Angelina well, and nobody had seen anything to make them believe she was about to run away from home. Every kid on the list of friends they'd been given had seemed genuinely surprised and frightened by her disappearance, and halfway through the day Jackson was convinced they were wasting precious time.

With one more student to go, he was champing at the bit, raring to get back on the streets where their chances of finding information suddenly seemed high by comparison. Lucy, on the other hand, sat through each interview with her hands locked in front of her and an encouraging look on her face, as if she actually thought these young girls might have something valuable to say.

He watched with growing frustration as the school counselor who'd been assisting them all morning led a coltish young girl with red-blond hair falling into her eyes into the room and introduced her as Erica Curtis.

Erica walked into the room slowly, her eyes so wide and uncertain she looked four instead of fourteen. When Lucy motioned her toward a chair, the girl sat quickly and tucked her hands beneath her legs.

Lucy smiled at her gently. "Hi, Erica. Please don't be nervous. We just need to ask you a few simple questions, okay?"

The girl nodded.

"You're a friend of Angelina's?"

Erica's gaze flickered toward the counselor, as if she wasn't sure she should answer. When the counselor nodded encouragement, Erica finally spoke. "Yeah." She slid a glance at Jackson, but looked away again almost immediately. "Is it true? Did Angel really get kidnapped?"

"We think it's more likely that she ran away," Lucy said. "We're hoping you can help us." She smiled gently and showed the girl her badge. "My name is Lucy. I'm a detective with the police department. You know Miss Peterman," she said with a nod at the counselor, "and this is Angel's Uncle Jackson. No one is going to be angry with you, so please don't worry about that."

Erica blew her bangs out of her eyes, but the hair flopped back almost immediately.

"Would you like a soda or something before we start?"

The girl brushed the hair away with her hand and tried to look brave. "No. I'm okay."

She was young and so obviously nervous, Jackson was torn between compassion and frustration. Angelina might be out there alone somewhere, more frightened than this, without someone like Lucy making everything all right.

"All right then." Lucy smiled again and picked up her pencil. "Can you tell me when you saw Angel last?"

"Friday, I guess. At school."

"Did you see her or talk to her over the weekend?"

Erica gave her head a shake. "No. We don't live near each other."

"Do you ever talk on the phone?"

The girl's gaze faltered. "Sometimes."

"But you didn't this weekend?"

"Uh-uh. Me and my mom were gone."

"I see."

Another waste of time. Jackson stirred impatiently and tried to catch Lucy's eye.

Either she didn't see him, or she pretended not to. Leaning toward the girl, she smiled as if they shared a secret. "Here's the thing, Erica…. Some people think that Angel ran away or that she went off with friends. Now, the truth is, we'd be really happy if that's what happened. At least we'd know she was safe. So if you know anything about where she is, or if you think maybe you know something, we'd really like you to tell us. But maybe that's not what happened. Maybe somebody took Angel away from her house. If that's what happened, we need to find her before she gets hurt. We need you to think hard and tell us everything you can remember. Does she have a boyfriend? Did she ever say anything to you about running away? Has she ever talked about somebody who bothered her, or has she ever acted afraid?"

The girl took all of that in without changing expression and remained unmoving for so long Jackson thought he might go crazy. Did she know something? If so, why didn't she just say so?

"I don't think she ran away," Erica said at last. "Angel wouldn't do that. And besides, all of her friends are here. If she was at somebody's house, they would have said something." She smiled uncomfortably and shifted so that she almost uncovered one hand. "And I don't think anybody was bugging her anymore. Not since Wayne moved away."

Jackson met Lucy's startled gaze over the top of Erica's head. After hearing so many people giving the same answers, he wasn't sure whether to believe this child or not. He moved his chair closer and forced words out past the knot of his suddenly tight throat. "Who is Wayne?"

"He's this guy who used to live near Angel."

"He doesn't live there now?"

She shook her head and looked to Lucy for guidance.

"Why don't you tell us about him," Lucy suggested.

Erica's gaze darted uncertainly between them. "He's just this guy."

"But he used to bother Angel?"

"Sometimes." Erica pulled one hand from beneath her legs and chewed her thumbnail. "He used to talk to her sometimes, but she thought he was creepy."

Jackson could hardly breathe, and it seemed as if time had slowed almost to a standstill. Erica's voice sounded strange to his ears, and the only thing he could clearly see was Lucy's face.

"Does he go to school here?" Lucy asked.

"No. He's too old."

"How old?"

The girl shrugged. "I don't know. Maybe the same age as my brother. He's twenty." She seemed to realize, slowly, that she'd said something important. Her face paled and her eyes grew even wider. "He was always bugging Angel. Asking her out and stuff. Walking by her house when her mom was gone. That's why she used to hang out with Hank, because Wayne left her alone when she was with Hank."

Ice and fire pulsed through Jackson with every heartbeat. Fear and determination. Disbelief and pain. Anger and hatred. "What is Wayne's last name?"

"I don't know."

"Do you know where he lived?"

"Not really. Somewhere near Angel is all I know." The class bell sounded through the closed doors and Erica finally showed a little animation. "Is that all? I have Geography next, and we're having a test. My dad will kill me if I miss it."

Still looking shell-shocked, Lucy nodded. "Yes. Of course. You don't want to miss your test."

Bolting to her feet, Erica scampered from the room,

leaving a stunned silence in her wake. Jackson recovered first, shooting out of his chair and heading toward the door, but Lucy was just half a step behind him. He could barely form a coherent thought around the anger clouding his mind, but at least now his anger had a target—and a name.

Now all they had to do was find him.

CHAPTER SEVEN

IT SEEMED TO TAKE FOREVER to make the short drive to Angel's neighborhood, and Lucy watched Jackson carefully as she drove. He was more agitated than ever, and no wonder. She could hardly breathe herself, and panic lurked just below the surface, waiting to drag her under. The only way she'd get through this was to focus on something other than herself, and that meant Jackson.

From the minute Erica mentioned Wayne's name, Jackson's mood had changed. All the energy that had gone into frustration and disappointment now poured into finding Wayne. She could feel the anger radiating from him. She could see the grim determination on his face. But she couldn't let his hatred run unchecked. Maybe Wayne did know something about Angelina's disappearance, but they were a long way from proving it, and she needed Jackson to keep his head until they had what they needed. If he didn't, she wasn't sure she could hang on to her own reason.

"Don't get ahead of yourself," she warned as she rounded the corner onto Angel's street. "This may turn out to be nothing."

He shot a glance across the seat and laughed sharply. "How can you say that? It's the first real lead we've found."

"We don't know what it is yet," she reminded him. "At this point it's nothing but a possibility." She pulled up to the curb and turned off the engine, shifting in the seat so she could see him better. "False leads turn up all the time in cases like this. This boy might be completely innocent."

Scowling, Jackson unbuckled his seat belt and reached for the door handle. "Might be. Then again, maybe he's not."

"All I'm saying is, we can't convict him on the testimony of one young girl. She might have been trying to sound important. Her imagination could have run away with her and turned something innocent into something wrong. We don't know anything yet."

Annoyance flashed across Jackson's face. "Look, Lucy, I know *you* have rules to follow and hoops to jump through, but I don't. If this Wayne character had anything to do with Angel's disappearance, I'm going to find out."

"You don't think I feel the same way?"

"I don't know. You have a job to do, that's all I know."

It was true, as far as it went, but for some reason his assessment stung. She opened her door and stepped out onto the street. "If you think I don't care about finding Angelina," she said when he joined her, "you're dead wrong. If you think I'll put in my time and move on without a care in the world, you're wrong again. I want to find Angel and bring her home as much as you do, but I'm not going to convict someone before I even talk to him."

"And I'm not going to let some twisted punk walk free if he's hurt my niece. I won't waste time jumping through hoops and fighting red tape when Angel might be in danger."

"Get real, Jackson. Even if Wayne *is* guilty, if you start playing vigilante he'll walk away and you'll be the one in jail. All we have is rumor and speculation, so cut me some slack, okay? I'll keep doing what I believe is necessary to make sure Angel is safe, but I'm not going to put my career in jeopardy because you're impatient."

He rolled his eyes in exasperation. "When did I ever suggest that you should?"

"If you want me to run after Wayne without taking time and care to find out what really happened, that's exactly what you're asking."

Jackson's eyes roamed her face for a long moment. She couldn't tell what he was thinking, and she prayed he couldn't read her mind. If he guessed how close she was to chucking it all in and walking away from the job, she'd never be able to control him. If he knew how she'd botched her last case, he'd never believe another word she said.

After a long time, he dipped his head and muttered, "Let's see what Hank says."

Almost sick with relief, Lucy led the way up the walk, but she was far too conscious of Jackson behind her, far too aware of his restless energy and his unspoken disapproval. She could only hope that she was making the right decision.

The door creaked open in response to her knock, and Hank frowned out at them. "Is this good news or bad?"

"Neither," Lucy said. "We'd like to ask a few more questions if you don't mind."

"I hope I have answers." Hank let them into the cool interior of the house and led them into a small living room filled with the tools of his trade. A few framed paintings hung on the walls, but many more unframed canvases leaned in stacks against the walls, and the heavy scents of paint and turpentine filled the air.

Hank motioned them toward the couch with the wave of one paint-stained hand. "Can I get you anything? Coffee? A soda?"

"No, thank you." Lucy sat at one end of the couch. Jackson somewhat reluctantly sat on the other.

Hank moved a canvas from in front of a well-worn re-
cliner and settled in. "How's the search going?"

"Slowly, I'm afraid. We've just come from Angel's
school. One of her friends mentioned a young man named
Wayne who used to live here in the neighborhood. She
seemed to think that Wayne caused trouble for Angelina
from time to time."

"Wayne?" Hank's expression sobered and he shook his
head thoughtfully. After a moment, his gaze shifted and his
eyes lit. "Wayne. Yeah. I think I remember him."

"You know him, then?"

"If I'm thinking of the right guy, he lived down at the
end of the block for a few years. I never had much to do
with him, but he seemed like the kind you'd want to keep
your eye on."

Jackson leaned forward, his face tight with worry. "Did
Angelina ever mention him to you?"

Hank tilted his head thoughtfully. "I don't remember her
saying anything about him, but she might have."

"She never told you that she was afraid of him?"

"No. I'd remember that. He was too old for her, so I suppose I never gave it any thought. Angel's a pretty girl, though,
so it's not hard to see how she might have caught his eye.
But I wouldn't put too much stock in what that girl told you.
If he'd been bothering her, Angel would have told me."

"You're sure of that?" Jackson asked.

"Positive."

Lucy hoped he was right. "Do you know his last name?"

Hank pushed up the footrest on his chair and crossed his
feet in front of him. "If I'm thinking of the right kid, his
dad's name was Fitzgerald. Ed. Kind of a rough guy.
Course, Ed might have been his stepdad. I never did know
the family well."

"And does the family still live around here?"

Hank nodded slowly. "I think the parents do. Wayne moved away a few months ago. Talk around the neighborhood is that they kicked him out, but you know how talk is."

Lucy felt a stirring of excitement. "Where do his parents live?"

"Green house down at the end of the block. I don't know the number, but you'll have no trouble finding it. There are always three or four cars on the front lawn."

"And you have no idea where Wayne is?"

"Not a clue. Sorry."

Lucy made a move to stand, but Jackson wasn't finished. "Have you remembered anything more about the argument Angel had with her mother?"

"Not yet, but I've been trying." Hank flicked dried paint from one finger. "It seems odd, doesn't it, that Patrice hasn't come back? I mean, wouldn't you think she'd want to work things out?"

Unbidden, Maria Avila's grief-stricken face flashed through Lucy's mind. She thought about all the things left unsaid between mother and son, and a desperate need to prevent that from happening to Angel and Patrice rose up inside her. Panic followed close on its heels. What if she couldn't prevent another tragedy? What if she couldn't bring Angel home? Couldn't help her reconcile with her mother and meet the rest of her family?

Needing to create some emotional distance for herself, she slipped her notebook into her pocket and stood to leave. "Thanks, Hank. You'll call me if you think of anything else?"

"I'll be on the phone the minute I think of anything." Bypassing Lucy, Hank crossed to Jackson and put a comforting hand on his shoulder. He didn't say a word, but he

communicated something that Jackson responded to, and
the despair on Jackson's face abated for one brief moment.

Emotion tightened in Lucy's chest, and she turned away
quickly. She couldn't connect with Jackson on that level.
She *couldn't*. The only way to salvage her career—assuming she even wanted to—was to remain disconnected.
Aloof. Strictly professional.

She stared blindly at the wall in front of her until she
heard voices again, then quickly turned toward the door
and led the way out into the heat. But the look on Jackson's
face tore her up inside, and she knew she'd have to work
a whole lot harder at keeping her emotions under control.

BEFORE THE SUN EVEN CAME up on Thursday morning,
Jackson was pacing the length of his mother's kitchen,
waiting for Lucy to call and tell him where and when to
meet her. They'd worked late into the evening for two days
trying to find Wayne Fitzgerald or pick up another lead on
Angel's whereabouts, but they'd struck out on every try.

It had been easy to find the house Hank described, but
no one had answered their knock—not the first time they
tried, not the second, not even the third or fourth. They'd
gone up and down the street questioning people, but only
a couple of neighbors admitted to knowing who Wayne
was, and nobody admitted to knowing where he'd gone.

Slowly, surely, the sun had slipped behind the horizon
on both days, and they'd had to call it a day. Logically,
Jackson knew they couldn't keep going nonstop, but he
hated every second of the delay. He hated having to put the
search aside while the city shut down and people slept, and
anger curled through him all night.

That people *could* sleep grated on his nerves. That they
could laugh, watch television, go on about their business

as if the world hadn't ground to a halt felt like a betrayal he couldn't explain, even to himself.

Unable to sleep, he'd gone back to Channelview last night and convinced Hank to let him into Patrice's house. After three hours of searching, he'd found a couple of slim leads he wanted to share with Lucy this morning—a few old bank statements, some phone numbers and a shoe box filled with receipts and check stubs from Truck Haven. Sure enough, the checks had stopped abruptly a few months earlier, and if Patrice was collecting a paycheck from anywhere else, she wasn't saving the stubs.

To make matters worse, he'd found himself fielding questions he wasn't ready to answer as he worked. He appreciated Hank's concern and the watchful eye he kept on Angelina, but his questions about Jackson's lack of participation in Angel's life had grated on his already frayed nerves.

His mood had been so sour by the time he left, he could barely stand to be around himself. Back at the condo, he'd spent hours combing through the telephone books. Not surprisingly, Wayne Fitzgerald wasn't listed, and if he lived with any of the other Fitzgeralds Jackson had called, they were covering for him. If Lucy faced these kinds of challenges with every case, it was a wonder she was still sane.

Jackson's nerves were stretched so tightly, he couldn't promise that he wouldn't snap. Yes, they finally had a break, but the sense of unreality that seemed to surround him all the time was growing stronger by the hour.

He hated being in this position—relegated to waiting on the sidelines while Lucy attended meetings. Waiting for permission to take the next step when he should have been helping Angelina. But that had been the story for years, hadn't it? He'd never been part of Angel's life. All his big talk about holding the family together, being there for Wiley, all his delusions about being some kind of rock were just a load of horse manure.

What had he actually done? He'd given up his dreams. He'd shoveled more horseshit than he'd ever thought he would. He'd taken a lot of orders, but he couldn't list a single accomplishment that he could call his own. He had no wife. No children. He hadn't even thought about the possibility in way too long—until Lucy asked him why he wasn't married.

He poured the last of the coffee and cradled the mug in his hands as he stared out over the backyard. He told himself there was plenty of time to build a life. He was only thirty-two, after all, and that was hardly ancient. And *nothing* was more important than the vow he'd made the day of his father's funeral. His father and Holden had made careers out of indulging themselves and hurting the family. Jackson was making one of being who and what his family needed.

At long last, the phone rang and he snagged the cordless receiver from the counter. Rush's familiar "Hey" caught him off guard.

Instinctively, he glanced at his watch. "It's a little early for you to be at work, isn't it? Is everything all right?"

"Everything's fine. Wiley's in a mood, but that shouldn't come as any surprise. What's the word on Angel?"

"There's not much word at all." Jackson carried his coffee to the table and tilted back in a chair. "We've only found a couple of small leads, but I guess something is better than nothing."

"You'll track her down," Rush assured him. "I've never known you to fail when the chips are down."

"The chips have never been this far down before."

"Don't lose heart, Jackson. It will cloud your judgment." The sound of something scraping across the floor came through the connection, and Jackson pictured Rush straddling his desk chair, arms resting on its back. "I wouldn't have bothered you at all, but there's a rumor going around that Terrence Knight may not run Sir Galahad next season. I thought you'd want to know."

Jackson seized on the distraction eagerly. Sir Galahad was a Thoroughbred who'd won twenty-five of his fifty-two races and set a couple of track speed records in the process. Breeders all around the country were salivating to get their hands on the horse, and an agreement to let him stand at stud for Crescent Valley would be a major coup.

Three years ago, Crescent Valley would have been a shoo-in to get him. Now, thanks to Holden, he wondered if they even stood a chance. "How true do you think the rumor is?"

"Hard to tell. So far that's all it is. I could put in a call, but I don't want to jump the gun."

Jackson nodded thoughtfully. "What about Art Smith? Do you think he'd know what Knight has in mind?"

"I wouldn't bet on it. Far as I know, Knight's not in the habit of confiding in his trainer."

"I don't want to approach him too soon," Jackson agreed. "I want the ranch to be stable before we do." It felt strangely good to think about something besides Angel's disappearance. He was lost when it came to finding his niece, but horse breeding…well, that was another story entirely. "If we go to Knight now," he said, "there's almost no chance we'll get Galahad."

"You can't be sure of that. The past couple of years have taken their toll, and we lost some footing when all that money disappeared, but we can thank God Wiley's the kind of man he is. His reputation gave us a chance to pay back what Holden took, and we're almost there. I think we probably have as good a chance as anyone. Maybe even better than some."

And worse than others. Jackson rubbed his face with one hand and let out a heavy sigh. "Knight was one of the hardest hit when Holden wiped out the trust account. And he was the first to take his business to someone else afterward. Even if I went to him on my knees, I doubt he'd be willing to take another chance on us."

"Well, we've gotta do something, man," Rush prodded. "We'll never pull ahead with empty stables."

"You don't need to remind me." Jackson moved his hand to the back of his neck and went to work on the knots there. Sometimes it seemed as if he'd spent his entire life cleaning up after Holden, and it had grown way beyond old. And what if Angel had run away? What if the cycle was starting all over again? He wasn't at all sure he had the energy or the patience to get through it.

Too irritated to sit still, he bounded to his feet and dug eggs and bacon from the refrigerator. "Okay, so we have work to do. If I want to convince Knight to stable Sir Galahad with us, we need to fix up the south barn. I know Knight, and he won't even consider bringing the horse to us unless that stable is in a whole lot better shape than it is now."

"You want me to put a couple of guys on it?"

Jackson cracked eggs into a frying pan and tossed the shells into the sink. "Do we have any to spare after the layoffs?"

"I can take Lopez and Hilton off the new fence in the back paddock if you don't mind letting that end lag a little. Or you could talk to your mother. If she's doing as well as you say, maybe she'd be willing to invest a little in the ranch."

Jackson laughed abruptly. "You want me to ask my mother if she'll invest in her ex-father-in-law's failing business?"

"No, I want you to ask your mother if she'll invest in her son's future."

"Not on your life." Jackson pulled a fork from the drawer and put his irritation into the art of scrambling. "She put up with enough from my old man, and Wiley would never forgive me if I asked her. He has his pride." And so did Jackson. He sprinkled salt and pepper over the eggs and turned up the heat on the burner. It was tough making decisions about the business from a distance, but that was exactly why he'd abandoned his career path in the first place. His *old* career path, he amended quickly. The ranch was his career.

"We can't let it lag too much," he said. "I promised Wiley we'd have that fence in before Christmas."

"Yeah, but for a chance at Sir Galahad, he'll understand if we have to extend the deadline a little."

"I'd have agreed with you six months ago." Jackson gave the eggs another whisk and tossed in paprika the way his mother had taught him. "But lately...I don't know, Rush. You've been around him the past couple of days, what do you think? Is he different, or is it just my imagination?"

"I haven't been around him a lot," Rush admitted. "He's holed up in the house and doesn't want to let me in. I don't think he trusts me, but he's okay with Annette and she says he's doing fine."

"That's my point," Jackson said wearily. "A few years ago, he wouldn't have pulled a stunt like that. He was one of the most reasonable men I'd ever met. Now, once he gets his mind set on something, he just won't budge."

"He's getting older, Jackson. Maybe he's entitled."

"It's not a question of entitlement," Jackson said. "I'm worried about him."

"I know you are, but he'll be fine."

Maybe for a little while, but not forever. No matter how hard they fought, some things were inevitable. And then where would Jackson be?

"Look," Rush said, interrupting his maudlin thoughts and dragging him back to the moment. "You just concentrate on finding Angel. Leave things here to me. I'll get the guys working on the barn. If I hear anything else about Sir Galahad, I'll let you know."

Jackson muttered agreement and disconnected, but he couldn't shake the feeling that he was racing toward disaster, and that Angel's disappearance was just the tip of the iceberg.

CECILY FONTAINE'S OFFICE was located in a three-story brick building six miles from police headquarters, tucked carefully away in a remote place, with the idea that anyone who had to use her services could come and go without being spotted by her colleagues. Much as Lucy resented having to be there, she did appreciate that.

She was already running late by the time she pulled into the parking lot and began winding her way through rows of parked cars, looking for an empty spot. Storm clouds hung low overhead, and a light rain had been falling for the past hour. Now puddles dotted the pavement and the rhythm of the windshield wipers as they slapped water from the windshield was the only thing that broke the silence.

She'd stalled too long in the shower and spent too much time reading the back of the cereal box, and now she was sorry. With just five minutes before she was due in the psychiatrist's office, she was trying to remain optimistic. If she could find a parking spot, and if the elevator gods would just smile on her, she could still make it, and nobody would be able to read any resentment—subconscious or otherwise—into her late arrival.

After minutes that felt like hours, she wedged her car into a tight spot, inched open the door and managed to extricate herself without earning more than a couple of bruises. Slipping her keys into her pocket, she jogged through rows of cars, darted in front of a slow-moving truck and reached the building with just three minutes to go.

Still determined to make it, she reached for the door handle just as it flew open to let someone else out. She was in such a hurry, she didn't recognize the other person at first, and she had only a dim realization that she was a woman. Completely focused on getting to the elevators, she started to slip past the other person and into the building, but a familiar voice stopped her short.

"Lucy?"

She turned and found herself looking into the wary brown eyes of Abby Carlton, one of the six-pack. Lucy hadn't seen her since the night their friendships had completely fallen apart, and running into her this morning—especially here—left Lucy off balance.

Shivering slightly, Abby stepped out of the rain and into the protection of the recessed doorway. Questions burned in her eyes, just as they must in her own, but, thankfully, Abby seemed as reluctant to admit aloud her reasons for being there as Lucy was.

A born nurturer, Abby had quickly become the "mother" of the group even though she was one of the youngest members. She'd been furious with Lucy for doubting Risa's innocence, but she smiled this morning as if nothing had ever happened. Lucy just couldn't tell whether she was genuinely glad to see her or putting up a good front, and she didn't have time to find out.

"I thought that was you," Abby said. "It's been a while."

Not wanting to offend, Lucy resisted the urge to glance at her watch. "Yes, it has. How've you been?"

"Fine. You?"

Of all the six-pack, Abby was the one most likely to relate to her feelings over Tomas Avila's death, but even if she'd felt right about unburdening herself, she didn't have time to do it now. "You know," she said with a shrug. "Same old, same old." Maybe the past few days were starting to get to her, but even with the seconds ticking past and her future on the line, she couldn't make herself just walk away.

Abby glanced behind her at the door. "We had an incident last night. Rough case. I'm…" She glanced at the door again and shrugged. "I'm just getting off."

Lucy wouldn't have questioned that explanation for anything in the world. After graduating the academy, Abby had followed her heart and not her head. She'd left Houston to marry, but they'd split before the wedding had happened and she'd eventually come back to her roots. Last Lucy heard, she was working Crisis Intervention. Either her failed relationship or her new job had brought something new to the table, and her eyes were filled with a hard-earned wisdom that hadn't been evident before. Lucy found herself wondering what kind of friendship they might have had if not for the mistakes they'd made. Now they were reduced to mundane small talk. The kind of exchanges generally reserved for people you didn't know well, or didn't care about.

A dozen genuine questions rose to her lips. Do you ever see the others? Have you talked to Risa lately? Do you think she'll ever truly forgive me for doubting her? Can we fix this awful rift between us? And what happened to drive you here? But she couldn't make herself ask a single one of them.

"So you're still working in Crisis?"

Abby nodded. "And you're still with Missing Persons. I saw your name in the newspaper." Her expression sobered and her voice dropped. "I'm sorry about the boy."

Just as they had too often in the past five days, tears pooled in Lucy's eyes before she could stop them. She nodded, but she didn't trust herself to speak.

But Abby didn't miss a thing. "Are you doing okay?"

Nodding again, Lucy did her best to look normal. "I'm fine. It's just hard to deal with."

"I can imagine." Abby's concern and compassion seemed genuine, but that only made Lucy feel worse—especially since it must be obvious why she was standing outside this building at ten o'clock on a rainy Thursday morning. "What are you doing to get past it?"

"Working," Lucy hedged. "What else?"

The corners of Abby's mouth turned down. "That's always been the answer for you, hasn't it?"

"Work's always there," Lucy said with a thin smile.

"Yeah, but there's more to life than work."

They'd disagreed so often in the past on that very issue, Lucy didn't want to go there. Abby considered Lucy career-obsessed; Lucy had always thought Abby could benefit from a bit more commitment. But Lucy couldn't argue with her today. For the first time in her life, work was not the answer.

She gave a little shrug. "I'll get through it. I always do." She just hoped she sounded more convinced than she felt.

Abby's lips curved gently. "I'm sure you will. But just in case…" She dug a card from her pocket and slipped it to Lucy. "It doesn't hurt to have someone to talk to." Her gaze flicked toward the door and her smile grew a shade warmer. "A friend."

The gesture both surprised and touched Lucy. She dropped the card into her pocket and tried to hold herself together. The last thing she wanted was to arrive for her appointment late and emotional. "Thanks, Abby. I appreciate that." And she was surprised to find how much she meant it. She caught a glimpse of a clock in the lobby, realized that she was now a full ten minutes late, and gestured toward the door. "I'm sorry. I have to go."

Abby nodded, and Lucy wondered if she only imagined the slight pulling back. "Sure. I understand. Call if you need to. I mean that."

"Yeah." Lucy reached again for the door handle and tugged it open, but before she stepped inside she met Abby's gaze once more. "Take care of yourself."

"You, too."

And that was that. Abby turned away, and Lucy forced herself to put the encounter out of her mind as she raced toward the elevators. For the first time since they'd drifted apart, she had the disturbing feeling that she wasn't going to be all right until she'd made an effort to patch things up with the others.

But she didn't have time to worry about that now. Cecily would probably read all sorts of things into her late arrival. Lucy couldn't explain the delay without dredging up her personal history—and that was something she had no intention of sharing with Cecily Fontaine.

CHAPTER EIGHT

CECILY WAS WAITING FOR her, of course. Lucy found her standing beside her assistant's desk, pretending to go over some paperwork. She was a pleasant-looking woman of about forty with short-cropped brown hair and a friendly smile that matched her telephone voice. To give her credit, she didn't show any sign of disapproval over Lucy's late arrival.

After shaking hands as if they were old friends, she led Lucy into a large office with wide windows, an abundance of plants and a fountain in one corner. It was so perfectly put together, Lucy decided Cecily either had a lot in common with her mother, or she'd paid someone a healthy sum to feng shui her workspace.

Cecily indicated a chair covered in pale blue leather so soft Lucy wondered how much the city gave her for a decorating budget. "I'm glad you decided to keep your appointment," she said, lowering herself into a matching desk chair. She sat back in the chair, almost pointedly refraining from picking up the pen that sat on an open notebook. "I was afraid something might happen to keep you away."

"I said I'd be here," Lucy reminded her.

"Yes, but you also made it quite clear that your case would come first."

Lucy stiffened. "Are you saying it shouldn't?"

"Not at all." Cecily crossed her legs and her friendly smile never wavered. "It's a pleasure to meet you, Lucy. Nick had a lot of good things to say about you."

"So you've already discussed me?"

"Briefly. You should be pleased to know that Nick considers you one of his best officers."

The compliment surprised Lucy. How was she supposed to respond to that? "I like what I do," she said after a pause that felt way too long.

"You're lucky. Not many people get to earn a living doing something they love." Cecily linked her fingers together in her lap and set one leg moving gently. "So, why don't you tell me what you'd like to talk about?"

"What *I* want to talk about?" Lucy laughed before she could stop herself. "That's going to be a short list."

"That's perfectly all right."

"I'd rather not talk about anything," Lucy admitted. "I don't see any reason to be here."

"I'm aware of that, too." Cecily smiled again, this time as if they shared a secret. "There's no need to be defensive. These sessions aren't designed so I can evaluate you as a human being. I just want to help you process what happened with your last case."

"Can you short-circuit the grieving process?"

"Would you like to?"

Lucy shook her head and shifted uncomfortably in her chair. "I don't think there's a good answer to that question."

"The truth is always good."

"Well, we'll stick with that, then."

"So would you like to short-circuit the grieving process?"

"What I'd like is to stop feeling guilty about Tomas's death." The admission surprised her as much as it seemed to please Dr. Fontaine.

"Why do you feel guilt?"

"Because I didn't save him, and I should have."

"In a perfect world."

But that was the point, wasn't it? They didn't live in a perfect world, but Lucy's job was to compensate for that. To take up the slack where the world fell short.

"Why don't we start at the beginning," Cecily suggested. "Tell me about Tomas."

"I don't see what good that would do."

"Maybe none. That's what we're here to find out, isn't it?"

Could she talk about it? Lucy wasn't sure. Just thinking about it made her edgy and nervous. "I'm sure you've read about it in the newspapers," she hedged.

"But that's not the story I want to hear." Cecily's smile softened slightly. "There's no hurry. Tell me what you feel comfortable with, or don't tell me anything at all. I want you to set the pace for these sessions."

Sessions. Plural.

Lucy's stomach turned over at the idea of repeated visits to the psychiatrist's office. One was bad enough. She had a feeling that despite Cecily's friendly demeanor, she wouldn't be satisfied until she'd learned far more than Lucy wanted to tell.

JACKSON HAD NEVER BEEN the fastest guy at reading other people's moods, but even he could tell that something was bothering Lucy. He'd waited half the morning for her phone call, and when it finally came she'd seemed strangely tense. Now that they were together, he was absolutely certain something was wrong.

Instead of the fluid movements and unflappable focus he'd grown used to over the past five days, she seemed disjointed and distracted. She'd put up no argument over tak-

ing his truck instead of her car. She'd been sitting silently
for blocks, staring out the window at nothing, and when
he spoke, she jumped as if she'd forgotten he was there.

By the time he drove halfway across town, he realized
the day would be a complete waste of time if she didn't
snap out of it. Besides, he hated seeing her like this. He
liked her energy and resolute determination. He'd been
touched more than once by her compassion, and her commitment to finding Angel and setting his world right felt
almost personal at times—and that had kept him going.

When he saw a sign announcing a city park up ahead,
he pulled off the street and found a shady place to park.
The rain had stopped and the sun peeked out from behind
innocent-looking clouds, so he figured they were safe—at
least for a few minutes.

Lucy didn't even seem to notice they'd stopped until he
opened his door to get out. Finally pulling herself out of
her daze, she managed a fair imitation of a scowl. "What
are you doing?"

"Going for a walk." He jumped to the pavement and
pocketed his keys. "Come with me."

Her eyes narrowed in confusion. "You want to take a
walk? Now?"

"Right now. Come on and keep me company." When she
didn't move, he shut his door, crossed in front of the truck
and opened hers. "Come on," he said again. "You've been
calling the shots for days. Now it's my turn."

Still obviously confused, she got out of the truck. But
when he took her hand and tugged her toward the walking
path that curved in and out of the trees, she followed without argument. He set an easy pace and walked for a while
in silence, waiting for Lucy to say something that might
explain her mood.

She left her hand in his, but she seemed so far away he was pretty sure it wasn't a conscious decision. He liked the feel of their fingers laced together—maybe a little too much—but he didn't let go or pull away. And when they'd walked for a while and she still hadn't spoken, he knew he was going to have to take the reins himself.

Knowing she wouldn't be happy, he drew her off the path toward a bench where she finally seemed to return to the moment. "Where are we going now?"

"Right here." He brushed raindrops from the seat, motioned for her to sit, then sank down beside her. It felt oddly natural to be here with her, but he tried not to think about that.

"Now you want to sit?"

"Sure." He ignored the moisture soaking into his jeans and concentrated on her eyes. They were pretty eyes. Soft and dark and compelling, and he suddenly wanted to understand all the secrets they held. But he told himself to be satisfied with one. "What I really want is to find out what's eating at you."

Her gaze shot to his, but at least he had her attention. "I don't know what you mean."

"Oh, come on, Lucy. You're a terrific cop, but you aren't exactly a world-class actress. Something's chewing on you, so let's talk about it."

She pulled back sharply, and he could see a denial forming on her lips.

"Don't insult me by saying there's nothing wrong," he warned. "I might not be the sharpest tool in the shed, but even I know a worried woman when I see one."

"I—" She cut herself off with a thin smile and stood, as if sitting beside him compromised her in some way. A light breeze stirred the leaves overhead and released a shower of moisture. She shivered in spite of the heat and wrapped her arms around herself. "It's nothing to do with the case."

"I never thought it was." And, strangely, he hadn't.

Her gaze slid toward him, but she didn't actually make eye contact. "It's personal."

"I kinda figured that, too." Instinct tried nudging him to his feet, and the urge to help her made him want to pull her into his arms. After all, he reasoned, that's what you did when a friend was hurting. But since there was nothing personal between them, he made himself stay right where he was. "How about we don't think of you as a cop working on a case," he said. "How about you just be Lucy for the next few minutes and I'll just be Jackson. Friends. I don't know how it works in your world, but in mine friends talk about things and even help each other from time to time."

Her gaze met his, and the mixture of irritation and amusement at the lines he'd stolen from her lifted his spirits considerably.

But she still couldn't seem to make herself speak.

"So what is it?" he prodded. "Trouble at home? Trouble at work? Trouble with the plumber?" Hoping to win a smile, he purposely deepened his drawl. "You might want to tell me, ma'am. I've been told I have quite an imagination, and I could get to thinking up all sorts of bad stuff if you leave me on my own."

She did smile, but it was a token gesture—the merest curve of a lip that didn't even come close to reaching her eyes.

"I know you mean well, but I really can't. It's—" Her gaze faltered and she took a deep breath. "Look, Jackson, I appreciate the offer, but I really can't talk about it."

The pain in her eyes pulled him to his feet. "It's more than an offer, Lucy. I know it's probably wrong a million ways from Sunday, but I think you and I could be friends under other circumstances." He decided to take a chance and admit something he'd hardly let himself think about. "Truth is, if we'd met under other circumstances, I'd be interested in seeing if we could be more than friends." He grinned and added, "You not being a troll and all."

She laughed, just as he'd hoped she would. "You are a charmer."

"You haven't seen anything yet." He stuffed his hands into his pockets to keep from reaching for her, but his arms itched to hold her and his heart ached from the agony he could see on her face. "It would be damn easy to care about you, Lucy. There are a dozen reasons or more why I shouldn't, but I think I could get around them without too much trouble."

Her smile evaporated and the shadows filled her eyes again. "Don't do this, Jackson. I'm not who you think I am."

"That's the point, isn't it? I don't know enough about you to think anything. All I know is what I see."

"Yeah, well, things aren't always the way they look."

She was shutting him down, but he had a gut feeling it wasn't because she wanted to. He touched her chin gently and tilted her head so she had to look at him. "I'd like to think that we've become friends, at least."

She moved away and put another couple of inches between them. "Please don't. I can't become involved with you on a personal level. Not even as friends."

"Why not?"

"Because you're involved in a case."

"Yeah. I am. So you can't get involved. Hell, I can't get involved, either. My niece is missing, and that's all I should be thinking about. So what kind of man does it make me when I catch myself thinking about the color of your hair or the fire in your eyes?"

She didn't speak, but she searched his face as he spoke and he thought her expression softened a little.

"Eventually, I'm going to have to leave here and go back to the ranch," he said. "I'll go back to spending my days thinking about horses and shoveling manure. I have no business even telling you this because even if everything else wasn't an issue, I have nothing to offer you. No home of my own, and a doubtful future. Thanks to Holden, the ranch is in such big trouble I'm not even sure I can save it."

He was on a roll now, saying things he hadn't even allowed himself to think. "I can't make promises. I shouldn't feel a damn thing for you, but here I am. I want to take you into my arms and make the world right for you when I can't even make it right for myself. So I understand all about why you shouldn't get involved with me, but do you really think I asked for this?"

To his surprise, a genuine smile tugged at the corners of her mouth and her eyes grew suspiciously bright. "No. I guess you probably didn't."

He moved closer, willing her not to pull away again. When she didn't, he let himself brush a stray piece of hair from her cheek and his fingertips burned where they touched her skin. "It's a fine mess we're in," he said softly.

"Yes." Her voice was little more than a whisper.

"I'm not sure I know the way out."

Her gaze dropped to her fingers. "I'm almost positive I don't."

"So what are we going to do about it?"

She lifted her gaze again, and her smile grew a little stronger. "I have absolutely no idea."

He let his fingers slide from her cheek to her chin. "Well, at least we're on the same page." Taking a huge chance, he leaned closer and touched his lips to hers—softly, in case it was too much for her.

Without warning, heat and need exploded together inside him, and he pulled away quickly. Even if it wasn't too much for Lucy, it just might be too much for him. He'd been looking for a soft place to fall, but he'd found a whole lot more.

Grinning sheepishly, he leaned back against the rain-wet park bench. "If I do that very often, Wiley's going to have one helluva time getting me back in the horse dung."

Lucy actually worked up an impish smile. "There you go, sweet-talking me again. I don't think I've ever been compared to horse dung before."

With a relieved laugh, he drew her into his arms and brushed a kiss to her forehead. "Lucy, there's one thing I can say with complete honesty. There is absolutely no similarity between you and horse dung." He chanced one more light kiss on her lips and decided he'd pushed enough for one day. "You don't have to tell me what's on your mind, but when you're ready, I'm here."

He felt a sigh leave her body. "Thank you."

"If looking for Angel is too much today—"

She cut him off before he could finish. "Don't even say it. No matter what else is happening, Angel comes first." She squared her shoulders and seemed to pull herself together in front of his eyes. "Angel is not going to suffer because of me. It's not her fault."

"If you're sure…"

"Of course I'm sure." She pulled away gently and dragged him to his feet with her. "Besides, if we stay here any longer, you might flatter me with some more of that sweet talk. I'm not sure I can take it."

He laughed and followed her back onto the path, and

his admiration for her surged. She was a complex woman and more than a little fascinating. He could spend a lifetime exploring all the facets of her personality and never get bored.

It was just too bad he would never get that chance.

TWENTY MINUTES LATER, they pulled up in front of the Fitzgeralds' run-down split-entry home and Lucy knew it was back to business. That interlude in the park had been idyllic, but she wondered if Jackson would feel the same way about her if she had taken advantage of his offer to talk about what was wrong.

Her appointment with Cecily had been predictable, but difficult. Talking about Tomas had nearly torn her in two, and Cecily had raised some tough questions about the future. Nothing Lucy hadn't asked herself, but coming from someone else made her doubts seem more real somehow.

Doing her best to stop thinking about that morning, she walked with Jackson past the makeshift parking lot on the Fitzgeralds' front lawn. Nothing had changed since their last visit. Boards were still missing from the fence, and someone had covered a broken panel of glass beside the door with a garbage bag held in place with duct tape. Weeds sprouted in places where even weeds shouldn't live, and the entire place had an air of sad neglect about it.

Somewhere inside a television blared daytime programs, and the bitter scent of cigarette smoke drifted out through open windows to meet them. Obviously someone was home this time, and her adrenaline kicked in with a rush.

Heavy footsteps on the stairs sounded in response to her knock, and a large dark shadow on the glass warned her a split second before the door swung wide. A burly man in his early forties glared out at them. His dark hair stuck out from his head as if it hadn't been brushed in a while, and at least two days' growth shadowed his cheeks and chin.

"Yeah? Wha'd' ya want?" When he moved farther into the light, Lucy noticed dark patches of sweat staining his shirt.

Charming.

"Mr. Fitzgerald?"

He looked down his nose at her. "Who wants to know?"

"I'm Detective Montalvo with HPD. This is Jackson Davis. We're looking for your son. Is he around?"

He sniffed and skimmed a glance over Jackson. "Which son?"

"We're looking for Wayne."

With a grunt, Ed Fitzgerald pulled a soiled bandanna from a back pocket. "Whatever you want, you're wastin' your time. Wayne doesn't live here no more."

"Do you know where we can find him?"

The man's eyes narrowed into wary slits. "What do you want him for?"

She could feel Jackson stirring behind her, and she willed him silently to remain patient. "We just have a few questions we need to ask him. Can you tell us where he is?"

"You here to harass him again?"

"No. We just want to ask him some questions. Can you tell us where to find him?"

A smirk curled the man's foul lips. "I don't remember."

And Jackson wondered why things moved so slowly. "Is your wife at home?" Lucy asked, still trying to sound pleasant. "Maybe her memory's a little better."

Fitzgerald leaned against the door frame and regarded her insolently. "She's working."

"Is there anyone else here who might be able to tell us where Wayne is living? Or even where he works?"

Fitzgerald wagged his head slowly, but the challenge in his eyes grew hard and cold.

"All we want to do it talk to him," Jackson interrupted. "So why don't you do the lady a favor and just tell her where he is?"

Still snarling, Fitzgerald pulled a toothpick from a pocket and wedged it between his teeth. He spent several seconds situating it just so. "We ain't seen Wayne in weeks," he said at last. "Months, maybe."

Irritated that he would answer Jackson and not her, Lucy shifted gears. She'd encountered chauvinistic attitudes before. Every female officer on the force did, and far too often. But men like Ed Fitzgerald never failed to grate on her nerves. "Was that before he went to jail," she asked, "or after?"

Fitzgerald moved the toothpick to the other side of his mouth. "Before."

"Then you haven't seen him since his release?"

He folded his beefy arms across his chest. "No. So like I said, you're wastin' your time."

"I think it's you who's wasting our time," Jackson said, his voice low and almost threatening. "We're trying to find a young girl who's been missing for nearly a week. We've been told Wayne knows her."

Fitzgerald's eyes narrowed even farther. "Wayne don't know that girl."

"How would you know that?"

"I just know."

"Yeah. I'll bet you do."

Afraid that Jackson would push too far, Lucy gave him a gentle nudge with her elbow and tried to regain control. "If Wayne doesn't know her," she said, "then I'm sure he won't mind answering a few questions for us." But both men seemed to have forgotten that she was even there.

Fitzgerald jerked his head toward Patrice's house. "You talking about that little girl who lives up there?"

"That's right."

"You think Wayne took her?"

"We never said that," Lucy said firmly. "We only want to ask him a few questions."

Fitzgerald snorted a laugh. "Oh, yeah. Just a few questions." He mopped his neck and face with the bandanna and returned it to his pocket. "I know what you people are like. Don't think I don't. You decide somebody done something, and then you twist facts around to make it look real. Happens all the time around here."

"It's not going to happen this time," Lucy insisted.

But Fitzgerald went on as if she hadn't even spoken. "Wayne may be in trouble from time to time, but there's no way he knows what happened to that little girl, and I ain't going to let you make it look like he does."

There had been whispers of corruption within HPD over the years, but Lucy had never taken them seriously. Even if some allegations were true, she resented having her integrity questioned by this oily piece of humanity. "Nobody's trying to make your son look guilty of anything," she said firmly. "We just want to know if Wayne has seen or talked to Angelina recently, and what she may have said to him if they did speak."

"I told you before, Wayne don't know that little girl. You want to find out where she is, try the mall. Ask some of those kids from down at the skating rink. Trouble's always brewing down there, and some of those kids are real bad news."

Lucy shot a glance at Jackson, but she couldn't read his expression. "Which skating rink?"

"The one over on Sheldon."

"And what makes you think they'd know anything about Angelina?"

"Because I see her there all the time when I go pick up my youngest boy." He scratched at his chest and spent another few seconds finding a new location for his toothpick. "Saw her there just last weekend, as a matter of fact. She was hanging all over some kid."

"Do you know who the boy was?"

He shrugged casually. "Those kids all look alike to me. Shaved heads and pants down around their ankles. All I know is it wasn't *my* kid, so go hassle somebody else. I've got things to do."

Before she could stop him, he slipped back into the house and slammed the door between them.

Jackson lunged for the doorknob, but she caught his wrist before he could turn it. "Leave it, Jackson. You can't force your way into his house, and it's pretty obvious he's through talking—at least for now."

"He knows where Wayne is," Jackson argued. "You saw that as plainly as I did."

"I think you're probably right, but he's not going to share that with us. He did give us a lead, though. One more place to look. We can be grateful for that."

"He could be trying to throw us off the scent."

"And he could be telling the truth."

"You really believe that?"

"It's possible."

"Come on, Lucy. You can't really mean to walk away—"

"That's exactly what I mean to do."

"When you know damn well Fitzgerald is holding back information?"

"I don't know that, and neither do you. I know you want it to be that easy, but it's not, and I'm not going to stand

around here while you take out your frustrations on someone who may be completely innocent. Get a grip on yourself, Jackson. You're an intelligent, reasonable man. You
know that pushing him isn't going to accomplish anything
except maybe help you release some tension. In the end,
it will only make things worse, and I know that's not what
you want."

"I *want* to find Angel."

"Then let's go about it the smart way. If we need to come
back, we will, and we may even get more out of him next
time. Maybe his wife will tell us what we need to know.
But he's not going to tell us anything right now."

He remained ramrod stiff and she could almost see the
argument he was having with himself playing out across
his face. Drawing on all of her patience and experience, she
waited silently for him to calm down. Little by little, she
saw his shoulders relax, then the muscles in his face, and
she knew the worst was over—at least for now.

"Come on," she said. "Let's get out of here."

He followed her down the sidewalk to the car, but she
could see by the set of his jaw and the fire in his eyes that
he still wasn't far from the boiling point. They both needed
a way to release tension before one of them erupted. After
those kisses they'd shared in the park, one idea danced ap-
pealingly through Lucy's mind, but she couldn't let herself seriously consider that. Becoming even *more* involved
with Jackson would only complicate everything. But
maybe they *could* be friends.

Friends, and just a little bit more.

CHAPTER NINE

EVEN LUCY COULDN'T LIE to herself about this one. She'd crossed a line and there would be no going back. Propped against a wall, she pressed a cool bottle of water to her forehead and let her gaze drift across the gym toward the weight bench. Long, lean and looking incredibly handsome, Jackson lay back on the bench and pressed the weights above his head. His muscles strained from the effort, and Lucy felt her mouth go dry.

What had she been thinking? Between her appointment with Cecily and yesterday's run-in with Ed Fitzgerald, Lucy had lost all sense of propriety. Yes, both she and Jackson needed something to help with the tension they felt, but this… Well, this was just a bad idea.

Maybe she was being ridiculous. She should just walk out there and go through the routine she knew almost as well as she knew her own name. But for some reason, she couldn't get one foot to move in front of the other.

Those kisses in the park had opened the door on something she wasn't ready to handle. After all, she'd known Jackson for less than a week. It had been an intense week for both of them, but that only meant that neither of them was thinking clearly. Her reaction to the sight of his almost-bare chest and solid legs was irrefutable proof that she wasn't.

But she couldn't stand in the corner all day. She'd just have to pull herself together and get her head on straight.

Clutching her bottle in one hand and a towel in the other, she made her way across the cavernous room toward the rows of treadmills. She tossed the towel over the bar, chose her program and focused on the way her muscles felt as they began to stretch. At least she tried to.

In spite of her stern internal warnings, Lucy couldn't stop herself from admiring Jackson—the way he moved, the glow of his skin, the curve of his smile as he talked to people around him. And the flicker of interest in her belly, the tickle that ignited a slow flame when he saw her and started toward her, killed the last weak, silent protest that she wasn't falling for him.

She forced herself to look straight ahead and concentrated on her run.

Climbing onto the machine beside hers, he said, "Much as I hate to say it, this was a good idea. Thanks."

She laughed at the grudging apology and treated herself to another quick glance. "You're welcome. I guess you probably don't have to use machinery to work out when you're home."

"Not this kind, that's for sure. Wiley would have a fit if he could see this."

"Really? Why?"

"Why walk on a piece of metal when there are plenty of real places under God's own sky you can walk?"

"Because not every place under God's own sky is safe, is open at six o'clock in the morning or stays dry when it's raining."

Jackson laughed. "Yeah? But they probably all smell better."

"I don't know about that. You think a cow pasture smells better than this?"

"Wiley would."

The program shifted and Lucy increased her pace. She fell into the rhythm after only a couple of steps and let her body move in time to the music playing over the loudspeaker. "I'm sure Wiley would," she said. "But what do you think?"

Jackson looked at her. "As long as my muscles don't atrophy, I'm fine with either choice."

His careful answer made her think he was holding something back. She couldn't fault him. She was holding back plenty herself. But she was still curious. "Do you always do that?"

"Do what?"

"Shove yourself down inside somewhere and defer to Wiley?"

His machine picked up the pace, and Jackson started to run faster. "Is that what you think I do?"

"It sure seems like it. You're working the job he wants you to work and you're living the life he wants you to live. You don't even have an opinion about where you exercise."

"I have plenty of opinions," he said with a sly smile. "I just don't feel the need to voice them all the time."

"You're a closed book, is that it?"

"Something like that."

She'd been accused of the same thing many times, so she had no business passing judgment on him. But she'd never really understood how frustrating her habit of keeping to herself must have been for friends and family. "And you're content with that?"

"I have a good life," he said with a shrug. "What's not to be content about?"

Lucy felt an urgent need to know what went on behind those hazel eyes. She knew how he felt about Wiley, his father, Holden and Angelina. She even knew how he felt about the ranch. But she had no idea how he felt about himself.

"So you're content, but are you happy?"

He lifted his shoulder again as if the answer didn't matter. "I'm happy enough. What about you?"

"The truth? I don't know." The honesty of her answer surprised her as much as it seemed to surprise him. "You and I are opposites in one way, but we're a lot the same, too. You've given up your dreams for everyone around you, and I've given up any other kind of life to have my dream. I'm not sure either solution is healthy."

Jackson didn't say anything for several minutes, and Lucy was afraid she'd gone too far. Then he asked, "So what would you do differently if you could?"

"I'm not sure," she admitted. "I suppose if I knew, I'd already be doing it."

He grinned and stepped off the treadmill and onto the sides of the machine as if he'd been using one all his life. "That's the problem, isn't it? You might know something's missing, but not what it is. It's a little hard to plug the holes in your life if you don't know where they are."

"And would you if you knew? Or are you too set in your ways to stir things up?"

"I suppose that would depend on what I found." He ran an appreciative glance along her body and the smile slipped from his face. "It would have to be something pretty special to be worth the trouble."

A delicious shiver of anticipation traveled the same path his gaze had taken. Lucy tried to laugh it off, but it settled low in her belly and coiled outward in slow, sensuous waves. It had been a long, long time since she'd felt this

way, and her step faltered as she ran, forcing her to grab
for the handrails to keep her balance.

Suddenly angry with herself, she stopped the treadmill
and grabbed her towel. She was making a big mistake to
let this attraction for Jackson take root. A big mistake.

But there was no denying that she felt more alive than
she had in years.

THE WEST-SIDE TRUCK HAVEN was a series of connected
buildings that housed a gas station, showers for road-weary
truck drivers and a large diner. It sat on a huge parking lot
dotted with cars, tractor-trailers and pickups. The scents of
gasoline and diesel fuel overpowered everything else, and
Lucy could see fumes rising in the heat as she parked her car.

After their conversation with Ed Fitzgerald, she was a
little reluctant to send Jackson off on his own, but they still
needed to check out the skating rink, and clues were already growing cold. She really didn't have much choice.
She just prayed that someone here would know something
about Patrice.

"Which do you want," she asked, "the gas station or the
diner?"

Jackson watched a couple of truckers push out through
a glass door, another who paused to tamp a new pack of
cigarettes against a concrete post. "I'll take the gas station."

"Great. Just find out if anyone remembers Patrice, and
if they've seen her or heard from her recently." She opened
her car door and started to climb out into the steamy heat.
"Maybe somebody has remained friends with her, or knows
where she's working. Anything at all would be a help."

With a brisk nod, he joined her outside. With so much
at stake, she shouldn't notice the way his shirt molded to
his arms and shoulders. The way it tapered sharply as it dis-

appeared into the waistband of his jeans. The way sunlight played in his tousled blond curls….

Turning away sharply, she slipped her fingers around the badge in her pocket to remind herself who she was and what she was doing here. "Meet back here when we're finished."

"What about the truck drivers? We're talking to them, too, aren't we?"

"Talk to anyone who'll listen, but don't expect much. The drivers are all over the country all the time, so there's no guarantee that any of them have been here before."

Jackson nodded and turned away, and the somber expression on his face made a profound sadness open up inside her. *Please,* she begged silently, *let us find something that will set his mind at ease.*

She watched him walk away, then turned resolutely toward the diner. Inside, the air conditioner cut the worst of the heat and the scents of hot beef and grease made her stomach growl. A waitress of about fifty with big blond hair and a bored smile looked up as she entered and jerked her head to motion Lucy inside. "Pick a spot, honey. I'll be with you in a minute."

Lucy passed a row of booths lining the wall, each of which came equipped with a bouquet of plastic yellow flowers and a telephone. Three of the booths were occupied by drivers who looked ready for a shower and a nap. The rest were empty and waiting.

She chose a stool at the counter and hummed along with the Shania Twain song on the jukebox. Just as Shania fell silent, the waitress, whose name tag identified her as Margaret, slid a glass of ice water onto the counter in front of her.

"You know what you want already?"

Leaning forward, Lucy produced her badge. "Water's fine. Food smells great, but I'm here on business."

Margaret's boredom vanished, but wariness replaced it. "What's wrong now?"

"I'm looking for a woman who used to work here. Her name's Patrice Beckett."

"Patrice? What do you want with her?"

Lucy's heart did a little tap dance in her chest. "I just need to ask her a few questions. Do you know where I can find her?"

Margaret glanced over her shoulder and rested her elbows on the counter, exposing her ample bosom. "I haven't seen her since she left here. What's she done?"

"I don't know that she's done anything. Do you have any idea where I can find her?"

"Not really. She came in for her last check a couple of weeks after she left, but that's the last I saw her."

"You haven't talked to her on the phone? E-mailed? Maybe heard how she's doing from a mutual friend?"

Margaret shook her head slowly. "No, but we weren't exactly close friends while she was here."

The answers were becoming predictable, and Lucy's frustration level rose sharply. "Did she have any close friends?"

"Not really. She barely spoke to the cooks. Course most of them hardly speak English. She was kind of friendly with Maya for a little while, but then they had a falling out." Margaret dug at something on the counter with her fingernail. "Patrice had an attitude, if you want to know the truth. Thought she was too good to work here. So what's she done?"

Lucy hesitated to tell her, but maybe letting word get out would help find Angelina or bring Patrice home. "We have a report that her daughter is missing," she said. "We're trying to determine if that's true, or if Angelina is with Patrice."

Margaret's eyes widened slightly. "So she finally did it?"

Lucy's hand froze on her glass. "Did what?"

"The kid finally ran off. Not that she hasn't before, but…well, you know."

"I'm not sure I do," Lucy said. "Why don't you tell me?"

Margaret pulled a piece of gum from her pocket and unwrapped it slowly. "I don't know a whole lot," she said with a shrug. "Just that Patrice was always complaining about having trouble with the kid. If it wasn't one thing, it was another."

"What kinds of things?"

"Patrice was always upset with her. Always looking for her. Always calling around trying to find her. Truth to tell, I think that's one of the reasons she lost her job. Her mind was always on that, not on what she was supposed to be doing."

Time seemed to slow as Lucy tried to wrap her mind around what she was hearing. Margaret's claims were so different from what Hank and Mr. Smith had told them, she could hardly take it in, and she had no idea how Jackson would react. "Has Angel ever disappeared for several days at a time?"

"Not that I know of," Margaret admitted, "but that doesn't mean she hasn't. She gave Patrice plenty of trouble, that's all I know. But Patrice wasn't exactly a fountain of information, if you know what I mean. She kept to herself, mostly."

Lucy felt the familiar buzz of excitement. "What kind of trouble?"

Margaret shrugged, seemed to realize she should be working, and began straightening straws in a glass container. "They were always arguing. I know that much. Patrice might not have liked the job, but she was a hard worker. Had to be, on her own that way. The girl didn't like her being gone, I guess. She'd take off wherever and whenever she wanted to. Just how her mother was supposed to keep a roof over her head without leaving home is beyond me, but you know kids."

Lucy struggled to hold on to her patience. "Do you know where Patrice would go looking for her?"

"Naw. Like I said, we didn't really talk much."

"And you have no idea where Patrice might be now?"

"Nope. Sorry."

"What about men? Was Patrice dating anyone?"

"Not that I know of. At least not anyone steady."

"And you don't know if she had another job lined up?"

Margaret shook her head. "She came in, got her check and left again."

And you don't know where Angel used to go when she left home?"

"Hung out with friends is all I know. Doing what kids do." The bell over the door tinkled, announcing a new customer, and Margaret's mood shifted abruptly. "Look, I don't know what to tell you. There just isn't much I can say. Now, are you gonna order something or just stick with your water?"

"The water's plenty." Lucy said. But as she watched the woman sashay across the room toward the heavyset trucker filling the entranceway, she wondered how two stories could differ so wildly. Hank was convinced Angel was a quiet, unassuming, respectful girl. To hear Margaret tell it, she was anything but. The truth probably lay somewhere in the middle. Lucy just hoped she could figure out soon.

BY EIGHT O'CLOCK THAT NIGHT, Rollerworld was jumping. A steady stream of cars pulled into the parking lot, paused near the front of the building long enough to disgorge groups of noisy kids and disappeared again. Still trying to digest what Lucy had told him after their visit to Truck Haven, Jackson followed her through the gathering darkness toward the building. Muffled music pulsed through the air, and each time the front doors opened, voices and laughter floated out to meet them.

Movement near the corner of the building caught Jackson's eye and he turned slightly just in time to see two kids, lips locked, shifting deeper into the shadows and away from curious eyes. Four boys, none of them much older than Angelina, came out from behind a parked car. Each of them held a lit cigarette between their fingers and walked with the calculated air of someone trying to look tough, no doubt to impress the clusters of girls who were all dressed in clothes too skimpy for their age.

The noise, the lights, the confusion all made his shoulders tense painfully. Or maybe it was the strain of realizing that Angel really may have run away. He tried to imagine Angel here. Had she been one of the young, innocent kids here just to skate with friends? Or was she one of the others?

So many questions remained unanswered. Had Angel run away? If so, why? How did Wayne Fitzgerald figure in to her disappearance, or did he figure in at all? Some days, Jackson was almost certain they were on the brink of finding her. Tonight, he wasn't feeling so optimistic.

When they reached the door, he took a deep breath, steeled himself for what they'd find inside, and held the door while Lucy passed through. Now that the ice between them had been broken, he was more aware of her than ever. Of the color of her hair, the clean scent of her shampoo. The curve of her cheek, the gleam of intelligence in her eyes, and the soft musk scent she wore that filled the space between them each time she moved.

It was wrong to let his mind wander from finding Angel and tracking down Patrice, even for that split second, but he couldn't seem to stop himself. He wasn't proud of that, but he did wonder what might have happened if they'd met in another time, another way.

Luckily, the noise inside Rollerworld wiped the question right out of his mind. Hordes of young teenagers waited in line to pay their admission fee. Music blared out into the entryway, and through an open door he could see strobe lights flashing into the darkness.

Lucy watched everything intently, as she always did. She had her game face on, ready to divide and conquer just the way they'd planned. Once inside, he'd move to the right and she'd move to the left, showing Angel's picture to kids and employees, searching for anyone who might know her, keeping one eye open all the time in case she was here tonight.

But would he even recognize her if she was? He hated knowing that he might not.

It took only a few minutes to work their way up in line and for Lucy to explain to the young man behind the window what they needed. And then they were inside, enveloped in the darkness, surrounded by the overwhelming noise, ready to begin the endless round of questions he'd asked so many times already.

He wasn't a bit surprised when the first few kids he approached gave the picture of Angel just a cursory glance before claiming not to know her. If he'd learned nothing else from Holden's frequent brushes with trouble, he'd learned that most people would rather not get involved. Even teenagers came equipped with that self-protective instinct.

Moving from table to table, he tried to look approachable, even friendly. Like someone the kids could trust. Someone they might want to confide in. After more than an hour of music, lights and kids who claimed not to know anything, Jackson was battling weariness and the growing belief that coming here had been a colossal waste of time.

Just when he thought he'd talked to everyone on his side of the room, he noticed a couple of girls he hadn't seen before and followed them past the snack bar and up a short ramp into a room lit with rows of black lights. The instant the girls hit the room, their white T-shirts became fluorescent and they blended in with dozens of other kids, most of whom were dancing in groups of two, three, four or more. There was no skating here, and some of the kids were curled up in couples, hidden from view of the employees who were doing their best to maintain order amid the chaos.

Slowly, Jackson made the rounds again, stopping to talk with anyone who would give him the time of day. Just as before, most of the kids either didn't know Angel or didn't know where to find her. But one young man, a kid of about fifteen whose dark hair fell in lank locks around his face and whose cheeks were flushed with red, did a double-take before handing back the picture.

"Sorry man," he shouted. "Don't know her."

Jackson might have believed him if not for the sly look on his face as he turned away. He caught the kid by the arm and held out the picture. "Why don't you take another look? Maybe it'll jog your memory."

"I said I don't know her. What do you want from me?"

"How about the truth?" Suddenly fed up with shouting to make himself heard, Jackson jerked his head toward the slash of light that marked the doorway. "Give me five minutes out there where I can hear you. I'll buy you a Coke or something."

The kid smirked unpleasantly. "Wow. Gee, mister, that'd be swell."

Smart-ass. "Maybe it's escaped your notice, but you're not old enough for anything else."

"That hasn't stopped me before."

"Yeah? Well it stops me." Jackson urged him forward, and though the kid looked unhappy, he didn't put up much of an argument. Jackson found a quiet corner—relatively speaking—and held up the picture again. "You know her, don't you?"

The boy very carefully avoided looking at the photograph. "I thought you were going to buy me a Coke."

"I will in a minute. How well do you know her?"

Maybe the kid figured out that Jackson meant business, or maybe the surly attitude just stopped being fun. He shrugged and raked hair out of his face with his fingers. "Pretty well, I guess. Why do you want to know?"

"I'm her uncle. I'm trying to find her."

"Her uncle?" The kid drew back slightly and looked Jackson over. "I didn't know she had an uncle."

Jackson slipped the picture back into his pocket. "Where is she?"

"What do you want her for?"

"I want to make sure she's all right."

The kid brushed back another lock of limp black hair and lifted one shoulder. "Sorry. I don't know where she is. I haven't heard from her for a while."

Jackson should have been used to disappointment by now, but every new failure still got to him. "Do you know anyone who might know?"

The boy shook his head. "Not for sure. She was talking a lot of trash about her mom last time I saw her, saying she was going to do this and that, but I didn't take her serious."

"What kinds of things did she say?"

"Oh, you know. She was going to leave home. Find somebody who cared about her. But she said it so often, nobody paid much attention anymore."

Find someone who cared about her. Was that how she'd learned about the ranch? If that's what she wanted, why hadn't she ever come to them? Was she on her way there now, or had she chosen to look for affection from someone else? There were so many possibilities, how could Jackson hope to cover them all? He had to force himself to stay focused on the boy in front of him and the questions he might be able to answer. "Do you think she finally did it?"

The boy shrugged again. "Who knows?"

That seemed to be the sixty-four-thousand-dollar question. "Does she have a best friend? Someone she might have confided in?"

"She has lots of friends, man. That's why nobody wants to talk to you. Everybody knows how her mom screwed her over, and nobody wants to help somebody else do it."

Jackson tried to keep his voice even. "How did her mom screw her over?"

"About her dad, man. You don't know anything, do you?"

He didn't need the reminder. "So tell me."

"I don't know everything," the kid said, backpedaling quickly. "I just know that Angel wanted to find out about her dad, but her mom wouldn't tell her. Said she didn't need to know. Like, you know, it was none of her business or something. It was rotten, man. That's all I've got to say."

Jackson's heart flopped. "You think she's gone looking for her dad?"

"Could be. She was going to get that one guy to help her since he had a car."

Everything inside Jackson turned to ice. "What one guy?"

"Wayne, I think. He's Toby's big brother."

"Wayne Fitzgerald?"

"I guess. All I know is he has a car and she was going to ask him to drive her if she could find her dad."

Jackson didn't know whether to be relieved or worried. The news alleviated *some* of his worries over her relationship with Wayne. Angel might have gone to Wayne for help, but if Wayne was the person Hank thought he was, it hadn't been a smart choice, or even a safe one.

And if Angel had found Holden? That possibility made him a little sick. Their meeting might start out well. Holden might even be able to play the part of caring father for a few days. But sooner or later, Holden would grow tired of the responsibility and what would happen then? He had a nasty habit of hurting people who stood in his way. "Do you know where we can find Wayne?"

The boy shook his head. "Not me, but Toby probably does."

"Is Toby here tonight?"

"Sure. He's outside, probably."

Getting information from people was like pulling teeth. "How will I know him when I see him?"

"He's about my size, I guess. Hair like mine. He's probably wearing a black sweatshirt. He usually does."

He'd just described more than half of the boys inside the skating rink, and probably all of them lurking outside. "Can you give me something more?"

The boy smirked again. "Yeah. He smokes Kools." A couple of kids came out of the dance room and the boy's demeanor underwent a dramatic change. Suddenly sullen again, he pushed away from the wall and swaggered past

Jackson. "You gotta feel sorry for a girl like Angel," he said, his voice low. "I kinda hope she gets what she wants."

Turning his back on Jackson, he jogged over to join his friends, said something under his breath and smirked back at Jackson when his friends burst into laughter. It was almost enough to make him wonder if the boy had just played him for a fool.

CHAPTER TEN

READY TO PUT THE NOISE and confusion of Rollerworld behind him, Jackson met Lucy near the skate-rental counter. "Anything?" he shouted over the deafening music.

"Nothing useful. What about you?"

"I think I found something," he shouted back. Grimacing, he jerked his head toward the door. "Let's get out of here. I can't hear myself think anymore."

With her lips so close to his ear and that scent filling the space between them, Jackson felt that now-familiar heat stir deep inside him. He would have given almost anything for just ten minutes to call his own. Without the worry that someone in his family had done something stupid. Ten short minutes to think about himself and his future. But this was the wrong time and the wrong place for that.

The music segued from one unbearably loud song to another. The strident guitar drove his headache up another notch, but the beat of the bass and drums filled the air with an almost sexual quality. No wonder kids were making out everywhere he looked. No damn wonder he was reacting to the soft swell of Lucy's breasts beneath her T-shirt and the nip of waist barely visible under her jacket.

"Come on," he said again. He could use some fresh air. Some space to think. A chance to get his head screwed on straight. Without waiting to see if she would follow, he headed for the door and plowed outside into the night, relieved to discover that the temperature had actually dropped by a few degrees.

"Jackson?" Lucy's voice sounded close behind him. "What is it? What's wrong?"

He stopped walking and turned to face her. "I talked to a kid in there who thinks Angel is looking for Holden. Says she was going to ask Wayne Fitzgerald to take her to him when she found him."

Lucy's eyes opened wide. "Is he sure?"

"It's a possibility, that's all I know." He glanced around at the groups of kids visible from where he stood. "He said Wayne's little brother, Toby, is probably out here somewhere. It might be worth a try to see if Toby can tell us where to look."

"Absolutely." She started to turn away but caught herself and ran an assessing glance over him from head to toe. "Are you okay?"

"I'm fine. Let's just do this." He was used to handling family crises on his own. He wasn't used to having someone else around to shoulder half the burden, someone to care about him, even for a second or two. It would be easy to get used to this. Too easy.

"Come on," he said, embarrassed to discover that his voice had grown gruff with longing. "We need to get Angel back before she finds herself in real trouble."

Lucy moved closer, touched his arm gently and set the dry kindling inside him aflame. "What if she's with Holden already?"

Jackson reached for her hand, needing the connection with her, wanting to believe it could last. "If she's with Holden, she'll probably be safe for a little while. But it won't last for long. He's too much like my old man. The first time Angel stands up to him, crosses him, argues with him…" He shuddered, reliving the memories. "We just need to find her, that's all."

Instead of getting back to business, Lucy twined her fingers through his and looked into his eyes. "We're going to find her."

"Better late than never, huh?"

"As a matter of fact, yes. Quit blaming yourself for this, Jackson. You're not doing yourself or Angel any good."

He rubbed the back of his neck and gave in to his anger. It was a whole lot more comfortable than this weakness and vulnerability that kept winding around him, threatening to knock him off balance. "Who else is there to blame?" he demanded. "I was just a kid when she was born, but even then I knew she was going to need me. Holden was too young and screwed up to be a decent father. I knew it. She knew it. Even as a baby. She took to me the first time I held her. She was only a day or two old, but she reached right up and touched my cheek, just like she was trying to tell me something."

He laughed in a vain attempt to hide the catch in his voice. "I know. I know. Babies so small can't do that. But she *did.* I knew right then and there that she and I had something special, but I let her down."

"What choice did you have?"

"I had a choice."

"Really?" Lucy planted herself in front of him. "Why don't you tell me what that choice was? What did you not do that you should have done?"

"I should have found her all those years ago."

"You were nineteen when she disappeared. Just how in charge of the world do you think you were? How in charge do you expect yourself to be now?"

He couldn't answer that, so he didn't bother to try. "All I know is, Angel wouldn't be out there right now if I'd done what I should have back then."

Lucy laughed harshly. "You don't know that for sure. There aren't any guarantees in this world."

"If she'd had the support of family—"

"Then maybe she'd still be home. And maybe not. Problems like this aren't confined to one type of family or one economic bracket, Jackson. Sometimes kids run away from good parents who do everything right. No matter what you and Wiley did, Angel might still have been curious about her dad. She might have run off even if you had been there."

He recoiled sharply. "We could have given her some roots so she wouldn't have to."

"You don't know if that would have made a difference."

"I do know. Angelina isn't like Holden."

A sad knowing filled Lucy's eyes. "Is that what you're afraid of?"

Jackson shook his head and looked away without answering.

"You're afraid she'll disappoint you?"

He clenched his jaw tightly enough to make something pop. "That's not it."

"Are you sure?"

"That's *not* it," he said again, but he wasn't sure which one of them he was trying to convince. "Even if it is, can you blame me for wondering? I've had this image of her since the day she was born. I've carried it with me for fourteen years. I've let that be what got me through the rough times. What if I—" He broke off, too disgusted with himself to say the words aloud. But Lucy didn't move and she didn't back away. She waited, eyes locked on his, until he made himself finish. "What if, when we find her, she's not…not what I've been making her up to be in my mind all these years? What if I don't love her? What kind of person will that make me? What will that do to her?" The idea hurt so much, he could barely force out the words.

"Do you really think that might happen?"

"I don't know." He pushed away from the truck, needing that space he'd come outside to find.

"Are you telling me you don't love your brother?" Lucy called after him.

He whipped back around to face her. "Don't judge me, Lucy. You don't know what he's put the family through."

"I'm not the one who's judging you," she said gently. "There's a big difference between unconditional love and unconditional approval. Just because you don't condone everything Holden does, that doesn't mean you don't love him."

"It's not that simple."

She smiled and moved close again. "Sure it is. You either love him or you don't. You either love Angel or you don't. From what I've seen of you the past few days, I don't think you're the kind of man to withdraw your love just because you don't like somebody's actions."

But that's exactly what he had done, over and over again since Holden began getting in trouble. "Holden wouldn't agree with you."

"Holden isn't in any position to judge." To his surprise, she leaned up and kissed him softly. Before he even had time to react, she'd stepped back and moved past him, as if she'd settled the matter once and for all. More than anything, Jackson wanted to believe that the solution could be that simple.

"GOT SOME BAD NEWS FOR YOU," Plumber Dave said the next morning about three minutes before roll call. "The support beams in your place are in bad shape. Worse even than I first told ya."

Groaning aloud, Lucy watched Orry Keenan and Darren Brady leave their desks and head toward the briefing room. Orry motioned for her to join them, but she held up a finger to indicate she'd be there in a minute. "So what are you saying?"

"I'm saying it might take me even longer than I first thought. And I'm gonna hafta work up a new estimate. I can't do the job for what I first told ya."

"That first quote was a minor fortune," Lucy argued. "Now it's going to be more?"

"Yeah, well, that's the joy of owning your own home. You want it safe, don'tcha?"

"Of course I do." But it would take her forever to pay off what he'd originally quoted. The thought of going even deeper into debt made her more than a little nervous.

"Hey, Lucy." Phil Babcock, returned at last from his mother's funeral, called out to her from across the bull pen. "Call for you on line one. I think it's your mother."

Without waiting for an answer, Phil headed for the door, leaving her alone—and late.

"I'm going to have to get back to you," she told the plumber. "Don't do anything until I talk to you again." Without waiting for a response, she punched the blinking light to connect herself to the second call. "Montalvo."

"Lucy, darling, I know you're busy, but I've talked with Marlene and Scott again. They can bring Janelle for dinner this Saturday. I'm calling to make sure that will work for you. Isn't that your day off?"

Still rattled from her conversation with the plumber, Lucy was defenseless against the sudden, senseless panic that hit her. She did her best to keep it from showing, but she knew her voice came out sounding almost strangled. "I can't do that, Mom."

"Oh, but I was so sure that's what I saw on your schedule."

"My schedule doesn't mean much right now. I'm in the middle of a case."

"You're not the only officer on the police force."

"No, but I'm the only one assigned to this case." The unnatural silence in the room made the panic surge higher. "I have to go, Mom. I'm late for morning briefing."

"Lucy—"

She hung up before her mother could prod further, and guilt only made the panic worse. She'd never hung up on her mother before, and the emotions warring inside made her feel fractured and unfamiliar, even to herself. Snagging a notebook from her desk, she raced into the briefing room and let out a sigh of relief when she realized Nick hadn't arrived yet.

Orry motioned for her to join him, and she made her way to his table gratefully.

"Hey, sunshine," he said with a grin. "I've got a present for you."

Smiling in spite of her frustrations, she sank into the chair beside his. "I hope it's a good one. I need something positive."

"What happened at the skating rink last night?"

She told him briefly about what Jackson had learned, and ended with "We spent another hour trying to find Toby Fitzgerald—no luck."

Orry wagged a thick file folder in front of her. "I'll make you a deal. You buy me lunch today. I'll give you this. A steak at Friar's sounds good, don't you think?"

"I'd say yes if my plumber hadn't just decided to finance

his European vacation out of my bank account." She snatched the folder away from him. "What is it?"

A pleased smile curved his lips and he folded his arms across his chest as he leaned back in his chair. "Wayne Richard Fitzgerald. Twenty-one years old. In and out of trouble for the past eight, nine years. Started off shoplifting when he was twelve and moved right on up the ladder to driving under the influence, possession and distributing controlled substances. Went to jail about six months ago and did ninety days. Got out the end of June."

Lucy had known some of that already, but she was stunned by the wealth of information Orry had found for her. A slow smile spread across her face. "If you weren't married, I'd kiss you for this."

Orry laughed and held up both hands with a teasing shudder. "Please! Don't threaten me."

Still grinning, Lucy leafed through more of the file. It was exactly as Orry had said—trouble from childhood right on to the present day. "Did you find any violence on his rap sheet?"

"A couple of domestic disturbances while he was living with his parents. His sister didn't like being pushed around and took matters into her own hands. Mommy bailed him out and sister dropped the charges. There's also an aggravated-assault charge two years ago. Got fired from a convenience store and went after his paycheck with a knife."

Everything inside grew cold at that. "And where is he now?"

"I don't know. He was living with his parents before he went to jail. Had an address near the docks after his release, but he's missed a couple of meetings with his probation officer and nobody knows where he is."

Lucy wondered what Jackson would think when he saw this. "If Angel's with him, do you think she's in danger?"

Orry shrugged. "The guy's bad news. No doubt about that. But there's no reason to believe he's going to deliberately hurt her—unless you count the possibility of getting her hooked on drugs or seducing her."

Lucy nodded slowly. "If all he did was deliver her to her father, she might still be all right."

"You think that's what happened?"

"That's what we're thinking at the moment," she said, closing the file. "But give us five minutes, and that could change."

Orry chuckled low in his throat. "Well, would you listen to that. You made a joke."

"Yeah? So?"

He leaned close and put a hand on her forehead. "Yep. The fever's broken. I think you're going to live, Montalvo."

She grinned in spite of her own doubts. "How do you know?"

"We've all been there," he said as Nick barged into the room and took control.

Lucy didn't have time to respond, but as Nick started the barrage of information, she wondered if Orry meant what he said. Had *he* been through therapy on the job? If so, she might have to rethink a few things. Because there was no one on the force she trusted more than Orry, and she'd fight anyone who tried to claim that he wasn't capable of doing the job.

ANGEL HAD BEEN MISSING for ten days when Jackson and Lucy finally got another break. After running headfirst into one brick wall after another, they found one guy on the docks who thought he remembered hearing that Wayne

Fitzgerald had a job with a shipping warehouse on the other side of town. It was hardly a solid lead, but for the first time in days, Jackson felt his hopes come to life again.

They pulled into the warehouse parking lot a few minutes past seven o'clock on a Wednesday evening, and he realized, a little late, that Lucy was waiting for him to say something. He just didn't have a clue what it was. His mind had been wandering while she talked. "I'm sorry. What?"

She turned off the ignition and slipped the keys into her pocket. "Are you ready?"

"More than ready. Let's just find out if the dirtbag is actually here." He opened the door and had every intention of getting out, but she put her hand on his arm to stop him.

"Even if he is, he might not know anything. Just remember that we are closing in. Now is not the time to lose hope."

Persistence, determination and optimism. A combination that was hard to beat and even harder to resist. He put his hand on top of hers. "I'm okay. You don't have to worry that I'm going to give up or grow discouraged." Grinning, he added, "Much. I just want to find the guy and hear what he has to say."

"There's no proof that he—"

"That he knows anything about her disappearance?" That ever-present knot in his stomach turned and Jackson managed a harsh laugh. "Believe me, that's one thing you don't need to keep reminding me of. There's no proof of anything. That's the hell of it."

He expected her to pull away and get on with business, but she let her hand linger, and though he was champing at the bit to find Fitzgerald and get some answers, he couldn't make himself move first.

"If he's in there," she said, "I want you to let me ask the questions." When he would have argued, she cut him off.

"I know all the things you want to ask him, but if he knows anything about Angel's disappearance, I want to make sure we do everything by the book. We don't want a judge throwing the case out of court based on some stupid technicality if we can avoid it." She looked him in the eye. "Right?"

Jackson hadn't spent much time thinking about court. The only thing he wanted was to pin Fitzgerald against the wall and convince him to start talking. But Lucy would never let him set foot inside that warehouse if she knew that, so he nodded and did his best to seem reasonable. "Right."

Still looking skeptical, she finally pulled her hand away. "Okay, then. Let's go see what we can find."

Jackson forced himself to follow her as she walked from their parking space to the open door of a cavernous building. All around them activity hummed as forklifts sped back and forth from the warehouse into the backs of several large trucks. Men shouted directions, but the heavy metallic clanging coming from inside the building made it difficult to hear what anyone said.

Before they'd gone more than a few feet inside, a large man wearing a hard hat, a sweat-stained T-shirt and jeans that hugged his hips but didn't have a prayer of actually spanning his waist planted himself in their path. "Whoa there, folks. You can't go in there."

He was at least twice as big as Lucy, but she lifted her chin and raised her voice to match his. "Where's the manager?"

The man jerked his head toward the inside. "Back there somewhere, but he's busy. What do you folks need, anyway?"

Lucy lifted the edge of her jacket to show her badge and identified them, just as she had a hundred times in the past ten days. "We're looking for someone we've been told may be employed here—a young man by the name of Wayne Fitzgerald."

The man's gaze flickered in the opposite direction toward a small group of employees who were loading boxes into a truck by hand. The glance was so quick Jackson might have missed it if he hadn't been watching closely. His pulse jumped in response and he could feel the quickening of anticipation in his veins.

The man blocking their way apparently thought he'd been subtle enough to fool them. He hooked his thumbs in his waistband and rocked up on the balls of his feet. "Fitzgerald," he said, shaking his head as if he'd never heard the name before. "And it's Wayne, you say? The name's not familiar, but that don't mean he's not here. What do you want with him?"

Lucy gave no indication that she'd noticed anything amiss. "We just need to ask a few questions."

"He in some kind of trouble?"

"Not that I know of," Lucy said, turning one of her most winning smiles on him. "But why don't you call your supervisor over and let us talk to him? Either that, or tell me which one of those guys is Wayne Fitzgerald and save us all some time."

The big man grinned like a kid who'd been caught with his hand in the cookie jar. "Gave it away, did I?"

"Just a little." Lucy took a few steps toward the crew, forcing their host to follow or let her go alone. Without a moment's hesitation he fell into step beside her, leaving Jackson to bring up the rear.

"So what do you want to talk to him about?"

Lucy treated him to another one of those smiles. "Not anything you need to worry about—unless, of course, you were with him on Saturday the fourteenth."

Some piece of machinery fell silent and the laugh that their guide belted out at the same moment echoed off the warehouse's tin walls. "Nope. Sorry. Saturday's my night off. I don't hang around this place unless they pay me to."

Jackson had remained silent long enough. "Are you saying that Fitzgerald was working that night?"

The man shrugged casually. "He works every Saturday."

"What hours?"

"We usually put in four tens, so he woulda been here from eight until six the next morning."

Lucy met Jackson's gaze and he saw disappointment in her eyes. But Jackson wasn't so sure. Somebody *somewhere* knew where Angel had gone, and he wanted to make certain Wayne was innocent before he walked away. "Are you sure he was here?"

The guide scratched with a finger above one ear. "Well, not one-hundred percent. Like I said, I wasn't here myself. But somebody could tell you fast enough." He came to a stop a few feet from the crew and nodded toward a skinny young man with a face full of dark stubble and a scraggly goatee.

Everyone there seemed well acquainted with hard work, but Wayne Fitzgerald looked dirtier than most—from the grease in his hair, to the dirt under his fingernails, to the stains on his bright yellow T-shirt. Bile rose in Jackson's throat at the thought of him anywhere near Angelina. Jackson had to force himself to stand still, hands clenched into fists at his side, while Lucy introduced them.

People like Wayne had been in Holden's path when he was younger, holding out enticements, shooting holes in Wiley's arguments, flattering, cajoling, pretending to care, while all the time they used him for their own personal gain. The decisions had all been Holden's, but he'd had help from pieces of scum just like the kid standing in front of them.

The machinery started up again, drowning out the sound of their voices. After only a few minutes, Lucy led Fitzgerald outside and away from curious ears, and Jackson trailed along once again, aching to do something constructive. He'd probably never understand why Holden couldn't see what kind of people he got tangled up with. He just prayed Angel wasn't following in her father's footsteps.

Fitzgerald scuffed along behind Lucy, hands in pockets, dragging his pants even farther down on his nonexistent hips. He appeared supremely uninterested in everyone and everything around him. Anger boiled up inside of Jackson, all the things he hadn't been able to say to Holden came rushing back, and he found himself wanting to wrap his hands around Wayne's scrawny neck, just to get his attention.

When they could finally hear each other speak, the kid flicked something from a tooth with the tip of his tongue and let out a resentful sigh. "So what's this all about, anyway?"

"We're told you used to live on Alder Drive across town," Lucy said. "Is that right?"

Wayne nodded uncertainly. "I haven't lived there in a while, though."

"When was the last time you were in that neighborhood?"

"I don't remember." He hitched his pants higher, but they immediately sagged back down again. "Why do you want to know?"

Lucy ignored his question. "Were you there on Saturday the fourteenth?"

"No."

"Are you sure?"

Tugging at the tangle of hair on his chin, Wayne took a

step backward. "I said no, didn't I? Whatever you're after, I can't help you."

The stubborn set of his mouth and the mocking light in his eyes were too much for Jackson. No way was he going to let Wayne walk away. He shifted to block his escape route and decided to try reaching him on a level he might understand. "Why don't you think again, asshole. Maybe you're forgetting."

Wayne's beady eyes flew to his and locked there. Jackson saw anger and uncertainty, but did he see guilt? He wasn't sure.

With a warning glance in his direction, Lucy switched gears. "Why don't you tell us what you know about Angelina Beckett?"

"Who?"

Lucy pulled a copy of Angel's picture from her pocket and handed it over. "You recognize her now?"

The boy barely skimmed the picture before handing it back. "Never saw her before."

"Why don't you look again?"

"Why? So you can pin something on me?" Wayne shoved the photograph at her and tried to put some distance between them. "I still have friends over there, and I've heard that she's gone. But if you think you're going to make *me* look guilty, you'd better think again. I haven't seen the kid in months. Don't want to, either."

"You didn't go over there last Saturday night and invite her to take a drive with you?"

Wayne's eyes darted from Lucy's face to Jackson's, and this time there was no mistaking the hatred burning in them. "What in the hell would I want to do that for? She's a kid."

"A kid who's been missing for the past ten days," Jackson growled.

"Yeah?" Wayne's lips curved into a smug smile. "Well maybe she doesn't want to be found. You ever think of that?"

"Did you take her somewhere? To meet her dad, maybe?"

"No way. A kid like that is nothing but trouble, and that's one thing I don't need more of."

"You didn't take her to meet her father?"

"I said no, but I wouldn't worry about her too much." The ugly smirk on his face grew stronger, and mocking laughter filled his eyes. "She knows her way around…if you know what I mean."

Maybe he didn't know where to find Angel, but he was cut from the same cloth as Holden and his friends. A parasite. A boil on the butt of humanity. "You'd better watch your mouth," Jackson warned.

"Why? Because you can't handle the truth? The girl's a skank, man."

The rage he'd been keeping barely contained came rushing to the surface and erupted in white-hot fury that nearly blinded him. With a roar, he lunged at Wayne, grabbed him by the shoulders of his scruffy T-shirt and shoved him up against the warehouse's outside wall.

He was vaguely aware of Wayne's shouts of protest and the sound of Lucy's voice behind him, but he could think of only one thing. He jammed his forearm against Wayne's throat and pressed hard enough to get the kid's attention. "Where is she, you little son of a bitch?"

Wayne bucked against the pressure, but he couldn't do much without hurting himself. "What the hell are you doing?" His voice came out tight and choked, and his eyes bugged out in surprise and fear. He looked for help from someone behind Jackson's shoulder, but a little more pressure got his attention back where it belonged. "Get off me, man!"

"Not until you tell me what you've done with my niece."

"You're crazy! I haven't done a damn thing with your niece. If she's not where she's supposed to be, it's not my fault. Dammit! You want to find her, check out her computer. She's always talking to people in chat rooms and stuff."

Jackson knew Lucy was saying something to him, but he wasn't ready to back off yet. She was shouting at him, warning him away, but Jackson didn't want to listen. He was sick to death of dancing around people. He wanted answers.

He leaned in close, inches from Wayne's face, to make sure the dirtbag didn't miss the point he was about to make. "You're making a big mistake," he said between teeth clenched so tightly he could feel the muscles in his own neck bulge. "If you've done anything to Angel, if you've so much as *touched* her, I'll prove it, no matter how long it takes, no matter how far I have to go."

"I mean it, Jackson. Let him go, *now!*" Lucy wrenched his arm away, and before he knew what was happening, whipped him around against the warehouse wall so hard it almost knocked the wind out of him.

"Go on," she said with a jerk of her head at Wayne. "Get out of here."

The scum hoofed it into the warehouse and disappeared, and Jackson could almost see his one hope of finding Angel disappearing with him.

CHAPTER ELEVEN

JACKSON DIDN'T EVEN HAVE time to catch his breath before Lucy rounded on him. "I thought I told you to let me handle the questions."

"He knows where she is."

"He was probably *here* the night she disappeared." She ran a hand across her face and turned away. Her shoulders heaved as she tried to catch her breath, but when she turned back toward him, her eyes still flashed fire. "What in the hell got into you?"

"He knows where she is," Jackson said again. "I could see it in his eyes."

"Oh, really? You could see that?" She propped her fists on her hips and glowered at him. "Well, I couldn't. In fact, I think that's what you wanted to see. And even if he does know where Angel is, you've just about guaranteed that the next time we want to talk to him, there'll be lawyers everywhere making sure he doesn't say a word."

She might have been right, but Jackson was still too riled to listen. "There's something wrong with a world where a young woman can go missing and nobody knows a damn thing, and all the rules in the books protect a son of a bitch like that."

"The system works," she snapped. "Just give it a chance."

"The system is a joke. It put Holden back out on the streets after his first half-dozen brushes with the law so he could keep hurting people. You saw Fitzgerald's rap sheet. He has no business being out here, walking the streets, spreading more of his poison."

"So what do you want to do? Lock him away for the rest of his life?"

"That would be a damn sight better than the way things are handled now."

Lucy's expression grew frosty. "Do you feel that way about your own brother?"

"You don't know my brother. You don't know what he's done, and you haven't watched your grandfather almost lose everything because of him."

"You're right. And I haven't lost my own dreams because of him, either." Lucy's voice was soft but it pierced him like a knife. "But you can't blame the system for that, Jackson. Ultimately, you made the choice to go back to the ranch."

He pulled away from her sharply. "I never tried to blame my situation on anyone else. But if the system had worked, Holden wouldn't have been able to commit fraud, wipe out my grandfather's life's work and walk away with a slap on the wrist. And that piece of filth in there would still be in jail, not out on the streets hurting people."

"If he has broken the law," Lucy said slowly, "he will pay. But you aren't judge and jury, and you can't make him pay for past crimes just because you don't think he's suffered enough. I'm warning you. Either you get a grip on yourself, or we're going to have to make some changes in how we're doing things. I know how much you want to find Angel, but I won't let you run around like a wild man attacking witnesses. If you keep that up, nobody will talk to us, and I'll be yanked off the case completely. Is that what you want?"

It was a stupid question, and she knew it. The fact that she'd even ask it got Jackson's blood boiling again. Never in his life had he felt so helpless, and he hated the feeling with a passion. But no matter how much he hated being dictated to, he couldn't let the police shut down the investigation.

"What I want," he snapped, "is to start looking in those chat rooms. You heard what Wayne said."

"Then that's the next place we'll look."

Slowly, the red began to fade, and with the return of reason came the realization that he'd lost control. Self-loathing rose like bile in his throat. He was no better than his old man.

This was the real reason he'd never married. He just hadn't been able to admit it to himself before. If there was even a chance that he'd take after his old man, he wasn't going to risk it. No wife of his would go through the things his mother had endured. His children would never suffer like he and Holden had.

And maybe it was a good thing he'd discovered a few basic differences of opinion with Lucy. Because the last thing he should be doing was indulging in daydreams he'd never dare act upon.

WHILE JACKSON WAS IN the other room ordering dinner, Lucy set up so they could get to work. Both Angel and Patrice had been missing a long time, and Lucy had finally received a warrant to their house, with Orry as backup. She'd been hoping to find Angel's computer so they could trace her activities, but if she had a computer at all, she'd taken it with her.

But for once, luck was on their side. A phone number

in Angel's room had led them to a girl named Paige, who'd tearfully admitted to letting Angelina use her laptop computer. Paige's mother had been wonderfully cooperative, and she'd given them use of the computer for the next few days to aid in their search.

Lucy had shown it to a couple of guys on the Internet Task Force. They'd recovered a list of names saved in the computer's recent Internet activity, pointing Lucy toward a couple of teen chat programs that seemed to be Angel's favorites.

Armed with this information, Lucy and Jackson were prepared to continue their search—this time virtually. With the laptop set up and the phone cords connected, Lucy started the computer and waited, stretching in the comfortable dining room chair. Here in his mother's condo she felt strangely comfortable. More comfortable than she'd ever expected to. More comfortable than she probably should.

As much as she resented her continuing sessions with Cecily, they had made Lucy rethink some of the ideas she'd once accepted without question. Her belief that she'd never marry was a big one.

As Cecily had pointed out, plenty of officers had successful relationships. Look at Orry. And Nick. Risa was apparently doing well with Grady. But Lucy had glossed over these examples and focused instead on the failures.

Why did she do that?

Tension had faded between her and Jackson since that afternoon, but things weren't quite back to normal and Lucy missed the easy camaraderie they'd begun to enjoy before their argument. While the computer booted up, she decided to take advantage of the moment to freshen up.

Though she'd probably never achieve her mother's fashion flair, she had been making more of an effort. For herself? For Jackson? She wasn't sure about that, either.

She slipped down the hall, found the bathroom and shut herself inside. The black slacks she'd bought during a free moment fit her well, but the sleeveless pink shell was more feminine than anything she'd ever owned. She wasn't used to her new look yet, and she wasn't sold on its practicality. If she had to chase down a suspect, she might be sorry, but at least for tonight it was kind of fun to feel feminine and pretty. Risa and the others would fall over if they could see her.

Remembering something her mother had once tried to teach her, she tipped her head over, ran her fingers through her hair and stood straight again. Better. At least it had a little volume.

She swiped at her lips with the tube of clear gloss she kept in her pocket, and reached for the door again with a sigh. But as she turned the knob, an overwhelming urge to talk to Risa came over her. If anyone would understand what she was feeling, Risa would. She knew Lucy nearly as well as Lucy knew herself, and she understood Lucy's hopes for her career better than anyone else. She'd somehow managed to balance career and her new relationship with Grady, and she would understand without being told why Lucy shouldn't mix business with pleasure in the middle of a case. She'd also know which of the arguments Lucy had been turning over in her mind were real concerns, and which were just excuses rooted in her insecurities.

But would Risa be willing to talk to her? That was the question that had been hanging over her for weeks.

She pulled her cell phone from her pocket and stared at the display screen for a long moment, then squared her shoulders and dialed Risa's number. There was only one way to find out if Risa had really forgiven her.

But as she listened to the phone ringing, her courage

began to fade. She told herself Risa may have turned her phone off, or maybe she'd left it somewhere. There might be many reasons why she didn't answer, but there was also the possibility that Risa had seen Lucy's name on the caller ID and chosen not to answer.

Her voice mail message started to play and Lucy nearly hung up. But she'd avoided this for too long already, and she was tired of feeling afraid.

"Hey," she said softly. "It's Lucy. I… It's been a while," she said before her courage deserted her, "and I was hoping maybe we could talk."

She hated being so uncomfortable with the woman who'd been her best friend. Hated the distance between them. Most of all, she hated knowing she was responsible. "There are a million things I need to say to you, Risa. Call me, please."

Feeling a little sick, she slipped the phone back into her pocket and hurried down the hall. She found Jackson standing in front of the computer, reading something on the screen. He looked up as she entered and his lips curved into a slow, sexy smile that wiped Risa right out of her mind.

His eyes darkened with appreciation and he observed her. "Have I mentioned that you look beautiful?"

She swallowed thickly and hoped she'd sound normal when she answered him. "Thank you."

He took a couple of steps toward her. "You should wear your hair this way more often."

What was she supposed to say to that? She laughed nervously, cut herself off before she sounded hysterical, and indulged in a long, luscious shiver of anticipation as he moved closer still. "Did you call for dinner?"

Still without breaking eye contact, he nodded. He was closer now, close enough for her to see the need in his eyes. She told herself that his need was spawned by frustration over the search for Angel, but she knew that wasn't entirely true. And she wanted, just for a minute, to believe that all was right with the world. She needed, even for one night, to feel the warmth of belonging to someone, real or imagined.

He stopped directly in front of her, so close she could see the tiny scar below one ear, the strands of dark and light that combined to create his wheat-colored hair, the lazy curls that lay on the back of his neck and brushed the collar of his shirt. His gaze dropped from her eyes to her mouth and lingered there. "Dinner will be here in about thirty minutes," he said, reluctantly dragging his eyes back to meet hers. "I, uh…I came in to see if you'd like something to drink."

She knew she should say no. Mixing alcohol with the emotions racing through her would be foolish. Irresponsible. *Dangerous!* But that didn't stop her from asking, "What did you have in mind?"

"There's a bottle of riesling in the kitchen. Or I could mix something if you'd like that. Mom keeps a well-stocked liquor cabinet."

"I'd love some wine." She wouldn't let herself ask for anything stronger.

He nodded slowly but didn't move away. "You're an interesting woman, Lucy Montalvo. I'd really like to know what you're like when you're not being a cop."

She tried to laugh, but the sound caught in her throat. And when she tried to speak, the words wouldn't come out above a whisper. "I'm the same," she said softly. "I don't change much."

His lips curved slightly. "I think that's one of the things I like most about you. It's a rare quality, you know."

"Is it?" Her voice sounded a bit stronger, but she couldn't be sure. Her heart was pounding so hard, she could barely hear herself.

"Yes, Lucy. It is. A woman who is what she is? No pretense? No illusions? Not many people like you really exist."

Was *he* real? The glow in his eyes made her breath catch, and he was close—too close. She couldn't think. Couldn't make sense of the emotions raging inside of her. Did he mean what he was saying? Did he—

Without warning, he dipped his head and brushed his lips across hers, wiping away the last bit of coherent thought in her head. He pulled back slightly and looked into her eyes for her reaction, but the shock of the contact, mingled with the growing need inside of her, gave him his answer.

He lowered his mouth again, and this time his lips demanded a response. One arm slid around her waist, pulling her close, the other around her shoulders, and she realized how long it had been since she'd felt like this—if she ever had.

Lucy was overcome by a burning desire. She tangled her fingers in his hair, drawing him closer, needing even more than he was giving.

With a low growl of pleasure, he responded, passing his tongue across her lips, teasing them open with gentle but insistent pressure. An answering moan filled her throat, and though she wasn't sure the sound actually materialized, Jackson seemed to feel it.

Something in the back of her mind whispered that she was making a big mistake, but she ignored it and gave herself to the sensations, the moment, the dream. She wasn't sure which of them came up for air first, she only knew that reality seemed to hit them both at the same time. Angel wasn't home yet. They couldn't put her second.

His arms fell away, and she took a quick step back at the same moment. He abruptly turned toward the kitchen. "I should… The wine."

"Yes," she said, moving toward the computer and trying to get her head on straight. "I need to—" Unable to put the words together, she broke off with a feeble wave toward the table.

With a nod, Jackson hurried from the room and left her clutching the back of a chair for support. He'd been right to pull away. They couldn't forget about Angelina and she couldn't forget that he really knew next to nothing about her. She still hadn't told him about Tomas, and despite what everyone else said, she was still terrified that he'd resent her and become angry with the department for putting her on the case. Jackson deserved someone who could do the job well, and Lucy still wasn't sure she was qualified.

And what kind of relationship could they possibly have anyway? Their lives were so different. Their needs were nothing alike. This was a relationship born out of crisis— it would be totally irresponsible to think that anything real or lasting could come of it.

It was merely a moment stolen out of time. And that's how it had to stay.

BY THE TIME THE FOOD arrived, Jackson had had time to move beyond that kiss by putting plates, bowls, napkins and the wine on the table. Lucy glanced up with a smile that made his heart melt, left the computer and switched chairs to sit across from him. "What did you order? It smells like heaven."

Removing the lid from the first takeout container, he

nudged it toward her. "Walnut shrimp, stir-fried beef, spring rolls with peanut dipping sauce and Thai egg roll, which, I am assured, is to die for."

Lucy laughed and reached for a pair of chopsticks. "You did very well. I'm impressed."

"Not bad for a guy who was raised on steak and potatoes, huh?"

"Not bad at all." She helped herself to a piece of beef and closed her eyes in appreciation. "Wow, it tastes great."

"And I love being around a woman who actually enjoys what she's eating." He lifted an egg roll onto his plate and passed the container. "Rush's wife is always on a diet. Always. I don't think I've ever seen real food pass her lips, and you can't sit down to a meal without hearing about what she's not eating this month." He glanced up, realizing how that must sound and added, "Don't get me wrong. I think the world of her, but…well, you know. It gets old."

"I'd probably be the same way if I didn't exercise every day." Lucy added a generous serving of shrimp to her plate and grinned up at him. "The treadmill is a glutton's best friend."

"Well, then, we'll just have to make sure you always have access to a treadmill, won't we?" Lucy's smile slipped and too late he realized what he'd said. He laughed uncomfortably. "Big talk for a guy without much of a future, huh?"

"Everyone has a future," Lucy said, her voice suddenly quiet. "Even you."

"I know. It's not that I don't see a future in front of me, just that I know what that future has to be, at least for the next few years. The ranch is teetering on the brink of bankruptcy. I can't just walk away and leave Wiley there to go down by himself—especially since it's my fault he's in this mess."

Lucy stopped eating and stared at him. "Your fault? Why do you say that?"

He chewed slowly, trying to figure out how to explain it. "Holden showed up one day about six years ago. He was wrung out, used up and dead broke. He swore up and down that he was ready to change his life, that he'd learned his lesson and wanted to get on his feet again. Wiley knew better, but I still had some kind of hero complex. Thought I could save my baby brother from the cruel world or something."

"That's not unusual."

"That doesn't make it smart." He concentrated on the spring roll for a minute before he could make himself go on. "Long story short, I talked Wiley into giving Holden a job. He did a good job for a while. Good enough to earn a little trust. Too much trust, it turned out. He wiped out our bank account one afternoon and disappeared. I've been trying to dig the ranch out of trouble ever since."

"That doesn't make you responsible. Holden's the one who stole the money."

"I'm the one who gave him access to it."

Lucy's brows drew together. "Okay, so it wasn't a smart move, but that *still* doesn't make you responsible for Holden's actions."

"Sure it does. I knew what Holden was. I just didn't want to see it. I kept wanting to see what he used to be. Before—" Almost too late, he realized how close he'd come to telling her everything, but he wasn't ready for that. Not yet. Not while the ugliness still churned inside of him.

Lucy lowered her fork to the table and looked him square in the eye. "Before what?"

"It's a long story."

"And I have lots of time."

He never talked about that time in his life. Never. He

barely even let himself think about it. But for some reason, the gentle pull of Lucy's eyes got the words moving before he could stop them. "My dad was an alcoholic. I've told you that. What I haven't told you is that when he got drunk, he got violent. Didn't matter who it was or what they did, if something didn't go his way, he started swinging."

"He hit you?"

"Me. Holden. My mom. Like I said, it didn't matter. When we were little, he had this piece of wood that he used whenever he wanted to discipline us. Called it his *chinga* stick. If we didn't make our beds right, haul out the trash fast enough or get him a beer when he thumped on the table, we got a *chinga*. If we talked back or tried to resist, he'd lash out even more. Sometimes he went so far, I thought he'd kill one of us."

Now that he'd unlocked the door, memories poured out. Holden hanging on to the bathtub and begging their dad to stop. Jackson's feeble attempts to protect his brother. And their mother's vacant responses when they tried to tell her. Anger and hatred twisted in his chest, but sorrow clogged his throat and burned his eyes.

Holden. So little. So young. So frightened. And nobody had been able to help him.

"My mom...I guess she was just trying to survive. I don't know. And Holden eventually snapped." He met Lucy's gaze again and laid his soul bare. "The thing is, Lucy, I have it, too. You saw me at the warehouse. I snapped. I lost it. And I hate that part of myself as much as I hated it in my old man."

"Violence is never the answer, but you lost your temper with a grown man whom you believed had abducted your niece. You didn't beat a child almost senseless. I think there's a difference."

"There's no difference."

Lucy pushed her plate away and locked her hands on the table in front of her. "Yes, there is. Do you think you and your family are the only people in the world to get angry? If you do, you're way off the mark. Everyone gets angry. *Everyone.* Having a temper doesn't make you some kind of twisted person. Being unable or unwilling to control it is the problem and, frankly, that's not a problem you have."

"You don't understand."

She cut him off with a harsh laugh. "I don't understand? *Me?* I'm a cop, remember? I see this kind of thing every day. I spent a year on the streets, four years working the Domestic Violence Unit, and I've been in Missing Persons for a year. Believe me, I've seen all kinds of temper- and impulse-control issues, and you do not have a problem. If you're locking yourself away at the ranch, hiding from the world, refusing yourself a life because you think you've inherited this thing from your dad, then you're being unfair to yourself and everyone around you."

Never in his life had he wanted to believe anything so much, but how could he? "What about Wayne Fitzgerald?"

"Did you hurt him?"

"I would have."

"You had every chance to hurt him right there, right then. You didn't have to let me stop you. You're bigger and stronger than I am, and we both know it. Yeah, I've had training, but if you'd been determined to hurt Wayne I'd have had to use force to stop you." She left her chair and came around the table to sit beside him. "Jackson, you're being so unfair to yourself. Please don't do that."

"And what if you're wrong? What if I believe you? Get married. Have kids? What if I find out then that you're wrong and I'm right?"

"Then you get help. You do whatever it takes to get yourself right." A flush crept into her cheeks, but she kept going. "The difference between your father and you is that he didn't want to become healthy. He gave in to his weaknesses and they became stronger. You won't do that. It may be a choice you have to make every day of your life, but you'll make it."

"How do you know?"

She touched his face lightly, stroked his cheek with her fingers and smiled into his eyes. "Because you're not him. You're you."

Torn in two, he gathered her into his arms and held her close. He needed so much for her to be right, but the beliefs of a lifetime were hard to ignore. For now, it was enough to believe he had a chance. That was more than he'd felt in a long, long time.

THEY SPENT THE NEXT FEW days alternating between spending time online and trying to rustle up a few more clues from Angel's friends. It seemed for every step forward they took, someone pushed them back two. Every time he began to feel hopeful, everything ground to a halt and left him feeling frustrated all over again.

Their forays into teen chat rooms hadn't produced any leads yet, and Jackson wondered if they were chasing another dead end. Driving home from a short trip to the grocery store, Jackson glanced at Lucy across the cab of the truck and realized she must be as frustrated as he was. But there was something more, besides. He still couldn't shake the feeling that there was something she wasn't telling him. Something she needed to talk about.

Their time together was starting to raise questions he wasn't sure he could answer, but he knew he cared about Lucy, and he knew he didn't want to see her hurting.

Acting on a whim, he pulled into the parking lot of a quiet restaurant and turned off the engine.

She arched a look at him across the truck's cab. "What are we doing here?"

"You're not hungry?"

Confused, she glanced over the seat at the traffic passing on the road behind them. "Well, yeah. A little, I guess." She turned back with a scowl. "But I thought you wanted to get back online before the kids sign off for the night."

"We need to eat, and I've been eyeing this place for days."

The confusion in her eyes deepened, but that was easier to look at than the sadness that cast shadows every once in a while. She gave the small brick building a once-over. It wasn't hard to tell that it had started life as a drive-through restaurant, and from the outside it hardly looked promising. "La Casa Familia? Have you ever eaten here before?"

"Nope. You?"

"Never. You must be in the mood for adventure."

"As a matter of fact, I am. And there's nothing wrong with a little adventure."

With a halfhearted grin, Lucy got out of the truck. "That depends. If you need Pepto-Bismol to get through the adventure, maybe it's not a good idea."

Rounding the back of the truck, Jackson grabbed her hand and tugged her toward the shabby building. "Don't judge a book by its cover," he said. "If it looks bad inside, we'll move on. How's that for a deal?"

"Promise?"

"Cross my heart."

Sighing in resignation, Lucy let him drag her toward the door. Inside, they found a pleasant surprise. Everything from the tables covered in white cloths to the colorful decorations on the walls seemed clean and well-cared-for, and the spicy aroma emanating from the kitchen made his mouth water.

"I guess it won't hurt to stop for a few minutes," Lucy said after they were seated. "It will give us a chance to re-group and decide if there's a better way to go about this chat-room search."

And Jackson wanted to get to that, absolutely. But there were other things that needed attention first. He poured water from the carafe their waitress had left on the table and slid a glass toward her. "How about telling me what's on your mind first?"

Lucy's dark eyes grew large.

"I know I said you could come to me when you're ready, but I'm beginning to think you'll never be ready. Besides, after the other night, I think it's only fair. I shared my shame with you, now you tell me what's on your mind. And don't play coy."

"Coy?" Her eyes narrowed and the smile that had been toying with her lips vaporized. "I don't play coy, Jackson."

"So what is it?"

"I don't play coy," she said again, "but this isn't really a good time to discuss my personal life."

"When will be the time?"

"I'm in the middle of a case."

"Technically, you're off duty. And besides, I care. Are you really going to shut me down? Do you have any idea how hard it is to see that look in your eyes and not be able to do anything about it?"

Her eyes roamed his face and disbelief lightened some of the shadows. "You don't have to say that just because we had a moment."

"And you don't have to play hard-ass just because you wear a badge." He tightened his grip on her hand and drew it closer. "What's up with you, Lucy? Why are you pushing me away?"

She laughed sharply and sent a pointed glance at their joined hands on the table. "I *can't* push you away. You won't let go."

"So then tell me. It's not going to kill you to open up to somebody, is it?"

Again, her eyes locked on his. "It's my concern, not yours."

"You and I have different definitions of friendship, then. In my book, being friends meaning you care about what's bothering the other person. It means caring enough to listen—and it means caring enough to talk."

A wounded look flashed across her face, but it disappeared almost as quickly as it came. Before he could find out what had caused it, a male server wearing tight black pants and a crisp white shirt came bearing a platter of corn chips and a bowl of salsa.

He fussed around for a minute, putting everything in its place, and stayed forever taking their order. Of necessity, Jackson had to release Lucy's hand so she could look at her menu, and she tucked it carefully on her lap afterward—out of sight, and out of reach.

But Jackson had news for her. He'd grown to care too much to let her keep hiding from him.

CHAPTER TWELVE

WHILE A SINGER BELTED OUT a mournful Spanish song on the jukebox, Jackson waited impatiently for the waiter to leave them alone again. "Look," he said at last, "I'm not trying to offend you, and I'm not trying to butt in where I'm not wanted. But, dammit, you're hurting and I need to do something."

Lucy studied him for a long moment without speaking. So long, in fact, he began to regret opening his mouth at all. Maybe it had been a mistake to push her, but if they had any chance at a relationship, it couldn't be one-sided, with all the confiding on Jackson's part and all the fixing on Lucy's. It wouldn't last a year under those circumstances.

Then again, who was he kidding? It wouldn't last a year under any circumstances. Maybe he should just put Lucy, her problems and the relationship that would never work out of his mind. Let her keep her secrets and get on with his own life the best he could.

Irritated, Jackson scooped up salsa with a chip and popped the whole thing into his mouth. Fire exploded in his mouth and tears filled his eyes before his mind had time to register how hot the stuff was.

Wishing he'd had the foresight to order a beer, he dashed the tears away with the back of his hand, felt his sinuses loosen and looked around frantically for something that would soak the heat from his tongue.

He was vaguely aware of Lucy leaving the table, and he felt a moment of panic, but she was back within seconds. "Drink this," she ordered, and shoved a cold glass into his hand.

He squinted to make sure she hadn't given him water, but when he realized that she'd somehow produced a tall glass of milk, he gulped it gratefully. Gradually, the fire in his mouth, nose and throat began to lessen and the tears dried well enough for him to see again.

Taking another swipe at his eyes with his sleeve, he sent her a wobbly smile. "Thanks." The word croaked out and left him sounding like an old man.

She grinned, and for a moment it was as if nothing had ever been wrong. "Hot?"

He cleared his throat and shook his head. "Hot? No. Are you kidding?" He took another long drink and coughed. "It's great. You should try some."

Lucy held up both hands to ward off the suggestion. "Oh, no. I can see how much you're enjoying it, and I'm not sure there's enough for both of us."

"What kind of gentleman would I be if I kept this all to myself?"

"What kind of lady would I be if I didn't let you?"

He grinned at her. "Compassionate?"

"Try stupid." With a laugh, she leaned back in her seat. Her smile faded. "Do you really want to know what's bothering me?"

The question nearly made him choke again, but he nodded. "I really do."

"And if you hate me when I'm through?"

"It won't happen."

She tried to smile, but failed miserably. "I probably should have told you this from the very beginning, but I just couldn't. Just before Angelina disappeared, I was working on another case. A little boy who'd been abducted out of his bedroom in the middle of the night." She faltered and spent a minute tearing one end of her napkin into a fringe.

The turn of the conversation confused him, but she was having such a difficult time talking, he didn't want to interrupt.

"We thought we knew who'd taken him, and we concentrated all of our efforts on finding that one person." She paused and took a deep breath "We were wrong. By the time we figured that out, Tomas was dead."

Her voice caught and her lip quivered as she smoothed her hand across the small pile of shredded napkin. "We found him the day before Angelina disappeared. I had to tell his mother that we'd failed her, and I lost it. My captain assigned me to this case and ordered me into counseling. I didn't want you to know. I wanted you to trust me. I wanted to trust myself." She gave him a sad smile. "I wanted to prove that I still had what it took."

"And you thought I might not trust you if I knew?"

"Why should you?"

He dipped his head so he could make eye contact. "Why shouldn't I?"

"Because I failed."

"You've never failed at anything before?"

She lifted her gaze to meet his, but she looked miserable. "Of course I have. But failure isn't allowed in my family, and you had to put your trust in me. You had to rely on me at a time when I had nothing to give you. Nick offered to let me take some time off, but I was so afraid of looking like even more of a failure I turned him down. That was wrong, Jackson. I shouldn't have done that."

"No harm done."

"Isn't there?" She sighed heavily and reached for her glass. "What if that's not true? What if I let my own self-ish concerns get in the way of the investigation?"

"You didn't."

"Are you sure?"

"Relatively sure." He leaned closer and shoved the salsa out of his way. "As sure as I need to be, anyway. You've been incredible, Lucy. You've gone above and beyond the call of duty."

"Someone else might have found Angel already, or at least a lead on Patrice."

"I thought you told me that these things take time."

"Well, of course they do, but—" She broke off, clearly frustrated. "To be honest, I don't know what I'm doing. I'm not sure I have what it takes to do this job."

He frowned, worried for the first time. "We've been pushing too hard. Maybe we should skip today. Give you a chance to breathe and then figure out what you want to do next."

She shook her head quickly. "Absolutely not! Whether I have a personal crisis or don't, Angel's still missing." She paused while their waiter settled large hot plates of food covered with *chile verde* and melted cheese in front of them. "I'll be all right," she assured him. "It's just been hard not telling you. But I promise, it won't affect my work."

"That's not even a question," he said. "But everything in life isn't about the case. Right now, I'm worried about you."

A shimmer of moisture filled her eyes a split second before she dipped her head. "Don't, Jackson."

"Don't what?"

"You *know* what. I'm a police officer. I can't cry, and especially not in public."

"Right now, you're a woman," he said simply. "A beautiful woman I happen to care about a whole lot."

She shook her head quickly, but he laced his fingers through hers and lifted her hand to his lips. "Is it really so hard to believe that I care about you?"

"What makes you think I don't?"

"Oh, I don't know. Maybe the way you have such trouble looking me in the eye whenever the conversation becomes personal."

"I'm on a case," she argued.

"And what excuse would you give me if you weren't?"

She lifted her chin defiantly. "What makes you think I'd need an excuse?"

"Call it gut instinct."

"I'd call it something other than that." She pulled her hand away and cut into her burrito. "I might not be good at relationships, but I'm not afraid of them."

"If you say so."

Her eyes narrowed and something dangerous flashed in their depths. "Gee, I wonder why I ever hesitated to confide in you."

"I'm sorry." He dug into his own burrito. "I didn't mean to upset you, but you have to admit you're not the most open person in the world."

"And exactly what do you see as the value of being 'open'?"

"I don't know. What do you get from your friends?"

Color crept into her cheeks and she looked away. "Bad example."

He blurted a laugh that got a couple of heads turning their way. "Oh come on," he said, lowering his voice again.

"You're not really going to tell me that you don't have any friends."

"I have lots of acquaintances," she said, "but friends? Close friends? Not really."

He lowered his fork and tried to read her expression. "You're not serious."

"Deadly." She spread sour cream over half of her burrito and smiled sadly. "Oh, don't get me wrong. It hasn't always been this way. If you'd asked me six months ago, I'd have told you that I had some of the greatest friends a person could have."

"So what happened?"

She shrugged as if the answer didn't matter. "There were six of us who went through the police academy together. A few months ago, my best friend was accused of killing her partner during a shoot-out. Everyone reacted differently to the shooting. Catherine, out of necessity, had to distance herself. She was an instructor at the academy and she's chief of police now. There was no way she could publicly support Risa without jeopardizing the investigation. The rest of us knew that standing up for Risa would only raise all those gender issues we work so hard to avoid. That was bad enough, but the evidence started mounting, and it really looked like Risa might have been guilty."

She put one hand to her cheek and took a steadying breath. "I never thought Risa was capable of murdering her partner, but I did wonder, in the face of the evidence, if maybe a bullet went astray in the confusion. She insisted that she was innocent, of course, but I— Well, I didn't exactly win the popularity contest."

"So what happened?"

"To Risa? She was innocent, of course, and she eventually proved it. And she said she understood my reaction."

The corners of her mouth turned down at the memory. "But we're not friends any longer. Not like we were."

"So fix it."

She laughed abruptly. "Fix it? Just like that? I never pegged you as being naive."

"It's not naive, it's realistic. There's nothing so wrong that it can't be fixed if you want it badly enough."

Lucy pulled her soda closer and took a drink. "I've tried. I left a message the other night, but she hasn't called back. I think it's pretty clear she's not interested."

"And that's okay with you?"

"No," she said with an exasperated sigh, "but what choice do I have?"

He laughed sharply. "You're an interesting woman. You'll stop at nothing if a case is involved, but you don't show the same tenacity with your personal life. Why is that?"

"You're jumping to conclusions."

"Am I? Tell me something, Lucy. The two of us… Would you fight for us if it came to that, or would you just let go?"

"That's an unfair question."

"Maybe so. But I'd sure like to know the answer."

Her eyes flashed. "I'd fight if there was something to fight for. But since we'll part company when the case is over, it's kind of a moot question, isn't it? But since we're asking, would you put us above your family if it came to that? Or would what Wiley wants always come first?"

The question stunned him for a moment, but when he realized what she was doing, he grinned. "Point taken. I have no room to talk. I come from a classic screwed-up family. My parents divorced. My grandfather's a wee bit controlling. My dad beat the crap out of everybody in his path and then drank himself into an early grave. My brother—" He broke off with a sharp laugh. "My brother could be the poster child for dysfunctional people."

"And then there's you."

"And then there's me. And I'm either crazy as a loon or more mixed up than all of them. I'm not sure which."

She studied him for a long moment before her lips curved into a sly smile. "I vote for crazy," she said at last. "If you're not, I might have to listen to your advice."

That was so unexpected, Jackson had to laugh. "God forbid!"

She forked another mouthful and paused with it a few inches from her mouth. "You can say that again."

"So I'll just shut up, then?"

"For now." But the smile in her eyes told him more than her words could ever say. Her eyes, so deep and dark, held untold promise, and his mouth grew dry at the prospect of discovering what else they held in store.

Before he had a chance to pursue it, her cell phone let out a bleat and the moment, like so many before it, was gone.

After a few minutes, Lucy glanced at him, and smiled. "She's back."

"Who?"

"Patrice."

His heart and stomach got all jumbled up inside of him and his voice cracked with the sudden emotion. "Is Angel with her?"

"Hank doesn't think so. He's pretty sure she's alone."

Just like that, Jackson's appetite disappeared and the food he'd already eaten turned over in his stomach. He'd never seriously considered the possibility that Angel was with her mother, but he'd obviously held on to more hope than he'd thought.

Shoving his plate away, he stood. "Let's go."

They were only two short words, but Lucy was on her feet before he could get them both out. "Let's hope she knows where Angelina is."

LIGHTS BURNED INSIDE the small blue house on Adler Drive when they pulled into the driveway and turned off the engine. Jackson had felt the anger growing as they drove across town, and now it had become a tight ball of sharp-edged tension that grated with every breath.

Almost before they stopped moving, he jumped from the car and started up the walk. He was halfway to the door when Lucy called after him.

"Wait a minute, Jackson. We need to talk before we go inside."

He wheeled back toward her. "If you're going to tell me to let you do the talking, forget it. I'm not going to let Patrice disappear again without answering a few questions."

"She's right inside. I don't think she's going to leap out a back window and sneak off. And you're jumping to conclusions. You haven't even seen Patrice in more than a dozen years. You have no way of knowing what she's like now."

"She's been gone for two weeks. Her daughter has been missing all that time, and she doesn't even know or care. What more do I *need* to know?"

He turned away again and would have kept walking, but Lucy caught him by the sleeve. Though he could have pulled away easily, he turned back. Even angry and nearly crazy with anxiety, he wasn't a complete jerk.

"We don't know any of that," she said. "You're assuming every bit of it. She might have taken Angel somewhere. She may have been in contact with her. You're assuming the worst, and if you approach her with that attitude, she won't tell us anything."

That possibility almost made his lungs stop working. "She'll tell us," he growled. "I'll make sure of it."

Lucy moved past him and took the lead position. "Why don't we find out if that's even necessary first?"

"Because people like Patrice don't change."

"Look, Jackson, I understand that you're upset and I know you *want* Patrice to know something that will help. But she may be as confused and lost as we are. And if she's not, then we have to be extra careful. Trust me. Let me handle this."

Trust me. She had no idea how much she was asking. Only two people in the entire world had his trust, and even they had never asked something so hard. Or maybe she did know. The confession she'd offered over dinner hadn't been easy for her, but in spite of her fears, Lucy's instincts had kicked in the instant Hank's call came in.

She had no reason to worry about her career. But would she devote as much energy to anything else in her life?

"You'll only make things worse if you barge in there like some lunatic," she said again.

Jackson's need to be in control went to war with his feelings for Lucy, and he finally managed a nod. Maybe she'd never devote one-hundred percent to their relationship, but he would never doubt her dedication to the case. "I'll do my best."

"I can't ask for more than that."

Lucy reached the front door first and rang the bell. Patrice answered almost immediately, and Jackson wasn't sure he'd have recognized her if he saw her on the street. Her hair, once nearly as dark as Lucy's, was now an unreal shade of blond, and she'd put on at least fifty pounds. Her hand trembled as she reached to hold the door, and it seemed to take forever for her to focus on them.

When she finally did, her eyes flew wide and the old hardness flooded back into her face. "What are you doing here?"

"I'm here to look for Angel," he told her.

"But how…? How did you find us?"

"Your neighbor called me when he couldn't find you."

She shot a look toward the house next door. "Hank? How in the hell did he know who you were?"

"Apparently, Angel told him."

"But how did she…?" Patrice sagged against the doorway and her eyes sought answers from Lucy. "I don't understand."

"We don't know the whole story, either, Ms. Beckett. We just want to make sure Angel is all right." Lucy introduced herself and showed her badge, then said, "Do you mind if we come inside for a few minutes?"

Patrice shook her head and moved away from the door to let them enter. "I'm sorry. I just heard about Angel a few minutes ago. I'm still in shock."

"You've been gone for two weeks," Jackson reminded her. "Maybe you'd have heard sooner if you'd come home or called."

"I *did* call. Angel was supposed to be staying with a friend. Until about half an hour ago, I thought that's where she was."

"Which friend is that?" Lucy asked with a warning glance in Jackson's direction.

"A girl she met at school. LaNiqua or something. Angel was supposed to be there."

Lucy kept her voice low and soothing, which was a whole lot more than Jackson could have done. "You don't know the people she was to be staying with?"

"No. I'm sure *he* thinks that makes me a horrible mother."

She got that one right. Jackson trailed the two women

into the living room, amazed that Lucy still didn't show a flicker of judgment. "Where have you been all this time?"

"Working." Patrice moved a pair of jeans and shoes that had been abandoned in the middle of the floor. "I got a new job that pays great. It's finally going to get us out of this rat hole and into something nice, but I have to travel two weeks out of every month."

"And Angel knew where to find you?"

"Of course. What do you think? I'd take off and leave without telling my kid where I am?" She caught the look on Jackson's face and laughed harshly. "Oh, that's rich. That's exactly what you thought, isn't it?"

For the first time since he'd known her, Jackson had to admit she was right and he was wrong. "Hank didn't know where you were," he said in his own defense. "Angel never told him you had a new job."

"So you figured I was out chasing men or tying one on." She dropped onto the couch and crossed her legs. "I always knew you hated me, but that's a little low, even for you."

Jackson held up both hands to ward off her attack, but he hated knowing he might deserve it. "I'm sorry," he said as he sat on the arm of a chair. "I didn't know. But why didn't you know that Angel was gone? Didn't *you* try to call her?"

"Wouldn't that be lovely? Haven't you been listening? We don't have that kind of money. I'm two months behind on the rent. The utilities are all thirty days past due. I've had creditors breathing down my neck for months, and we lost the phone two weeks ago. I can't afford long-distance phone calls just because." She paced for a minute and then seemed to regain control. "I'm hoping she's just in a snit. That she'll get over it and come back."

"I'd love to agree with you," Lucy said, "but we've talked to so many of her friends, I'm having trouble with that theory."

Patrice smiled almost gently. "That doesn't mean anything. Her friends are very loyal. They'd cover for her if she asked them to."

That was hardly news. Jackson leaned up eagerly. "Why do you think she's in a snit?"

"Angel?" Patrice laughed and brushed the hair back from her face with one hand. "When *isn't* she in a snit these days? Everything's fine one minute, and the next nothing's good enough for her. I'm not good enough. This house isn't good enough. I mean, this place *is* a dump, but she doesn't have to get nasty about it."

"We were told you had an argument before you left," Lucy said. "Can you tell us what that was about?"

"It was just more of her dramatics. She wanted to be on the pom-pom squad and I told her no. We can't afford things like that, and I don't take charity. I'm not going to get one of those fee-waiver things just so she can jump up and down at some silly games."

"You don't need to take charity," Jackson reminded her. "Wiley and I would be happy to help."

"And you don't think that's charity?"

"Angel's family."

Patrice tossed her fake blond head defiantly. "We do okay on our own. We don't live fancy, but we do okay. I don't get welfare. I don't use food stamps. And I don't beg for anything."

Once again, they were straying from the point. Jackson tried to steer her back. "Even if she is in a snit and ran away, she's just fourteen years old. She's not equipped to be out there on her own."

"Well maybe after she's been out there for a while, she'll figure that out and stop taking me and everything I do for granted."

"One of her friends said she might be trying to locate her father," Lucy said. "Do you know anything about that?"

That certainly got Patrice's attention. "Holden? Are you kidding me?"

"That's what we've heard, but we don't have any proof to back it up."

Patrice stood and walked toward the window. She fumbled in her pocket, pulled out a cigarette and lit up with trembling fingers. "She's asked about him in the past, but I thought she'd gotten over wanting to know."

"Apparently she hasn't. We're starting to think maybe that's where she's gone."

Patrice's eyes filled with tears and she looked so frightened, Jackson almost softened toward her. "But she can't do that. You know what he's like."

"Yeah, I do." He paced back and forth in front of the couch for a few minutes. "The key still has to be with her friends. We've talked to everyone we can find, but maybe you know someone else. Like this LaNiqua. She probably knows exactly where Angel is."

"If we can find her."

"Surely you must know something. Doesn't Angel talk about her friends or mention things that have happened at school?"

"You don't know a whole lot about teenagers, do you? They like their privacy."

"If a kid can run away without a trace, maybe she has a little too much privacy."

"And maybe I'm doing my best."

Lucy signaled Jackson to be quiet and took over the

questions. "Just think for a minute, Ms. Beckett. Do you know where LaNiqua lives?"

"No. I should, I guess, but Angel worked things out with her and her mother. I talked to her mom on the phone, but they were going to pick Angel up and bring her back, and I never went over there."

Jackson had never expected much from her, so he didn't know why he was surprised by their arrangements. Patrice had turned out just like the aunt who'd raised her. The apple didn't fall far from the tree. But that's what scared him most about himself.

"We've learned that Angel spent quite a bit of time on-line," Lucy said. "Do you know who she talked to?"

Patrice shook her head slowly. "I don't know. When Angel's home, I'm at work. I hate it, but that's how it is right now. I don't know what else to do. Even when I ask her to stay with friends, she ignores me—obviously."

Jackson was torn between old anger and the reality in front of him. Patrice might not win any parenting awards, but she wasn't exactly the person he'd been expecting, either. Even he had to admit she cared about Angelina. "We'll work all of that out later," he assured her. "Right now, let's focus on finding Angel and bringing her home, okay?"

Patrice nodded wordlessly and dashed a couple of tears from the corner of her eye. "I don't like you, Jackson. You know that. But maybe you're right. Maybe I do need your help."

The sudden change of heart made him almost weak with relief. "Thank you. So let's start at the top. Tell us about her friends. Her school. About your neighbors. I don't want to leave any stone unturned—agreed?"

She gave another nod and crushed out her cigarette. We

don't know many people in the neighborhood, but I'll tell you what I do know."

He felt the yawning chasm of hopelessness grow a little smaller. Maybe he'd been wrong about her. Maybe they could actually come together, if only for Angelina's sake. And maybe Patrice would finally let them play a part in Angel's life. At least there was hope.

CHAPTER THIRTEEN

LATE THE NEXT NIGHT Lucy popped a piece of caramel candy into her mouth and closed her eyes in appreciation as the creamy taste spread across her tongue. The detectives assigned to the Avila homicide case had left a message requesting clarification on one of her earlier reports, and she'd been poring over witness statements for hours, trying to refresh her memory. The small of her back felt cramped and tight, her head hurt, and the smell of someone's dinner from a nearby trash can turned her stomach.

If only there were something that would help clear her mind. To release some of her tension, she pulled the elastic from her hair to relieve the pressure on her scalp.

On the other side of the room, Orry rolled away from his computer and nodded toward the case file that sat open on her desk. "How's it going?"

Lucy shifted her shoulders to get rid of the knotted muscles between them. "I think there's something wrong with me. A few weeks ago, I would have moved heaven and earth to assist with this investigation. Tonight, all I can think about is Angel Beckett. If she's hurt because I can't find her, I don't know what I'll do."

Orry crossed the distance between them and perched on one corner of her desk. "Come on, Luce. You know what this job is like. Sometimes you find 'em. Sometimes you don't. You do everything you can, but you don't blame yourself if the outcome isn't what you want it to be."

She knew he meant well, but his words were hardly reassuring. "She's a fourteen-year-old girl, Orry. A kid with a mother who cares but doesn't know the first thing about being a parent. She's had a rotten life, and the thing is, there's no need for it. She has a great-grandfather and an uncle who'd give her the moon, but she's never even had the chance to know them."

"And you want to fix it all for her?"

"I want her to have a chance to know her family. What's wrong with that?"

"Not a thing—as long as that's all it is."

"What else could it be?"

Orry gave a nonchalant shrug. "Anytime you're working with kids it's hard to keep yourself from getting personally involved. But you can't get wrapped up in their lives or the worry and aggravation will kill you. And if you lose your objectivity, you can't do the job."

She knew he was right. God only knew she'd heard the same advice more times than she could count. Sighing heavily, she rubbed her temples with her fingertips and nodded reluctantly. "I know. I know."

"So what have you got?"

"We've got a kid who's missing. A mother who didn't even know her kid was missing. A guy named Wayne who's been in and out of trouble since he was young. A dozen people who say this guy routinely bothered her and one who claims she was going to ask him to help her get to her father—who, by the way, makes Wayne look like a choirboy. I've talked with Wayne's supervisor and good ol' Wayne can prove that he was at work the night she disappeared, so all those stories mean nothing."

"Maybe."

"Maybe." Lucy rolled her head from side to side. "And if she actually *found* her father, I want to know how she did it, because even with all this technology we have here at HPD, I can't find anything on him." She slumped down in her chair and kicked her feet onto her desk. "I'm lost."

"You want to talk about it?"

A slow smile curved her lips and Orry jumped up a notch on her list of favorite people. "Do you have time?"

"Sure. I'm in the middle of a report, so let me just finish up with that and then we can go over what you've got."

Dropping her feet to the floor again, she dug change from her desk drawer. "You're on. I'll head down and get Cokes and chips. Any special requests?"

"You know what I like." Orry headed back to his desk, and since it was late and the building nearly deserted, Lucy left her shoes under her desk and padded down the hall to the break room in her bare feet.

Stifling a yawn, she fed one machine enough coins for two Cokes and hit another for chips. Halfway out the door, she turned back and bought a candy bar. Sugar and caffeine. Together, they ought to keep her awake for a while.

Clutching the goodies, she headed back toward her office. Her shadow stretched in front of her in the dimly lit corridor, and a shiver skittered up her spine as she walked. She was used to working late, but tonight the eighteenth floor felt unusually deserted.

Laughing at herself, she rounded the corner by the bank of elevators. Just then, the elevator let out a high-pitched ding that sounded unnaturally loud in the silence. Acting solely on instinct, she whirled around on the balls of her feet and watched the doors swish open.

It took only a heartbeat to recognize Mei Ling, one of

her friends from academy days, but it took a moment longer to decide what to do. She hadn't spoken to Mei since shortly after the shooting that had put Risa on the chopping block, and their last conversation had been so strained Lucy wasn't eager to repeat it.

Seeing Mei tonight brought back memories of when things had been good between them, and a tight knot of longing welled up inside her. If they'd still been friends, she could have told Mei about the case, talked with her about her fears of disappointing her parents and even confessed her confusion over Jackson. Though she'd been trying to tell herself for months that she was doing all right on her own, she knew it wasn't true. Oh, sure, she'd move on. She'd make new friends and life would change. But she didn't want to lose those old friendships completely.

The old elevators frequently stopped on floors for no apparent reason, and that must have been what happened tonight. Mei was staring at the lights above the door in consternation and, with an agitated flick of her wrist, swept back a lock of midnight hair as she reached out to punch the number for the floor she wanted. When she saw Lucy standing in the middle of the hall, she froze.

Still clutching the two cans of Coke, Lucy lifted her hand in something resembling a wave. A gesture, but nothing so overt that Mei couldn't ignore it if she wanted.

Lucy held her breath, waiting, hoping, wishing, while Mei stood like a statue in front of her. The elevator dinged again and Lucy's heart sank. Then slowly, almost imperceptibly, just before the elevator doors swished closed, Mei lifted one hand and curled her fingers slowly into her palm—a wave of acknowledgment.

The elevator door closed. Juggling all the goodies in her hands, she tried to ignore the stinging in her eyes. Lucy wasn't comfortable with strong emotion. Never had been. But the possibility that the doors to her friendship with Mei weren't completely locked gave her more of a boost than caffeine and sugar ever could.

"EITHER ANGEL'S ONLINE friends aren't chatting," Lucy said the next evening, "or they somehow know I'm not her."

Jackson glanced up from the counter where he was working on dinner. They'd ordered in every night this week, but tonight he wanted to do something different. Special. Something to show Lucy how much he appreciated all the hours she'd devoted to finding Angel.

"Maybe we're just hitting the Internet at the wrong time," he suggested.

"Maybe. But it's hard to believe that with all the hours I've spent online, none of her friends have logged on even once. And if Holden's out there, he's not saying anything. I keep wondering if we're chasing the wrong lead again, but she must have found a lead on Holden this way. Why else would she have run off?"

"Maybe we should log on right after school, or maybe we should stay on later. Maybe the good stuff happens after parents go to bed."

Lucy shrugged and rolled her shoulders. "Maybe, but most kids going to school would be in bed, wouldn't they?" She thought about taking the computer home with her, but she didn't have the heart to keep Jackson out of the loop. Or maybe she just wanted an excuse to be here. "I have an appointment in the morning, but I'll try to get here shortly after lunch. I should be able to make it by one-thirty or two. Maybe someone she knows will be online then."

"If she's made contact with Holden, there's no telling what time of day will be best." He poured two glasses of merlot and carried one to her. She'd taken off her jacket hours earlier, and the soft swell of her breasts had him spellbound—like a kid who'd never seen a woman before. "Last time Holden was at the ranch, he spent a lot of time surfing the Net. All he needs is access to a computer, and that's easy enough with libraries and Internet cafés around. But how did she find him if we can't?"

"If she's with him, he knows we're not the real thing and he's not going to let us see him." Lucy took the glass and slid down in her seat, arching her feet and stretching like a cat luxuriating in the sun. "So what's this secret you're fixing for dinner?"

Jackson followed the shift in the conversation without batting an eye. Sometimes thinking about something else, even for a few minutes, made it easier to concentrate when they went back to work. "Oh, it's some secret. Steak. Baked potatoes. Corn on the cob. Real exotic fare."

Lucy laughed and reached for a handful of the candy corn he'd picked up on a whim earlier. "There's nothing wrong with a good old-fashioned steak. I'm a Texas girl, too, you know. But when did you learn how to cook?"

"When my dad was drunk out of his head and Mom was too busy looking after him to think about us, my cooking was the only thing that stood between us kids and an empty belly." He grinned and helped himself to the candy, as well. "I took a hit-and-miss approach when I was little, and some of the combinations I came up with were…well, let's just say they were imaginative. When I got older, I decided to read a few books and learn some real techniques." He indulged himself and bent down to give her a brief kiss. A reminder that life had changed for the better. "Next time it's your turn. Just don't show me up too badly."

To his surprise, a faint pink tinge crept into Lucy's

cheeks. "Oh, I—" She pulled her bottom lip between her teeth and sent him a sheepish grin. "I don't think you really want that. I'm not much of a cook. My mother tried to teach me, but the lessons never took."

"So you have other talents," he said with a shrug.

"None of them in the home-and-garden department."

Abandoning the computer, she carried her glass into the kitchen, and Jackson watched her, appreciating the sway of her hips, the beauty of her movements, and wondering if she was as fluid and graceful all the time. "There are other things that are important," he said, letting his eyes linger on a few of his favorite places. "Dusting and vacuuming aren't everything."

"Yeah? You only say that because I'm not in charge of cleaning your house. My cousin Tony once told me that I'd make some man a great husband."

Under other circumstances, Jackson might have laughed. But there was something beneath the laughter in Lucy's eyes that stopped him. "Some cousin. I hope you set him straight."

Lowering her glass to the counter, she sat on one of the breakfast stools and picked up the bottle of Cajun seasoning he'd left sitting there. "I'm never going to be wife material, Jackson. I work too much, hate being stuck in the house, and I'm never going to love the smell of Mr. Clean."

"That's your definition of a wife? Kind of narrow, isn't it?"

She opened the bottle and took an experimental sniff. "Are you saying that's not what you want in a wife?"

He shrugged as if they were talking about the weather, but he knew the topic was anything but casual to her. "The whole time I was growing up, my mother stayed home with Holden and me. She took care of my daddy whenever he needed it—and believe me, he was one man who needed taking care of. When I was little, I remember Mom being fun. She loved to play games with us kids, loved to go camping and riding, and she could pitch baseball with the best of 'em. But every year, it seemed like she shrank a little bit and lost a bit more of herself.

"She all but disappeared on us, and I wasn't real fond of her for a while there. Maybe that's affected me. I don't know. But I'd never ask my wife to be anything she didn't want to be."

"You're going to stay on the ranch, aren't you?" Lucy asked.

"As long as Wiley's around," he said into his wineglass. "After that, who knows?"

"So if you want to get married, you'll need to find a woman who loves ranching life."

He glanced up sharply. "I never said that."

"There's some other piece of the picture I'm missing?"

"Well, I live on the ranch, yes. But we're not *that* far out of the city. Nacogdoches might not be Houston, but it's still civilized."

Again, that faint flush crept into her cheeks. "I didn't mean to imply that it wasn't. But you're right. It's *not* Houston."

She couldn't have made her opinion more clear if she'd written it on the wall. She wasn't any more interested in Nacogdoches than she was in the scents of household cleansers. "I suppose I would have to hook up with someone who appreciates the simpler life. A simple life with a simple man."

"That's not what I meant," Lucy protested. "You're certainly not simple."

But Jackson had heard her loud and clear. "Well, I'm sure as hell not complicated." He jerked a thumb toward the stupid bowl of candy corn and wished he hadn't given in to the urge to buy it. "You won't find caviar and crème brûlée on my table. Halloween candy's more my speed."

"There's nothing wrong with that." Lucy stood and put some distance between them. "This isn't about candy, Jackson. Don't pretend that it is."

"All right. What *is* it about?"

"It's about two different people with different lives."

She turned back to face him, and only the fact that she looked as miserable as he felt kept Jackson from ending the conversation. "I really care about you," she said. "Probably more than I should. But we have to face reality. Once we find Angel, you and I aren't going to cross paths again."

"We could if we wanted to. Crescent Valley isn't that far away. There's e-mail and a little thing called the telephone."

"Yeah." She lifted those huge brown eyes to meet his. "But you're as busy as I am. When do you think we'd ever find time to talk?"

"I suppose we could make time if we cared enough." But maybe she didn't. Maybe that's what she was trying to tell him.

"And that would be enough for you? A conversation now and then? An e-mail once a day?"

She'd created the distance between them, but Jackson needed to get rid of it. He moved up behind her and slid his arms around her waist. "No. But it would be better than nothing. I'm falling in love with you, Lucy. I'm not willing to just turn my back and write you off because a relationship might be a touch inconvenient."

Eyes wide, Lucy spun around in his arms. "Is that what you think I'm saying we should do? Because it's not. You're the first man I've wanted a relationship with, but I'm so afraid I'm not up to the challenge. That I'll let you down."

"You can't be any more afraid of that than I am," he assured her. He brushed the hair from her cheek with the fingers of one hand. "Both of us have been running from life for a long time, Lucy. But I don't want to do that anymore."

She pressed her cheek into his palm and closed her eyes. "Neither do I."

"I'm willing to take a chance on us if you are."

He watched the mood shift in her eyes, watched the clouds of fear part and hope shine through. "It's an awful big chance."

"Yeah, but I think we might be worth it." Cradling her face in his hands, he leaned close. He needed to belong to this incredible woman with the fierce determination shining in her eyes.

He stopped, his mouth just above hers, and watched as determination changed to anticipation. A soft breath escaped her lips and that told him all he needed to know. He brushed his lips across hers once. Twice. The third time, he lingered, kissing her softly at first and then with more urgency.

Every beat of Jackson's heart sent heat coursing through him, and when she finally relaxed against him and gave herself to the moment, the fire inside ignited. She shifted slightly and slid her arms around him. Ran her hands lightly up his back, tracing shivers and heat in their wake. He groaned softly and deepened the kiss, parting her lips with his tongue and abandoning himself to the sensation.

To his delight, she responded in kind, meeting him, matching him, asking him for more. He cradled her against him, relishing the softness of her breasts against his chest, the smooth curve of her hip beneath his hands. Need burst to life and consumed him, but he did his best to hold on to the reins and let her set the pace.

Before either of them could see where the moment would lead, the telephone jangled. Jackson told himself to ignore it, but his concentration was shot, and after a couple of more rings, its sheer persistence shattered the mood.

With an apologetic smile, he released Lucy and dove for the phone, answering it with a silent vow to kill whoever was on the other end.

"Jackson? It's Rush. Don't get upset, but we're on our way to the emergency room with Wiley."

Sensation died and the moment with Lucy faded into the background. "What's wrong?"

"We're not sure, but he's been complaining of a sharp pain in his eye and he's having some trouble seeing. We've called Dr. Crandall and he's going to meet us at the hospital."

Jackson collapsed in a nearby chair and cradled his head in his hand. "How bad is it?"

"Bad enough for Wiley to call Annette and ask for me."

"It must be serious, then. I'm coming home."

"Wiley figured you'd say that, but he wants you to stay where you are and do what you can for Angel."

"There's not a whole lot I can do to help Angel tonight," Jackson snapped. "I don't want Grandpa to be alone."

"I know, buddy, but he made me promise not to let you come back. We don't know that it's anything to worry about, and he says he'll never forgive himself if you bail out of there before Angel's home."

Jackson let out a growl and turned to find Lucy back in front of the computer, her eyes locked on the screen in concentration. Rush was there for Grandpa Wiley. Lucy was the one who could help Angel. And he was completely useless. Powerless and unnecessary.

"Jackson?"

Rush's voice pulled him back to the conversation. "Yeah?"

"Just stay there, okay? I'll call again as soon as I know anything."

"Yeah," he said. "Sure."

But even after he disconnected and tossed the telephone onto the table, he knew he couldn't stay. Wiley had been everything for him for as long as he could remember. He couldn't abandon the old man in his hour of need.

Rubbing his face with his hand, he turned back to face Lucy. "I have to leave."

"Something's wrong at home?"

"It's Wiley. They're taking him to Emergency." He looked around the room without seeing, trying to get his head working again so he could do something. The laptop on the table made his stomach knot with guilt. How could he leave with Angel still out there somewhere? But how could he leave Wiley alone after everything the old man had done for him?

The choice wasn't easy, and he wasn't at all certain he was making the right one. But leaving Wiley alone just wasn't an option.

LUCY WATCHED THE EMOTIONS tear across Jackson's face and wished, not for the first time, that knowing what to say in tough situations came more naturally to her. Obviously, he needed comfort. Obviously, he needed someone to tell him that Wiley would survive, that Angel would come home safely, and that everything was going to be all right. But promising him any of those things would have been foolhardy, so Lucy did the only thing she could do.

Pushing aside her personal disappointment, she closed

the distance between them and caught his hand in hers. "It's all right," she said gently. "Go. Do what you need to do. I'll keep working on the case, and I'll let you know if I find anything."

All the uncertainty he'd been fighting flooded his eyes and his shoulders sagged as if someone had dropped the weight of the world on them. "I shouldn't leave," he said, but there was no real conviction in his voice.

Lucy ached to lift some of the burden from him. "Your grandfather needs you," she said, tightening her grip on his hand and locking eyes with him. She ignored the similarities between the promises she'd made to Maria Avila and the assurances that rose to her lips now. The situations were different. "I promise I'll keep looking for Angelina."

Nodding, he pulled her into his arms. He couldn't seem to speak, but his gratitude was easy to read in his choked silence.

He really was the most remarkable man. Solid. Steady. Responsible. Warm, caring and affectionate. Ready to laugh even in the most trying circumstances, but sensitive enough to know when laughter wasn't appropriate. For the first time in her life she'd found a man who might have held her attention longer than a few days, but she wasn't even going to get a fair chance to see where things could lead.

She shook off the selfish thoughts and focused on what was important. "What can I do to help you get ready?"

He shook his head and stepped away from their embrace. "I didn't bring much. It will only take a few minutes to pack."

"I'll shut down the computer, then. I'll take it with me

and see what I can find while you're gone." She wanted desperately to believe that he'd be back, but she couldn't shake the hollow feeling that if he walked out that door, she'd never see him again.

He brushed her cheek with the backs of his fingers and briefly touched his lips to hers. "Thank you, Lucy."

"Of course."

With a lump in her throat, she watched him stride down the hall. When he disappeared into the bedroom, she turned away with a sigh and told herself again that it wasn't about her and what she wanted. That their friendship was tenuous at best, and their relationship... She laughed harshly at herself and dropped into the chair in front of the laptop.

Their relationship was a product of the investigation, born out of their heightened emotions and fed by her confusion. Nothing more. She had to believe that, or it would hurt too much to lose him.

Still fighting melancholy, Lucy moved one finger over the computer's mouse. The screen saver stopped swirling, and the Internet chat room she'd been logged into popped back onto the screen. Row after row of type in various colors and fonts scrolled up the screen as the nonstop conversation continued.

To be certain no one had said something important, Lucy scrolled backward as far as the software program would let her and read quickly. She could hear Jackson moving around in the other room as he packed, but she refused to let herself think about him leaving again.

Just as she was about to leave the chat room, a soft chime rang from the computer's speakers and an instant message from someone called BRANDONSGURL popped onto her screen.

Where have u been?????

Lucy's hand froze on the mouse and her heart began to race with anticipation. Sure enough, one of Angel's contacts had logged on while she was away from the computer. This was the first hit they'd had, and she couldn't afford to blow it. She decided to stick with short answers to lessen the chances that she'd give herself away. She could allow BRANDONSGURL to assume she was Angelina, but one false move might get the case she was building tossed out of court.

Busy.

Is your mom giving u trouble again?

Lucy smiled grimly and typed Yes.

What's her problem, anyway?

Chewing one thumbnail, Lucy carefully considered her answer before writing Same as always.

Did she find out?

Find out? Lucy's mouth grew dry and her hands clammy. She glanced toward Jackson's bedroom again and wondered if she should let him know what was happening. But he had enough to worry about, and there was still no proof that this conversation would lead them anywhere.

About what?

About u and your dad. U did meet him, didn't u?

Lucy wiped her sweaty palms on the legs of her jeans and tried to decide on her next response. Better stick with the truth as much as possible.

Yeah, she found out.

I thot so. He hasn't been around. I thot maybe u 2 were together still. What was he like?

At the realization that Holden talked with Angel online, Lucy's heart pounded so hard she was surprised Jackson couldn't hear it all the way down the hall. That question wasn't going to be so easy to answer, but she couldn't let too much time elapse. She decided to take a risk with What do you think?

I think u r being mean. U promised 2 tell me everything.

Lucy drummed her fingers on the tabletop and toyed with different ways to answer. Luckily, BRANDONSGURL saved her the trouble.

Did u have trouble finding it?

Finding what? Was she being too obtuse?

Sid's Lounge, duh! Did u get lost?

A flush of excitement spread through Lucy and a slow smile curved her lips. Angelina had been planning to meet Holden at a place called Sid's Lounge. It was the clearest lead they'd found so far, and for the first time, she believed they might actually find Angel and bring her home again.

No, she wrote, and tried desperately to contain her elation. I didn't. She thought frantically, searching for some way to ask what screen name Holden had used. Almost any question she could ask would risk blowing her cover.

Did he send u a picture finally?

No, she wrote, still stalling. What could she say? That her mother had erased her addresses? BRANDONSGURL wouldn't believe for even a second that Angel didn't have her father's address memorized. Lucy certainly didn't believe it. She chewed a thumbnail, acutely aware of the seconds ticking past on the clock, but completely baffled about what to say next.

So was he nice?

Yeah, Lucy typed. That seemed safe enough.

Do u look like him?

Lucy hesitated over that one. Not really.

U R sure quiet. What's wrong w/u tonite?

Nothing, Lucy wrote. Just tired. Surely even teenagers used that excuse.

And then, blessedly, before Lucy had to come up with anything intelligent, an emoticon showing surprise appeared on her screen and BRANDONSGURL wrote, My mom's home. Gotta go. Lucy didn't even have time to say "okay" before she'd logged off and the sound of a door closing came through the computer's speakers.

She sat back hard in her chair and stared at the conversation on the screen. Had she blown it? Had BRANDONS-GURL been suspicious? Or had her mother really come home? She might never know, but at least they had somewhere to look—somewhere they *knew* Angelina had been going before her disappearance.

Would Jackson stay to pursue this lead? Could she even ask him?

She sat there for a long time, arguing with herself over the right way to handle this. He was already torn between his duty to Wiley and the need to find Angelina. She couldn't add to the pressure he felt.

But how could she keep something like this from him? If he found out she'd kept this a secret, he'd never forgive her. And that was all it took to get her on her feet.

She found him standing in the center of the bedroom, his bag nearly packed, his face a mask of worry. Her heart melted at the sight of him, and she ached to make things easier for him.

"Jackson?"

"Lucy. Are you—are you finished?"

"Almost." He seemed so distracted, she nearly changed her mind. But she stepped through the door and nodded toward the bed. "Sit down for a minute, okay?"

He shook his head, tossed another shirt into his suitcase and turned back to pull socks from a drawer. "I really need to get on the road. As it is, I'll be lucky to hit Nacogdoches before midnight."

"I realize that, but I just found a lead on Angelina."

He froze over the suitcase, and the only thing in the

room that moved was a pair of socks that fell through his fingers to the floor. "Where?"

"A friend of hers was online when I went to shut down the computer. It looks like Angelina was going to meet Holden at a bar called Sid's Lounge. I logged the conversation if you want to read it."

He dropped the rest of the socks into the suitcase and headed toward the door. "Show me."

Lucy followed him into the living room, opened the log she'd kept and moved out of his way so he could read. It only took a few seconds before his eyes lifted to hers. "Where is this place?"

"I don't know, but it shouldn't be hard to find. I can follow through on this while you go back to Nacogdoches. We can stay in contact every step of the way."

Jackson nodded slowly, but she could tell that he wasn't really listening. "This could be it," he said. "This might really be it." He whipped back, eyes wide and filled with excitement. "I need to call Rush."

Lucy sank into a chair and waited. She didn't want to do or say anything more to influence his decision. Either choice he made would leave him feeling guilty. It was a choice he had to make on his own.

But try as she might, she couldn't ignore the flicker of anticipation or the overwhelming relief that they were closer to finding Angel.

CHAPTER FOURTEEN

IT WAS NEARLY TWO O'CLOCK in the morning when Lucy closed the door of her car with a soft click and silently made her way up the front walk toward her parents' front door. She was bone-tired yet so excited she wasn't sure she'd ever get to sleep.

Holding her breath, she slipped her key into the front door and tiptoed into the house. She moved cautiously as she latched the door and turned the lock, slipped off her shoes, and started up the stairs.

"Lucy?" Her father's disembodied voice came out of the darkness behind her.

Stifling a startled gasp, she turned back. "Dad? What's wrong? Why are you still up?"

He moved out of the shadows into the dim light of the foyer. "Come in here a minute, sweetheart. I'd like to talk to you."

Those words had always struck terror into her chest as a girl, and Lucy gripped the banister. Memories of poor report cards and the fender-bender she'd tried unsuccessfully to keep from them after graduation filled her with dread. It must be serious if he'd waited up this late. "Is something wrong?" she asked again. Then more hopefully, she added, "Is it something at the condo?" She *had* been woefully negligent about following through.

He gave her a sad smile. "I don't know if something's wrong, sweetheart. You're going to have to tell me."

Inside the living room, he turned on a lamp and waited for her to take a seat. The expression on his face worried her as much as the lateness of the hour, but if there was a problem, she'd rather deal with it when her mind was clear. "Can this wait? It's late, and I need to be up early."

"I think it's waited long enough already." He motioned her toward the couch and sat after she'd perched on the edge of one cushion. "Someone called here for you this afternoon, Lucy. A woman named Cecily Fontaine."

Her heart dropped to her feet, but she tried not to panic.

"She left a message on the answering machine, and your mother was trying to be helpful."

"Mom *called* her?"

He nodded. "Of course, Dr. Fontaine wouldn't tell your mother anything, but you know Mom. She did some digging and found out what Dr. Fontaine does for a living."

Lucy sank back into the couch and curled her legs under her. She didn't need Cecily to point out her body language was an attempt to make herself a smaller target. "I guess Mom's pretty upset."

"*Worried* might be a better word. Why didn't you tell us?"

"Because I didn't want to talk about it."

That sad smile curved his lips again. "Well, I can certainly understand that, I guess. Tell me why you feel the need to see a psychiatrist."

Feeling all of twelve again, Lucy wrapped her arms around her knees and drew them up in front of her chest. "I still don't want to talk about it."

"I think we need to. If something's wrong…"

"Nothing's wrong," she said quickly. "Nothing serious,

anyway. I just finished with a rough case, and Nick felt it might help me to talk it out with a professional."

"And you agreed with him?" Her dad's forehead puckered and confusion went to war with annoyance on his face. "Is there something so wrong we can't deal with it within the family?"

The old fear of failure pulsed through her, but Lucy knew she couldn't let it slow her progress. She'd been a prisoner to it far too long. "I love you, Dad. I love Mom, too, but neither of you has any experience with what I've been going through."

"We have experience being your parents. We've known you since the day you were born."

"Of course you have, but you've never knelt in the wet grass outside a construction site and stared into the face of a little boy who's been murdered because you failed at your job."

"Because you failed?" Her father stiffened and his face grew tight. "Who told you that? Who's trying to blame that on you?"

"Nobody told me that," Lucy said, pleading silently with him to understand. "But it's true." Her father opened his mouth to argue, but Lucy was quicker. "For a while, I thought I didn't have what it takes to do this job. I thought that needing help was a sign of some serious failure on my part. But it's not, Dad. And as long as I do this for a living, I'm probably going to need to decompress from time to time."

"You can decompress by talking to your family." He stood and towered over her. "Montalvos don't air their dirty laundry in public."

"This isn't in public. I'm seeing a professional in her office. What happens there is strictly confidential."

"So she says."

"Millions of people see psychiatrists every day—"

"But not *us!*" Her father glared at her, angrier than Lucy had ever seen him. "Nothing good can come from what you're doing, Lucy. Nothing."

"I disagree."

"Well, you're wrong. And if you're smart, you'll stop those visits and deal with things the way we've always done it. At home."

"If I stop those visits," Lucy said quietly, "I'll lose my job."

Her dad recoiled ever so slightly, but his surprise didn't last long. "Well, if that's the way HPD wants to play it, maybe it's just as well."

Lucy laughed in disbelief. "You'd rather have me get fired than talk to a doctor? This isn't like you, Dad. Where did this archaic attitude come from?"

"I've worked hard to create a certain image for this family, and so has your mother."

"And if I'm the least bit flawed, I'm going to mess that up?"

"You're not flawed."

"I'm human. Of course I'm flawed." The stress of the past few weeks suddenly caught up with her, and she knew she didn't have the energy or the patience to continue the conversation. If she stayed, she'd only say something she'd regret. She might have gone upstairs to bed, but when she heard the soft tread of her mother's footsteps overhead, she panicked. She couldn't face both of them together. Not tonight, when she was so exhausted.

Stuffing her feet into her shoes, she grabbed her keys and yanked open the front door. "I need to go," she said, closing the front door and racing down the driveway before he could stop her.

She heard the front door open. In the spill of light on the lawn, Lucy heard her father calling after her. But she slid into the car, cranked the engine to life and drove away without looking back.

She thought about Jackson's question. Would she fight for their relationship if she had to? She wanted to believe she would, but maybe he was right. From the six-pack to her parents, Lucy had a bad habit of running when things got tough.

If her father needed any more proof that she wasn't perfect, that was it.

SHE DROVE AIMLESSLY for more than an hour, before it dawned on her that she had to find somewhere to spend the night. As she saw it, she had four choices. She could go back to her parents' house, but she didn't consider that a real option. She could phone one of the six-pack—or could she? She could get a motel room, but she never carried her credit cards with her on the job so she'd have to go back to her parents' house to get them. Or she could go back to Jackson's and ask for sanctuary on his couch.

Five options.

She could sleep in her car. But that felt a little too pathetic, even for her.

Ignoring the internal whisper that she was justifying the decision she wanted to make, she drove back through the quiet streets toward Jackson's condo. Just as she'd suspected, every light in the place was still on. He was no closer to settling down for the night than she was.

She was crossing yet another line by coming back here, but any direction she turned she'd be crossing a line, either professional or personal. Of all the imaginary lines out there daring her to step over them, this one seemed the least frightening—or maybe it was simply the most appealing.

Walking quickly, she hurried to the front door and pressed the bell before she could change her mind. She heard his footsteps coming toward the door and saw his shadow through the window. Her courage nearly failed her.

What did she want from him? Why was she really here? Did she want a temporary bed on his couch, or was she really searching for something more? Would she have the courage to see this through?

The door flew open and he stood there, framed by the light. His broad shoulders and lazily curling hair got her heart racing in ways that had nothing to do with sanctuary.

"Lucy? What's wrong?" He pushed open the screen door and stood aside to let her enter.

She breathed in deeply as she stepped inside, catching the coolness of the scent he wore and wrapping herself in the energy that poured from him. All her life, she'd thought of herself as a strong, self-reliant person, but never had she been more aware that it wasn't true. She felt vulnerable and weak, certainly not the kind of woman who could plow through life on her own.

"Nothing's wrong," she assured him when she realized he was waiting for an answer. "Nothing about the case, anyway."

"Are you all right?"

She nodded, shook her head and cut herself off with a thin laugh. "Yes. No. I don't know. I just…" It was harder than she'd imagined to lay herself bare, but she couldn't keep going the way she had been. "My dad was waiting for me when I got back to my parents' house," she said. "They found out that I've been seeing the department psychiatrist for the past few weeks."

"And that was a problem?"

"Apparently." She let out a shaky laugh, realized it

sounded more like a sob, and gave up. "I couldn't stay there. I'm too tired and emotional, and I was afraid I'd say something I could never take back."

To her surprise, Jackson moved close and slid an arm around her shoulders. "What did he say?"

She leaned into the strength of his embrace. "I know he loves me. They both do, but they've created this image of me that I just can't live up to. I'm not perfect. I'll never be perfect, and I don't know how to live up to their expectations."

His fingers moved on her shoulder, gently massaging her. "You don't trust them to love you in spite of that?"

"I didn't say that." His hands worked magic, and in spite of her agitation, Lucy closed her eyes and gave herself over to the moment. "*My* expectations aren't the issue."

He brushed a kiss to the side of her neck. "Why do you think he feels that way?"

Lucy shook her head slowly. "I don't know. I've wondered the same thing. I guess maybe he was just raised that way. I don't remember my grandparents well, but I do have memories of Grandpa shutting down any time someone showed any emotion." She laughed uncomfortably. "He must be turning over in his grave watching me."

Jackson's hands slipped lower and set off another round of fireworks inside her. "Some people are more private than others. And I think there's a generation gap, too. Wiley probably feels a lot like your dad does, but that doesn't make them right."

"Try telling *them* that."

Jackson laughed softly. "I'd rather saddle a wild mare. There are just some arguments you have to realize you're never going to win. Then you have to decide whether you want to keep fighting, or just quietly go your own way."

Lucy soaked in the comforting sound of his voice. "So is this why you don't offer your opinions on things?"

"I just don't see any reason to keep arguing. Wiley's set in his ways, and I'm never going to change him. I realized that a long time ago. I could keep arguing, but I'd rather be happy than right."

Lucy pulled back to look at him. "So your advice is to do whatever my dad wants?"

"No. I'm saying you should do what you think is best. Just don't let yourself get dragged into an argument over it. Your dad can't argue with himself, and you don't need to justify yourself to him. The only other reason to argue is to prove yourself right, and that's a lost cause."

"That's easy to say," Lucy said with a sigh. "It's not so easy to do."

"Hey, I never said anything about easy." He kissed her softly and moved his hands back to her shoulders. "It's just that at some point you have to decide. If being right is all you care about, you're going to be very lonely."

That hit a little too close to home. Was that what she'd done with Risa and the others? Had her determination to be right driven them away?

"It's funny, isn't it?" Jackson said. "I never considered how my expectations of Angel might affect her until tonight. I don't want to be guilty of the same thing your parents are doing. Am I expecting too much out of her? Am I setting her up so that she has no choice but to fail?"

Lucy searched his face, loving how it was so familiar to her now—the cut of his jaw and the strong line of his cheek, the scar below his ear and the dark shadow of his beard at the end of the day. "You won't do that," she assured him.

"How do you know?"

"Because you're aware of it now, and you won't let it happen. You'll deliver what Angel needs. And tonight, I'm hoping you'll deliver a soft place for me to crash. Do you mind?"

"Mind?" He laughed softly and pulled her close. "You seriously underestimate your charms, Detective."

Excitement fluttered low in her belly, but she tried not to let it overwhelm her. She was emotional and vulnerable—but so was he. Neither of them was thinking clearly, and together they were a dangerous mix.

Keeping his arm around her, he turned toward the bedroom. "You might as well take the comfortable bed. I'll sleep out here."

She battled a flash of disappointment that was nearly as strong as her relief. "I'm not going to put you out of your bed."

"Well…" He stopped walking and grinned down at her. "There is another alternative if you're interested."

If she was interested? She moved her arms to his waist and met his gaze solidly. "If you have to wonder about that, I think maybe you're the one who underestimates his charms."

With a low growl, he bent and covered her mouth with his own. His arms tightened around her convulsively and his tongue brushed her lips, teasing them open. She responded eagerly, needing him as much as he needed her, wanting him as much as he wanted her. There was no room for pretense between them.

He slid his hands down her back, cupped her bottom and pulled her against him snugly. She pressed into him, aching, needing, wanting. It had been too long since she'd acknowledged that there was a woman inside of her.

His hands brushed across her back, skimmed her hips and moved up her sides to her breasts. Conscious thought flew out of her head, and she was nothing but physical sensation. He trailed kisses across her jaw and down her neck, nipped at the soft skin on her shoulder, then lifted his mouth to hers again.

New flames ignited wherever his hands and lips touched. Jackson slid his hands beneath her T-shirt and she gasped in shock at the touch of his fingers on her bare skin. He was murmuring something in her ear, but she was too far gone to understand more than a few words. She only knew that he called her beautiful, and that tore away what little resistance she had left.

Burning with eagerness, she tugged his shirt up over his head and tossed it onto the floor beside them. She ran her fingers across his chest and followed them with her lips. Words filled her throat and spilled into her mouth. Words she knew she shouldn't say, but she had no power to hold them back. "I don't want you to leave," she whispered.

He trailed tiny kisses along her jaw to the corner of her mouth. "I'm not going anywhere."

"I mean ever. When I thought you were going back to the ranch tonight, I realized that I don't want you to leave. Not tonight. Not tomorrow. Not ever."

He drew back slightly, but it was enough. The moment was gone. "Lucy—"

She'd seen that look before, and she couldn't bear seeing it tonight. Shaking her head, she slid away from his embrace. "Don't say it, please. I don't think I can take hearing that now." She tried to recapture the strands of hair that had pulled loose from her ponytail, but her hands were trembling too much. "Look, Jackson, I know you have to go back home when this is all over. And I'm not asking you to stay in Houston. I just wish you could, that's all. It would be nice to get to know you under normal circumstances."

He stood to face her, held her cheek with his hand and

brushed a quick kiss to her lips. "You have no idea how much I wish I *could* stay for a while."

"But you can't."

Tenderly, he smoothed the backs of his fingers across her cheek. "Not as long as Wiley needs me on the ranch."

With Wiley sick, they both knew that would be forever.

"You could always come to the ranch and stay for a while," he suggested.

She smiled sadly. "That sounds nice. I'd like that." And she would. But a week here and there wasn't what she'd had in mind. Still, she should be grateful they could do even that.

He checked his watch and made a face. "It's nearly three o'clock already. I should show you to your bed and let you get some sleep."

Sleep wasn't what she had in mind, either. But she knew he was right. Much as she wanted him, they'd be smart to wait for some time when they hadn't both been through an emotional wringer.

They spent a few minutes arguing playfully over which of them got the bed and which would sleep on the couch, but the air was still charged between them, and there was never any real contest. Jackson gathered a few things from the bedroom, kissed her once more and left her alone to spend the night in the massive king-size bed.

But even though she told herself repeatedly that they'd done the right thing, she wasn't really convinced. Wearing one of Jackson's shirts, she lay down on the cool sheets and tried not to notice that his touch had left every inch of her skin ultrasensitive. But the ache of longing kept her awake, and her ears picked up on every sound as quiet descended on the house. Sleep would be a long time coming—if it came at all.

MORNING DAWNED HOT, muggy and far too soon. Every muscle in Jackson's body ached as he stumbled to the kitchen to start the coffee, and his eyes were gritty because he could have counted on his fingers the number of minutes he'd actually slept. When he wasn't thinking about Angel meeting up with Holden, he was far too aware of Lucy in the other room in that big bed all alone. When he wasn't thinking about Lucy, he was worrying about Wiley and wondering if he'd made the right decision to stay in Houston for now.

He'd been so relieved to see Lucy standing on his doorstep, he hadn't mentioned the phone call he'd received from Rush only minutes before she rang his bell. Wiley's doctor would be performing surgery this morning, and the wait was killing him.

He couldn't have foreseen how tough this would be. Until he came to Houston, he'd been sure that he'd put those old longings for another life behind him. He'd been certain that working on the ranch with Wiley was his future. But now—

No doubt about it, this was going to be a long-ass day.

Still fighting sleep, he measured grounds, filled the coffeemaker with water, popped a frozen waffle into the toaster and sat down with the newspaper to wait. But his attention was so splintered, he read the opening paragraph of the same article four times and still couldn't remember what it was about.

Just as the aroma of coffee began to fill the air, he heard Lucy coming down the hall toward the kitchen and his senses jumped onto high alert. Setting the paper aside, he steeled himself for the jolt of awareness that was becoming commonplace whenever Lucy walked into a room… but nothing prepared him for the sight of her with her hair tousled, her body encased in the shirt she'd borrowed from him, and long, bare legs stretching beneath it.

She was always beautiful, but she was utterly breathtaking this morning. Knowing that he was one of the rare people who got to see her this way made the moment feel intimate and special, and almost rendered him speechless.

With a yawn, she sat across the table from him. Sweeping the hair out of her eyes, she glanced toward the coffeepot. "I will love you forever for waking me up this way."

Unable to resist, he leaned across the table and kissed her. "Gee, if I'd known it would be so easy, I'd have made you coffee a long time ago. What would a waffle get me?"

She laughed softly and crossed her legs, unconsciously exposing a little more thigh to his view. "Two will get you almost anything you want. I'm disgustingly easy when I'm hungry."

"I'll make a note of that." He dropped two more waffles into the toaster, filled two mugs, grabbed a couple of spoons and carried everything back to the table. He'd never been a fanciful man. Not one for big dreams. Never had believed in fate. But sharing the morning with Lucy felt so right maybe he'd been wrong before. He could almost see a lifetime of mornings just like this one stretching out in front of him—but unless one of them underwent some big change, that wasn't likely to happen.

Ignoring the flush of disappointment, he slid one mug in front of her. "How did you sleep?"

She rolled her eyes but her gaze settled on his chest and a faint flush brushed her cheeks. "Sleep? Is that a word I should know?"

"You didn't sleep, either?"

"Not even a wink. I was sure you were out cold."

Wanting to keep the moment light, he shook his head

and grinned. "After last night? Are you kidding?" He could have left it at that, but he didn't feel right keeping the truth about Wiley from her. Sobering, he straddled his chair and rested his arms on its back. "Rush called last night just before you got back here. The doctor says one of the blood vessels in his retina burst. They're doing emergency surgery on his eye this morning."

Her smile faded immediately. "Oh, Jackson. Why didn't you tell me?"

"You had concerns of your own…and I got a little distracted."

"Is he going to be all right?"

"I won't know until after the surgery—and maybe not even then. The doctor thinks the problem was brought on by high blood pressure, so that's also an issue. Wiley can't see a thing out of the eye now, and only time will tell if he ever will again."

She slid her hand over his and gently squeezed. "I'm so sorry. I know how much he means to you. You must be worried sick about him."

"Yeah. I am." Jackson held on to her hand tightly, but he wouldn't let himself tell her how much *she* meant to him. It wasn't as if he had a choice. He'd made commitments to Wiley that he couldn't break, not for any reason. Doing his best to shake off the melancholy, he forced a thin smile. "Rush has my cell number, though, so there's no need to stick around here all day. Let's figure out where Sid's Lounge is and get over there before it's too late."

Lucy's eyes roamed his face, but she accepted the abrupt change of subject without question. "Why don't you see if you can find it in the phone book while I go downtown. I need to be there for the morning briefing and I have another appointment with Cecily before I can get away. I'll call when I'm finished and we can decide where to meet."

Jackson nodded and let go of her hand. "Sounds fine to me." Last night had been almost magical, but today real life had returned with a vengeance. He just hoped one night of magic wasn't all they'd ever know.

CHAPTER FIFTEEN

THE NEXT TWO HOURS PASSED with agonizing slowness
while Jackson paced around the condo and tried to distract
himself with odd jobs that needed attention. He tightened
knobs on cupboards, installed a new washer in the kitchen
faucet, tacked down a loose section of carpet and replaced
a couple of lightbulbs that had burned out since his arrival.

After what seemed like days, the call finally came. Just
as he feared, the news wasn't encouraging. The doctor
couldn't predict the future, but at least for now Wiley's days
behind the wheel of his beloved truck were over, and he
had a long healing period ahead of him.

Almost immediately after Rush disconnected, the phone
rang again. He snagged it eagerly, needing to hear Lucy's
voice. "Hello?"

"Jackson? Oh, I'm so glad I caught you at home. I was
afraid I'd miss you and I misplaced your new cell phone
number."

"Mom?" He rubbed the bridge of his nose and tried not
to resent the interruption. His mother's timing couldn't
have been worse—but that was nothing new. Beverly had
always moved at a pace Jackson couldn't understand. For
twenty years she'd tolerated her husband's drinking and
abuse, then she'd bailed out right when Holden needed her
most. "Where are you calling from?"

"We're in Chania. I'm telling you, Jackson, Greece is quite possibly the most fabulous place on earth. I just wish I could enjoy it. What's the news about Angelina?"

Jackson leaned against the counter. "We haven't found her yet, but we did learn that she's been talking to Holden in an Internet chat room. Looks like she made plans to meet him."

His mother let out a sigh of frustration. "This is pure hell, I just want you to know that. I really should be there doing something to help."

Unless she'd recently had a personality transplant, she'd be more of a distraction than a help. And her new husband…Jackson shuddered at the thought of having to deal with Lloyd on top of everything else. "I'll let you know if there's anything you can do. Until then, you might as well stay there and keep Lloyd happy."

"But what about you? You shouldn't have to do everything alone."

"I don't know why this should be any different." He'd meant the comment to sound lighthearted, but even he couldn't miss the bitterness in his voice.

His mother didn't miss it, either. "Jackson? Are you all right?"

He nodded, even though she couldn't see him, and rotated his neck on his shoulders. "I'm fine. Just tired and frustrated. I got off the phone with Rush right before you called. Wiley's just come out of surgery and it looks as if he may have lost the sight in one eye."

"Oh, Jackson, I'm so sorry."

"Rush is doing everything he can, but if I don't get home soon, the ranch is going to suffer. I feel like we're close to finding Angelina, but not close enough. It's been a rough couple of weeks, that's all."

"And, as usual, you're shouldering everything yourself."

"Who else?"

"What about me?"

He snorted. "First of all, Wiley and the ranch aren't your responsibilities. And you have a new husband to think about, remember?"

"That's true, but you *are* my responsibility, and I'd like to see you happy. I don't know why you continually push me away, especially when you need me."

Jackson ran a hand along the back of his neck. "I'm fine, Mom. You don't have to worry about me."

After a pause, his mother released a heavy sigh. "Honestly, Jackson, do you have to be so prickly with me? I know I haven't always been the best mother, but I did try."

Old resentments he'd thought long dead rose to the surface. He tried to brush them away, but they were there, alive and breathing and fueling every move he made. Those feelings made him angry—and very, very tired.

He thought about Lucy and her argument with her parents, about Angelina running away from a mother she thought didn't care about her, and a soul-deep sadness filled him. His mother wasn't a bad person. Lucy's parents weren't bad people. Even Patrice was trying her best to give her daughter a better life. They all believed they were doing the right thing.

But how was anyone supposed to know what the right thing was?

"Jackson?"

He shook off his thoughts. "I'm sorry, Mom. Just distracted. Tell you what. Let me follow through on this lead today. If this doesn't pan out, I'll let you know, and if you really want to come home to help, I won't argue."

Maybe it would sound like nothing to a stranger, but he

and his mother knew just how big a concession this was. A long silence stretched between them before she whispered, "Thank you."

"Sure."

"You don't know how much this means to me. Maybe… Maybe we can finally put the past behind us?"

"I think maybe we can," he said. And for the first time in his life, he believed it.

"WE JUST GOT WORD THAT the Amber Alert issued by the Cheyenne police department at 0230 this morning has been canceled. The girl and her father were found just outside of Rock Springs and the girl is on her way back to her mother."

As always, the news of a found child spurred a round of applause among the members of the Missing Persons Unit. Good news was hard to come by in their line of work, and they celebrated whenever some came their way.

When the cheering subsided, Nick settled his gaze on Lucy. "What about you, Montalvo? You ready to call off the search for your missing girl?"

"I'd like to stay on the case a few more days, Captain. Last night, we picked up some critical information. I have good reason to believe that the girl left home to meet her father after chatting with him online."

Lucy briefly filled Nick in on the conversation she'd had with BRANDONSGURL. "I'm planning to check out Sid's Lounge after I leave here. See if anyone knows where to find Holden, or remembers seeing Angelina the night she disappeared."

"All right. Why don't you talk to one of the guys on the Internet Task Force before you go. They might have a line on this guy already." Nick looked at the group. "Anything else?"

Orry lifted one finger and got the nod from Nick to go ahead. "I want another crack at the mother in the Donny Williamson case. I don't think she's telling us everything she knows."

"Then take it." Nick leaned back in his chair and tapped the eraser end of his pencil on the table in a gesture that always indicated agitation. "Nothing we can take to Homicide yet?"

"Not yet. But I'm working on it."

Nick nodded and pushed to his feet. "All right. If that's everything, let's get going."

Lucy didn't waste a second. Intent on making her way to the ninth floor where the Internet Task Force was headquartered, she slipped into the crowded elevator and pressed the button for the eighth floor. The elevator stopped on every level as it descended, letting people in, letting people out, but by the time the doors swished shut on the twelfth floor, the elevator was almost deserted.

Just before the doors closed, someone slid inside and Lucy recognized Crista Santiago, one of the six-pack. Crista had been particularly vocal about Lucy's reaction to Risa's troubles, but the two of them had never seen eye to eye on many things—especially the justice system. Lucy's strong belief that the system worked clashed with the cynical attitudes about law and order Crista had developed living in the barrio. When all the evidence had pointed to Risa's guilt in Luke's murder, Lucy had been convinced that justice would prevail, while Crista had been adamant that they couldn't trust the system—especially not when it affected a friend.

One particularly heated conversation had essentially put an end to their friendship, and Lucy hadn't talked to her since. Seeing her now threw Lucy for a loop. Neither of them had been willing to concede their point, and Lucy had lost a dear friend. She thought of the conversation she'd had with Jackson last night, and it made Lucy's whole argument feel childish. Could she admit to Crista that being right had been more important than their friendship? It wouldn't be easy.

Crista recovered from the shock first. She brushed a lock of brown hair from her cheek and managed a smile that looked almost genuine. "Hello, Lucy."

"Crista."

"It's been a while."

Lucy had forgotten how stunning Crista could be when she smiled. She was stunning anytime, really. Her long brown hair and curvaceous figure had caught more than one male eye during their monthly lunches, and Crista had never been left sitting alone at the table when they'd gone clubbing.

Lucy nodded. She longed to open up to her old friend—to talk like they used to—but she was unsure how to do that. "Yeah, it has been a while. How have you been?"

"I've been all right. How about you?"

The temptation to tell the truth rose sure and strong, but all that came out of her mouth was a noncommittal "Fine."

"You're still in Missing Persons?"

"Yeah. And you?"

"I was transferred to Homicide a few weeks ago. The Chicano Squad." An uncomfortable silence fell between them as Crista studied the numbers above the door. After only a few seconds, her gaze dropped to meet Lucy's again. "Have you talked to any of the others lately?"

"I saw Mei a couple of days ago, but we didn't speak." She couldn't bring herself to mention Risa.

But Crista obviously didn't suffer from the same uncertainty. "Have you talked to Risa?"

Lucy shook her head and fought the urge to break eye contact. "No, I—" How was she supposed to finish that sentence? No, I haven't had the nerve? No, I've been too afraid? She shook her head weakly. "No. Have you?"

"A few weeks ago."

"So everything's okay between you?" Lucy hoped it was. She didn't want her mistake to ruin the friendship for everyone.

But Crista merely shrugged. "I don't know if 'okay' is the word I'd use. I'd say things are tentative between us. But the two of you were always so close. It's hard to believe that you're not friends any longer."

"We *were* close," Lucy said with a sad smile. "But I took care of that."

Crista's eyes roamed her face for a long moment. The elevator jerked to a stop and the doors swished open. The moment was over, the conversation still unfinished, yet there was nothing more for either of them to say.

"It was good to see you," Lucy said as she stepped in front of the sensors to keep the doors from closing again. And she was surprised to discover how much she meant it.

"You, too." Crista stepped farther into the corner, prepared to let the elevator move on, but at the last minute, she darted through the doors into the corridor with Lucy. "All right, I give. You don't seem like yourself. What is it?"

"It's nothing. Just the case I'm working on."

Crista laughed softly. "I've known you for six years, Lucy. I've seen you working tough cases before, but I've never seen that look in your eyes. What gives?"

Her genuine concern was hard to resist—but Lucy gave it hell. "It's just life. You know how that is."

"Yeah, I do." Crista was a good cop and she obviously wasn't ready to back off yet. "Do you have time to grab a Coke?"

"I'd love to," Lucy said honestly, "but someone is waiting for me and I need to talk with the guys on the Internet Task Force."

With a shrug, Crista pressed the elevator call button and Lucy sensed the moment was slipping away. There had been too many moments lately and she suddenly realized she couldn't afford to let another one go. "What you said before—about me not being myself? Well, you're right. I'm not."

Crista turned back, her face awash with curiosity. "I knew something was wrong."

Lucy slid her hands into her pockets, needing to feel her keys, her phone, the change and lint there to ground her. "We lost an eight-year-old boy three weeks ago, and I've had a hard time dealing with it. I've been talking with Cecily Fontaine, and I think that's helping, but my parents found out last night and they're fit to be tied."

Crista's eyes grew sad. "They're still expecting you to be their golden girl?"

"I'm afraid so." Lucy had forgotten how nice it was to have friends who knew her history, who didn't need an explanation for everything.

"Well, I'm sorry. I know that's tough for you, and I hope they figure it out someday. But what about you? Are you really doing okay?"

Her concern touched Lucy more deeply than she could have expected. "I think so. For a while, I wasn't sure I had what it takes to do this job, but I'm starting to rethink that now."

"You?" Crista laughed in disbelief. "You're one of the

most dedicated officers I've ever known. If *you* have doubts, what should the rest of us be feeling?"

"I don't know if *dedicated* was the right word," Lucy admitted. "*Obsessed* might be closer to the truth. And you're a great cop, Crista. I know we've come at the job from different angles for the past few years, but I've always known you were good at what you do."

Crista's lips curved. "That can't be easy for you to say."

Stung, Lucy tried to laugh. "It's not *that* difficult," she said. But she was glad Crista knew how hard she was trying.

A man at the other end of the corridor moved away from the clock and Lucy realized with a start how long they'd been talking. She really didn't want to end the conversation, but she couldn't be late for another appointment with Cecily.

"I really have to go," she said with a weak smile. "This case I'm working on—" That could have been another lengthy conversation in itself. "I have to—"

Crista waved her off with a flick of her wrist. "Yeah. Go. I understand."

But she didn't. She couldn't know about the longing that melted through Lucy, the need to put an end to the rift that had kept them all apart. "Crista, I—" she began, but the words still wouldn't come. She finally managed a weak "Thanks."

"Sure. What are friends for? Just don't let anyone make you question what you're supposed to be doing. Not even your parents. Even the best of us fail sometimes. That's life, you know?"

With one last grateful smile, Lucy turned away. But she had blown it again. And she had no one to blame but herself.

TWO HOURS LATER, LUCY pulled out of traffic into the parking lot of a low cinder block building. Jackson had found a listing for Sid's Lounge in the phone book, and his directions had brought her right to it. She wondered how long Jackson had been waiting. The sun had already climbed high in the sky and heat undulated in waves from the road in front of her.

Her appointment with Cecily had gone well, and Cecily had seemed pleased with their progress. She'd even indicated that she might give Lucy the all-clear soon. That was enough to have Lucy smiling as she spotted Jackson's truck in a stall near the front door.

She parked as close as she could to the place he'd chosen. He was out of the truck and moving toward her before she could shut off the engine, and in spite of the morning she'd had—or maybe because of it—a warm rush of relief poured through her.

She'd grown so used to seeing him every day, to hearing his voice, to breathing the scent of his soap, and even to enjoying the rare rumble of his laugh. The more time she spent with him, the more in love with him she fell. She didn't even want to think about what she'd do or how empty her days would feel when he went home again, but he seemed to be there in her thoughts all the time.

He embraced her quickly and picked up the conversation they'd been having when she called from the station. "The place is pretty full. It's surprisingly popular, in spite of the way it looks."

Lucy ran her gaze along the low lines of the building. Even in the daylight, neon beer signs glowed from long, narrow windows near the flat roofline. A battered red metal door led the way inside.

Her spirits sank at the sight. This certainly wasn't the kind of place where kids met for burgers and fries, and it wasn't the kind of place where respectable fathers met their daughters. That put a bad taste in her mouth, but she didn't want to worry Jackson any more than he was, so she tried to keep her voice light. "Have you been inside?"

"Yeah. The old boys in there aren't what you'd call the friendly type."

"Well, let's just hope one of them is." She stepped through the door while Jackson held it open, and she paused for a moment on the faded red carpet to let her eyes adjust. If anything, Sid's Lounge was worse inside than out—though it was hard to imagine how that was possible.

Cigarette smoke hung in the air, and its bitter scent mixed with something else Lucy didn't want to identify. Two men sat at a long bar, a few others clustered at small round tables near the deserted dance floor.

Every eye in the place looked up when they entered, and Lucy could almost feel the walls go up around them. Interviewing them one by one, would take a little while. Impulsively, she decided on a different approach.

She pulled the picture of Angelina from her pocket and held it aloft. "Can I have your attention, gentlemen? I'm Detective Montalvo from HPD, and I'm searching for a missing girl. We have reason to believe she met someone here the night she disappeared, and I need to know if any of you have seen the girl in this picture or know where we can find her."

A few murmurs went up and a couple of the guys shifted uncomfortably on their chairs. Lucy watched them all carefully, looking for signs of guilt. "We're also looking for the man she was supposed to meet. His name is Holden Davis. If any of you know where we can find him, we need you to tell us immediately."

A hushed silence fell over the group and the men exchanged glances—some cautious, some suspicious. Were any of them guilty?

"We're going to bring this around to each of you," she continued. "I want you to take a good look at it and tell one of us whether or not you've seen this girl around here—either inside this bar or in the vicinity."

The bartender, a husky man of about forty with deep-set eyes and a disapproving expression, stepped out from behind the bar. "Who is this girl?"

"Her name is Angelina Beckett. She goes by Angel. She's only fourteen years old, though she may try to pass herself off as older."

"We don't allow fourteen-year-old girls in this bar."

"I'm sure you don't, but she may not have looked fourteen when she was in here." She crossed to the bar and slid the picture toward him. "I'm not here to shut anyone down for underage drinking. I just want to find this girl and get her back home where she belongs."

The man examined the photograph and shook his head firmly. "Never saw her before."

Jackson stepped forward, his face clouded with worry. "What about a man talking about meeting a young girl? Have you heard anything like that?"

"I hear all kinds of things working in this place. Some asshole planning to meet a girl wouldn't even make a dent."

He was probably right about that, but Lucy nudged Angel's picture closer, anyway. "Then take a good, long look at this picture, and think real hard, okay? Have you ever seen this girl? Or have you heard anyone talking about meeting up with someone? A father, maybe, getting set to meet his long-lost daughter."

The man's eyes shot to hers so quickly, Lucy had a feeling she'd hit pay dirt. "Well, now, I do remember something about that. There was a guy in here a few weeks ago. Said he'd found his little girl after…hell, I don't remem-

ber how many years, but it was a long time. Said she'd
come looking for him, just like he thought she would when
she got old enough."

"Where is he now?" Jackson demanded.

"I couldn't tell ya. He was new around here. Hung
around for a few days and then disappeared again."

"Can you tell us what he looked like? What kind of car
he drove?"

"What he looked like?" The bartender gave that some
thought. "He's tall. About your height," he said, with a nod
at Jackson. "Wore a cap most of the time, so I never saw
his hair. Had a beard…one of them goatees."

"Anything else?"

The bartender thought for a moment. "Yeah. A scar
right here on his chin. But I don't think he drove a car. I
got the feeling he was on foot." He turned to the end of the
bar where a couple of guys sat nursing their drinks. "Hey,
Tyce, didn't you give that guy a ride somewhere once?"

Tyce, a small-framed man with skin the color of hot
chocolate, nodded slowly. "Yeah. That day I had to pick
up the lumber out in Channelview."

Lucy's fingers grew numb and her heart raced so fast
she could hardly breathe. "Where in Channelview?"

"He just had me let him out near the McDonald's. That's
all I know."

It was enough. Holden had been in Houston—in *Channelview* around the time of Angel's disappearance. Any
doubts Lucy might have had before had certainly been laid
to rest. Now she just hoped he was still around.

CHAPTER SIXTEEN

ON HER CELL PHONE, LUCY put in calls to friends at the Department of Motor Vehicles and the Driver License Division in case Holden had actually paid off his DUI fines and recovered his license, while Jackson worked through traffic and road construction toward Channelview. They'd agreed to start with Patrice to see if she'd remembered anything about Holden's whereabouts or Angel's desire to find him. If they came up empty there, they'd pay Hank another visit. And if he couldn't help, they'd spread out again and talk with Angel's school friends.

The sun was already low on the western horizon and storm clouds had gathered when they pulled up in front of Patrice's house. Jackson breathed a sigh of relief when he saw Patrice's car in the driveway.

He should know where to look for Holden. Holden was his brother, after all. But it had been far too long since they'd had a conversation that wasn't made up of shouting and accusations. Too long since they'd parted company with anything less than hatred boiling between them thanks to their father's legacy of excess and anger.

Would they ever be rid of it?

Patrice must have seen them arrive because she met them at the door, and this time she seemed less cocky, less certain, and even a little frightened. "Have you found her yet?"

"I'm afraid not," Lucy said crisply. "But we have an idea about where she might be."

Relief that even Jackson couldn't deny filled Patrice's eyes.

"We'd like to ask you a few more questions if that's all right."

Nodding with an eagerness that shocked Jackson, Patrice stepped aside to let them enter. The house seemed even more cluttered as they were led into the tiny living room, and Patrice perched on the edge of one couch cushion like a bird ready for flight. She looked young and frightened, and Jackson had a hard time reconciling the woman in front of him with the one he'd carried around in his head all these years.

He leaned against the wall and vowed to let Lucy do the talking. Much as he hated to admit it, she knew what she was doing and her methods usually met with better results than his.

"So what is it?" Patrice asked. "Where do you think she is?"

"We're almost certain she's made contact with her father."

Patrice's gaze shot to Jackson, and she nearly lost her perch. Raindrops spattered on the window behind her and a gust of wind rattled the glass. "But why? Why would she want to find him?"

"He *is* her father," Lucy said.

"In name only. It's not as if he's ever done anything for her."

"That doesn't change the fact that he's her father." Lucy smiled, and sat in a chair close to Patrice. "Maybe she's curious about who he is and what he's like."

"I've told her what he's like."

"Maybe she wants to see for herself. She's at that age

where girls struggle with their identity. You remember how it was, I'm sure. You want so much to be an adult, and you're trying to distance yourself from your parents—your mother, especially."

Patrice let out a tight laugh, but a flash of lightning and the rumble of thunder made her sober again quickly. "Yeah, I do remember. That's when I moved in with my aunt. I just never thought I'd be on the other side."

"We're trying to locate Holden now," Lucy said, "but it may take a while to track him down. We still don't know if Angel has actually made contact with him, but we're fairly certain that's the direction she's heading."

Still obviously shaken, Patrice ground out her cigarette and leaned back into the couch. For the first time in years, she looked at Jackson without hatred. "Will he hurt her?"

Hearing her voice aloud his greatest fear and seeing the obvious worry on her face made it hard to stay detached. "I don't know," he admitted, but he hated having to admit that about his own flesh and blood. "You probably know him as well as I do. What do you think?"

She pulled her legs up and wrapped her arms around her knees. "He found me accidentally about two years ago. He came into the restaurant where I was working. He's the same as he ever was," she said quietly. "Especially if he's drunk or high and he doesn't get his way."

The weight of the knowledge staggered him, but he straightened slowly. "Are you saying that Holden used to hit you?"

"Are you saying you didn't know?"

Jackson's stomach turned over. "Of course not." He should have known. He should have at least suspected, but he'd naively assumed that Holden had hated the beatings their father had administered with as much passion as he had. "You never said anything."

Patrice laughed without humor. "I didn't know you well enough to say anything. And according to Holden, you were worse than he was."

That knocked the wind out of him. "And you believed him?"

"Why shouldn't I? Every time the two of you got together, all you did was fight. All I ever saw was you acting just like him. And Wiley…"

Jackson gaped at her. "Wiley never laid a finger on either one of us. He was the one place we could turn when Dad was in one of his rages."

"Then why does Holden hate him so much?"

"Not because Wiley hit him." Jackson sank into a chair and leaned forward, resting his elbows on his knees. It was a surreal moment, but for the first time in years the world around him made some kind of sense. "Holden's a lot like my father. Volatile. Temperamental. Selfish. Everything is all about him, all the time. You must know that. It's about what Holden wants, what Holden needs, what Holden didn't get."

Memories came at him from every side, but he didn't look away. How could he after asking Lucy to face her own issues? "Holden hated the way Dad was, but he hated the way Wiley made him stand up and take responsibility even more. He wanted excuses to make his life easier, and Wiley's never been big on excuses. Holden figures a rough childhood entitles him to skate through the rest of his life, and Wiley sees things a little differently."

Everything Lucy had tried to tell him suddenly rang true. He really wasn't responsible for Holden's decisions, or for the hurt he'd caused. Holden had made those choices himself.

Patrice rested her chin on her knees and took a shuddering breath. "I still don't understand why she's looking for him. It's not like her. She's never seemed all that interested in him before."

"She's never asked questions?" Lucy asked.

"A few, but she hasn't acted as if she wanted to find him. She seemed satisfied by what I told her until just a little while ago."

"Maybe she didn't want you to know what she was planning."

Patrice shook her head with force. "No. That's not Angelina. She's too open for that. She'd be far more likely to get in my face and tell me everything than to sneak around."

"Sometimes parents aren't the people who know their children best," Lucy suggested.

Patrice rubbed her arms as if she was cold. "Angel must have planned this. Holden certainly doesn't plan things. He does what feels right at the moment. There's never any thought about tomorrow."

"She's probably safe for the time being," Jackson said. "At least until Holden gets drunk or high and she talks back to him or doesn't do something he wants."

Lucy nodded. "Then we have to find her before that happens."

"How do we do that?" Patrice asked.

"We check the hotels in the area," Lucy said. "We take Angel's picture into every restaurant and every store we can. Holden's picture, too. If they're around here, someone will have seen them."

"I have pictures of Angelina," Patrice said, obviously relieved to have something concrete to do. "But I burned all of my pictures of Holden."

"We have pictures at the ranch," Jackson told her. "If need be, I can get Rush to fax some to me, but I'm pretty sure Mom will have some here in Houston. I'll just need to dig around until I can find them."

It felt strangely good to be working at Patrice's side. He just hoped they could continue once Angel was home again.

RAIN WAS POURING DOWN in sheets by the time Lucy pulled into Jackson's driveway. Even though they still didn't know where Angelina was, the relief inside the car had been almost palpable during the drive home. For the first time since she'd known him, Jackson seemed to be almost free of the tension that had kept him tied in knots since Angelina's disappearance. Angel might still be in danger, but at least they knew who and what they were looking for.

It should have been a great moment—and it was in every way but one. Once they found Angel, Jackson would go back to the ranch, and this brief idyllic time together would be over. Never, never, never would Lucy want to drag the case out or leave Angel twisting in the wind, but she couldn't shut down the whisper of disappointment that came with the thought of Jackson returning to his life and leaving her here with hers.

Over the past few weeks she'd been able to delude herself into thinking she had more than her career to hold on to, but without Jackson, her early-morning workouts would just be exercise. She'd lost her friends and she was barely speaking to her parents. It was getting harder all the time to convince herself that her life was chugging along smoothly.

She sensed Jackson watching her and turned to look into his concerned eyes. "What is it?"

"Nothing." She forced a smile and allowed herself to be drawn into the warmth of his embrace. She watched the rain making patterns on the windshield for a minute. "Maybe it's because we're so close to finding Angelina, but I've been thinking about all the unfinished things in my life and wondering how long I'm going to let this go on before I do something about it."

Jackson kissed her lightly. "What do you think you should do?"

With a shrug, she nestled against him. "I don't know. I guess it's time to go see Risa. I don't want to wait so long that I miss my chance." She paused, then added, "I'm not going to lie and tell you I'm not nervous. What if she won't forgive me?"

"You'll never know the answer if you don't try."

"I know." She trailed one finger along the buttons of his shirt, wanting to hold on to this moment forever. Another bolt of lightning lit the sky and a clap of thunder made her glad she was safe inside the car, cradled in his embrace.

"Just talk to her. See what she has to say. Tell her how you feel."

"I don't know how to say it."

"Practice on me."

She laughed and shook her head. "I don't think so."

"Why not? It's important to you, isn't it?"

"It's very important," she admitted, sobering. "But I can't let myself grow too reliant on you, Jackson, and I'm afraid that's exactly what I'm doing."

"Reliant? You?" His chuckle filled the space between them. "Becoming dependent on anyone else will never be a problem for you. And what's wrong with relying on someone else once in a while? Nobody gets to be in charge all the time."

"You do."

"Me?" He brushed a kiss to the tip of her nose and

shook his head. "I haven't been in charge for one minute since I came to Houston. It's been hell, having to wait and letting someone else call the shots. It helped that you're a great person with a level head, but it was still hell."

"You had your moments," she reminded him.

"And got chewed out for them every time." He grinned and drew her close again. "All I'm saying is, if the friendships are important enough to you, maybe you should let go a little. Take a chance. Do something different and see what happens. It's pretty clear that what you've been doing isn't working."

And that was the problem in every area of her life. What she'd been doing *wasn't* working. Not even a little.

He caressed her shoulders gently and sent delicious shivers of anticipation through her. "Are you coming inside?"

Every cell in her body urged her to say yes, but if she stayed, she wouldn't sleep alone, and being with Jackson tonight would only add another layer of complications neither of them needed right now. She leaned up and kissed him, putting everything she couldn't say into the contact. "Not tonight. I think I'll stop by Risa's on my way home."

"Do you want me to go with you?"

"More than anything in the world, but I think this is something I need to do on my own. Can I call you later if I need to?"

"You know you can. I'll stay up until I hear from you."

One more kiss, and he let himself out into the night. She watched him pound up the sidewalk and let himself in the door before she drove away. It was a monumental step she was considering. She just hoped she had the strength to go through with it.

LUCY COULD HARDLY BREATHE as she made the long walk from the street to Risa's door. The rain had let up for the moment, but puddles lined the sidewalks and the lights shimmered in the moist air. Her heart hammered in her chest, and a thousand thoughts raced through her mind. What should she say? Would Risa be glad to see her, or would she turn her away?

Maybe she should wait until tomorrow. Maybe she should call first. But if she didn't knock on that door now, she might never find the courage to do it at all.

Her stomach lurched as she climbed the steps, and she could have sworn her heart stopped beating entirely as she pressed the doorbell.

It wasn't too late to change her mind. She could turn around and run away. But the past rose up every day to haunt her, and ignoring it wouldn't make it go away.

After only a few seconds, the door opened and Risa stood in front of her. Right away, Lucy noticed subtle differences in Risa—small changes, as there had been in Crista and Mei. Her hard edge had been blurred, either by her ordeal after Luke's death, or her relationship with Grady. Whatever had caused it, the change wasn't a bad one.

She was obviously stunned to see Lucy standing there, and neither of them could find their voice for a long time. Finally, Lucy regained control.

"I hope I'm not interrupting," Lucy finally managed to get out. "I just came to apologize."

Risa's eyes narrowed. "I thought we'd been over that."

"We have, but this is different. This time, I'm not here to convince you I was right. I was wrong to ever doubt you. I should have stood by you, and I was wrong."

"There was a ton of evidence against me," Risa said, but she'd always been good at playing devil's advocate.

"Yeah, but you were my friend. My *best* friend. I should have trusted you. There's no excuse for what I did, and I'm not here to offer one. I'm not even here to ask for your forgiveness. I just needed to tell you that I was wrong."

It was the hardest thing she'd ever said, and getting the words out left her feeling used up and exhausted. She didn't have the energy or the desire to prolong the encounter, so she turned away.

"Lucy?"

"Yeah?" She turned back to find the door standing wide open and Risa on the porch.

"Do you want to come in? You haven't really met Grady, and I think it would be nice if you two could become friends, too."

Friends? Lucy's lungs burned and her vision blurred. She gasped once, trying to get some air, but that only opened the valve on the tears she'd been trying to hold back.

Risa grabbed her hand and pulled her onto the porch, out of the last bits of the storm. "I've missed you."

"I've missed you, too." Lucy was an emotional wreck, but she didn't care.

"Come on," Risa said, but when they stepped into the porch light, she stopped walking and stared at Lucy as if she'd never seen her before. "What *is* that on your cheek?" She reached out to touch it and drew her hand back with a shout of laughter. "You're wearing mascara?"

"A little."

"Lucy Montalvo, get your butt in the house this minute and tell me everything."

JACKSON SEARCHED FOR an hour the next morning before he finally found his mother's photo albums lodged high in the back of the coat closet behind lightbulbs and an iron he'd bet she hadn't touched in years. There were just three books, but he would have recognized them anywhere. The remnants of their life together, the memories of his childhood.

Suddenly almost afraid to touch them, he drew his hand away and stared at the cracked leather bindings. Maybe he should call Rush and have him find a picture at the ranch. It would be easier than leafing through the yellowed pages of these scrapbooks on his own.

He turned away, fully intending to call Rush, then caught himself and turned back. Those pictures were from long ago. Another lifetime. One he'd successfully put behind him—almost. Looking at a few pictures wasn't going to hurt him, and they'd have a better chance of finding Holden if they had the originals instead of faxed copies.

Still, it took courage to lift down the scrapbooks and carry them to the table. And he had to fortify himself with a beer—just one—before he could open the cover on the first book.

It was the wrong one. He could see that immediately. Pictures of his mother in her wedding dress leaped out at him, but he couldn't let himself look at the man beside her. He closed the book, shut his eyes, buried his face in his hands. It seemed that where family was concerned, he had just two emotions—fear and anger. How could it still hurt so much after all this time? Why did the memories still have the power to haunt him? He'd lived almost as long without the abuse as he had lived with it, and he was so tired of it hounding his every move. Gritting his teeth, he flipped open the book again and took a good long look at the man who'd been his father. Tall, blond and handsome. Charming enough to sweep his mother off her feet in the beginning. Holden looked a lot like him. Hell, *he* looked a lot like him, too.

But that's where the resemblance ended.

Jackson would probably never know what had driven his father's rages. It couldn't just have been the booze. The whiskey had been the fuel, but the fire had already been lit. Wiley had never seemed to know what demons had haunted his son, but maybe Wiley just wasn't talking. Or maybe Wiley had never understood, either.

Jackson pushed aside his half-empty beer bottle and turned the pages, one by one. He saw his mother's spirit die in front of his eyes. Saw the birth of Holden's anger and the beginning of his own resigned acceptance of life. He watched his grandmother grow old, and he teared up at the pictures of that first Christmas without her.

Suddenly, amid the painful memories, he found a picture he remembered fondly. Jackson and his brother stood on either side of Holden's first horse, a gift from Wiley on Holden's twelfth birthday—before the trouble had started.

Holden looked at the camera wearing a wide, toothy grin filled with hope and promise. Smiling, Jackson trailed a finger over their faces and felt years of anger and resentment drop away. He might never be able to trust his brother, but he would always love him.

Slowly but surely he worked through all three albums and carefully chose a couple of pictures they could work with. One taken on Holden's last visit to the ranch before the money disappeared. One taken a few years before that, and one of Holden holding Angelina shortly after her birth.

Just as he picked up the albums to put them away, the phone rang. He dropped the books and grabbed the phone as he had a hundred times over the past three weeks. Always hoping for good news. Always disappointed.

"Jackson Davis."

"That you, boy?"

"It's me, Wiley. How are you feeling?"

"Like somebody ran over me with a mule. Twice."

Jackson laughed and sank back into the chair he'd just vacated. "Nobody has a mule that brave."

"Well, they used something on me. I'm a mess."

"You'll get better."

"The Good Lord willing. I can't see a damn thing out of this eye."

Jackson's heart dropped. "Nothing?"

"Not a blamed thing. Doctor doesn't hold out much hope, either. Too much damage, I guess. I don't know. You'll have to talk to him. I don't follow a blasted thing he's saying. I only know I ain't gonna be much use on the ranch after this."

"So we'll adjust." Jackson turned the bottle he'd left on the table in circles, watching the pattern the condensation left. "We've adjusted before. We'll just do it again."

Wiley made a noise low in his throat. "Dagnabit, boy, I don't want to adjust. I'm old. I'm tired. I've done this for too long, and I don't have the heart to keep on."

Jackson's hand froze. "What are you saying?"

"I'm saying, I'm through. This has finally beat me."

"You just had surgery," Jackson reminded him. "This isn't the time to be making big decisions like that."

"Doesn't seem like there's a much better time to me."

"Just give yourself a chance to rest. You'll feel better, I'm sure."

"You're not listening to me, boy. I've held on as long as I could. I know how much you love the ranch, and I've tried to keep it running for you, but I don't know anymore. We're flat broke, and we'd have to renovate up the yazoo to get much business."

Jackson's heart began to beat faster. "Are you saying you want to sell the ranch?"

"Now, don't go getting upset with me. I'm an old man, and I've had doctors messing around in my eye. But yes, that's what I'm saying."

"Are you sure?"

"I'd sign the damned thing over to you right this minute, but it's not worth as much as we owe. A stack of bills isn't the inheritance I wanted to leave you, that's for sure, and the truth is, I've been thinking about this for a long time. I just didn't know how to tell you."

Jackson laughed. "Are you kidding me?"

"No, and I'm real sorry, boy. I know you love the place, but frankly it's been a burr under my saddle for years."

Leaning back in his chair, Jackson grinned up at the ceiling. Maybe miracles did still happen. "You know what, Wiley? I don't want you to worry about it for one more minute. If you want to get rid of the place, then that's what we'll do. We can talk it all out when I get home again. You just be thinking about where you'd like to live instead."

"Someplace that don't have horseshit, that's all I know."

Jackson closed his eyes and slid down in the chair. He felt sixteen again. As if his whole life stretched out before him and the possibilities were endless. His heart felt lighter than it had since he was a boy, and love for his grandfather almost overwhelmed him. "So what do you think about Houston?"

"What's in Houston?"

"The future, Grandpa. The great big beautiful future."

CHAPTER SEVENTEEN

LUCY TOOK HER TIME showering the next morning and decided at the last minute to leave her hair loose. It had been a while since she'd done anything different with her appearance—but maybe it was time to shake things up and try something new.

She'd made only small changes, and they were more symbolic than anything else, but they felt monumental to her. The absence of a hair elastic. The addition of some soft eye shadow and mascara. One quick brush of color on her cheeks. She looked exactly the same, and completely different at the same time, but inside she was shaking like a leaf.

Until recently, she'd never deliberately made herself vulnerable to another human being. Now it was becoming a habit.

Jackson was watching for her when she pulled up in front of the condo, and she indulged her senses as he walked toward the car. His long legs ate up the distance and she realized how familiar everything about him had become in the past few weeks. His smile, the sound of his laugh, the restless energy that filled the car when he was with her. She would miss everything about him when he went back to Nacogdoches.

Determined not to become melancholy and ruin their time together, she pasted on a smile as he opened the car door. He slid in beside her and seemed to notice the change immediately. Slowly, he picked up a lock of hair that fell on her shoulder. He rubbed it between his fingers and his eyes met hers, but there was no question in them, only a quiet knowledge and the kind of acceptance she had hoped for.

"You're beautiful," he said an instant before he brushed a kiss across her cheek. "I think I'm in love with you."

"You think?"

He grinned. "I'm playing hard to get. Waiting for you to say it first."

"You're chipper this morning."

"Yes, ma'am."

"Are you going to tell me why?"

"Not yet. But I will soon."

Smiling uncertainly, she turned the key in the ignition and put the car in Reverse. "Did something good happen?"

"Yep."

"But you're not going to tell me?"

"Not until I'm one-hundred-percent sure that it's official."

"You realize that's not fair."

"Yes, ma'am, I do." He grinned again and winked. Winked!

Completely dumbfounded, Lucy pulled into traffic. She'd never seen this teasing, flirtatious side before, but she couldn't say she didn't like it. "All right, then. If you won't talk about your night, we'll just have to talk about mine. I went to see Risa."

He sat up quickly and his teasing grin faded. "Things went well, apparently."

"Very well. Things aren't back to normal yet, but I think we're going to be all right. How was your night? Were you able to reach Wiley?"

"I talked to him."

"And?"

"And we worked some things out."

"You did? Oh, Jackson, that's wonderful."

"He's changed a bit since this surgery. He said a few things that surprised me."

"You'll need to get back to him soon, won't you?" It was inevitable. She might as well start preparing herself for it now.

Jackson shook his head slowly. "Not yet. Rush and Annette are with him. Angelina still needs me more."

"We'll find her," she said, but she wasn't sure whether she was trying to reassure him or herself. "Holden can't stay holed up forever. One of these days he'll make a move."

With the return of reality, some of Jackson's good humor seemed to fade. "Yeah? But when? And where? He could be across the country by now."

"He could be, but I have a feeling he's still nearby. I was thinking about it on the way over here, so tell me what you think about my logic. First, if he came here to meet Angelina, there has to be a reason. We all agree on that, right?"

"Right. We're pretty sure he didn't come after her so he could suddenly start buying school clothes and attending PTA meetings."

"Okay. So if he's using Angelina to get something, it's a safe bet that the person who can give whatever it is to him is someone who also values Angel. That means you, Wiley, or Patrice. Now, why would he run across country if he wants to use Angelina to manipulate one of you?"

Jackson nodded almost grudgingly. "I guess he wouldn't."

"Right. On the other hand, if he did want something from one of you, chances are he would have made contact by now."

He frowned thoughtfully. "So you really think he came just to meet Angel?"

She shrugged. "Even the most unlikely people can occasionally act like a parent. And it might not be money he's after. It might be something else."

"Such as?"

"I don't know. Maybe a shot at impressing another person. A chance to feel good about himself. The chance to have someone look up to him, even for a little while. Holden doesn't see himself the way you see him. He probably thinks he's done the best he can do. I'll bet dinner at the noodle house that he sees himself as a victim—of his past, of his childhood, of his circumstances, of rotten luck. You name it, he's probably a victim of it. Am I right?"

Jackson's mouth thinned. "You're right on the money."

"So maybe he's just here to get a little sympathy from someone who needs him. If Angel tracked him down and started asking questions, maybe the appeal of looking like the good guy for the first time in his life was too strong to ignore."

"I sure hope you're right."

"So do I. Wiley knows to direct him to you if he calls?"

Jackson nodded. "But I think Holden would rather chew glass than talk to me."

"Well, he's going to have to talk to you if he calls. Patrice and Wiley have to make sure of that."

"And in the meantime, we pray for a miracle and hope somebody has seen one of them?"

She nodded. "In the meantime, we pray for a miracle." It wouldn't be the first miracle she'd asked for, and it wouldn't be the last. She just hoped this time someone would be listening.

IT WAS LATE AFTERNOON when Lucy and Jackson pulled into the parking lot of the Channel-Vu Motel, yet another in a long series of run-down motels along the shipping lines. This one was a two-story L-shaped building with a half-empty parking lot, potholes in the pavement, and a sad-looking neon sign with a couple of burned-out letters. How many more of these places would they have to check before they finally found Holden? Or were they once again chasing the wrong lead?

One after another, they'd checked motels, restaurants, fast-food establishments, Laundromats, convenience stores and anything else that looked promising, but nobody any-where had seen Holden or Angel—at least, nobody was ad-mitting to it. Lucy had been trying to keep their spirits up, but even she was fatigued and growing discouraged.

Doing her best to stay motivated, she walked with Jack-son toward the office at the front of the building. Inside, a couple of vending machines hummed against one wall.

A buzzer sounded somewhere when they entered, and a second later a tall woman in her late thirties poked her head out from the back room and took their measure. Her red hair fell in corkscrew curls to the middle of her back, and the spandex top she wore looked as if it had been made for a much smaller woman.

When she saw Jackson, her eyes lit and she strode to-ward the counter running a tongue across lips covered with bright red gloss. She leaned onto the counter, pushing her breasts into the V of her shirt, and locked eyes with Jack-son. "Well, hello. What can I do for you?"

If they hadn't been so tired, and if they hadn't been worried about Angel, the situation might almost have been comical. "We'd like to ask you a couple of questions," Lucy said.

Shutters dropped over the woman's eyes when she turned to look at her. "What are you, a cop?"

"As a matter of fact, I am." She produced her identification and slid the pictures of Holden and Angel across the counter. "We're looking for either of these two people. The man is a few years older than in the picture, and either of them might have changed their haircut or hair color."

"I might have seen them," she purred at Jackson, "but I can't be sure."

Jackson kept his eyes on her face. If he was tempted to check out her ample charms, he didn't give in. "What would it take to make you sure?"

"Well, I don't know." She wriggled a little and her breasts popped up a bit higher. "What's it worth to you to know?"

Lucy really wasn't in the mood for this. "Listen, miss, we've been at this a long time, and this is really important."

Once again, the woman tore her gaze away from Jackson's and settled it on Lucy. Funny how the purr got lost in the process. "I got that, but if you aren't willing to make talkin' worth my while, it must not be worth all that much to you."

Jackson dug into his pocket and tossed a wad of bills onto the counter. "Have you seen them?"

Slowly, the woman straightened and her hungry gaze settled on the money. With a small laugh, she stuffed a handful into her pocket and another batch into the already-crowded neckline of her blouse. "They're in room 23 up on the second floor."

Lucy's heart skipped a beat. After all this time, all the questions, all the long nights, she wasn't sure she'd heard right. "They're here?"

"I said they was."

Jackson glanced through the window toward the metal railing that lined the second-floor walkway. "Are they up there now?"

"Far as I know. I haven't seen him leave today."

"And the girl?" Lucy asked. "Have you seen her?"

"Couple of times."

"Did she look all right? Was she healthy? Unhurt?"

The woman scratched lazily at a spot just beneath her bra strap. "Well, I didn't take inventory if that's what you're askin', but yeah, I thought she looked okay."

Relief nearly took the legs out from under her and she could see the stunned disbelief on Jackson's face. "What about the man? What kind of shape is he in?"

"Strung out, probably. I'd be careful if I was you."

"Strung out on what?"

"How would I know that? I didn't get it for him."

Lucy wouldn't have put money on it. "Do you have any ideas what he might have taken?"

The woman grinned. "Honey, there are so many drugs around this neighborhood, he could be on anything or everything. He tosses out enough beer bottles every day to keep half of this neighborhood happy. But like I said, if you're planning to go in there, you want to be careful. He's got one gun for sure, and I seen a knife in his boot the other day. I can't swear that's all, either."

Lucy's relief quickly turned to caution. She glanced at Jackson to make sure he was still breathing, and took another look at the layout of the rooms and the approaches available to them. "If you're smart," she told the woman, "you'll get into the back room and stay there. And don't get any ideas about calling room 23."

"You got it."

Lucy hoped she was telling the truth. All of their lives could be in danger if she wasn't.

Keeping away from the windows, she moved to the other end of the foyer and pulled out her cell phone to call for backup. Before she could complete the call, Jackson crossed to her and took the cell phone out of her hands. "Don't call yet, Lucy. Please. Let me talk to him."

His request didn't surprise her. She'd have been surprised if he hadn't asked. "I'm not going to let you walk in there, knowing that he's high on whatever and armed. That's crazy."

"Look." He took her arm and tugged her away from the ears of the curious hotel clerk. "We're talking about my brother, here. I know him better than anyone else, and I know he won't go quietly if a bunch of cops show up and start issuing orders. If he blows, Angelina could get hurt, and I haven't spent all this time and gone through everything we've done to lose her now."

"I know how you feel, Jackson—"

"How can you? That's not your brother in there, and it's not your niece, and you're not the one responsible for making sure they both come out of there in one piece."

"No, it's not my brother. And no, Angelina is not my niece. But I love you, Jackson, and if you still think this is just a job to me, you're sadly mistaken."

"Then let me go up there. Let me try," he said, handing back her cell phone. "If I'm not back in a few minutes, you can come in and get me."

She understood his need, but he was asking too much. Unbelievably, he walked out of the office and into the parking lot, leaving her no choice but to follow. "I can't do that," she told him as she followed him toward the staircase. "Not only is it completely against regulations to let a civilian walk into a dangerous situation, but I don't want something to happen to you. What if Holden *is* whacked out on drugs? What if seeing you sets off something inside of him? He could take you and Angelina out together. How could I ever live with that?"

He reached the bottom step and turned back to face her. "If your backup arrives, Holden might not make it out of there alive. How can I live with that?"

She growled in frustration and raked her fingers through her hair. "Jackson—"

"Twenty minutes." He climbed a couple of steps and grinned down at her. "He might just open the door and ask me inside for a beer."

She wasn't about to let him go upstairs alone. "Do you honestly think that will happen?"

"Look at it this way. We've been fighting with each other for years, but we haven't killed each other yet."

Even his grin couldn't wipe away the ominous dread. "Do you know what could happen in twenty minutes?"

He started climbing again and spoke over his shoulder. "I have to try."

"And if I lose you?"

"You won't."

"You can't promise that," she snapped. "You have no way of knowing how he'll react to seeing you."

"Lucy—"

"No. *No!*" They reached the second floor and she quickly stepped in front of him to block his way. "For a dozen different reasons, I can't agree. It's crazy, Jackson. It's irresponsible and far too dangerous." She had no way of knowing whether or not she was getting through to him, and she would never know. Before either of them could speak again, the door to room 23 burst open and a young girl raced out onto the walkway. A split second later, a tall man with dirty blond hair stumbled outside after her.

Grabbing the girl's arm, he jerked her roughly toward the open door. He said something Lucy couldn't hear, and Angel shook her head frantically.

"Holden!" Jackson's voice echoed and brought both of their heads up in a snap.

In horror, Lucy watched Holden grab Angel and hold her in front of him like a human shield. "What the hell do you want?"

If he had a weapon in his other hand, Lucy couldn't see it, but she couldn't take chances. Trying to avoid startling him, she pulled out her cell phone and began dialing.

"Drop it!" Holden shouted. "You're not calling the cops on me. I'm not going back to jail. Not ever again."

Jackson shot a pleading glance at her and Lucy argued with herself for only a moment. She should make the call, but she couldn't take the risk. Holding her cell phone in two fingers so he could see it, she drew on all of her strength to keep her voice calm and steady. "I'll just put it away."

"No! Drop it. Right there where I can see it." His eyes were wild and frightened, but not nearly as frightened as Angelina's.

Lucy bent slowly and lowered her phone to the ground, praying for a distraction so she could grab it again. She took a mental inventory of the weapons at her disposal. She didn't routinely carry her sidearm, especially when working so closely with a civilian, so her revolver was in the locked glove box of her car—too far away to reach. Her phone was out of commission, and she was facing a potentially armed suspect alone.

She'd screwed up royally this time. She just hoped Jackson and Angel wouldn't pay the price for her mistakes.

Carefully holding both of his hands in plain sight, Jackson took a step closer to his brother. He drew one breath after another and willed himself to remain calm. "Come on, Holden. Let her go so we can talk."

"I don't have anything to say to you."

"How do you know? I might have something to say that you want to hear."

Holden let out a drunken laugh and spit over the railing. He must have tightened his grip on Angel because she let out a frightened whimper and her terrified eyes met Jackson's. Those old memories came back to haunt him. Holden young and frightened and looking at him just like that, begging him silently to make everything all right.

"When have you ever had something to say that I wanted to hear?" Holden shouted.

"Look, I know it's been a while, but things change. People change." He inched another step closer and shifted a little to his right, hoping he could block Holden's view of Lucy long enough for her to grab her phone, just in case. He'd seen Holden in rough shape before, but never this rough and never this angry.

"I came to tell you about Wiley," he said, grasping at every thought that ran through his head. "He had surgery the other day and he's in bad shape. How about the two of us go somewhere and grab a beer so we can talk?"

"I don't care about him. When has he ever cared about me?"

"He cares. He's just Wiley, you know? Remember when he bought you your first horse?" Jackson somehow got a laugh out of his throat. "I was looking at old pictures last night and found that one. You remember the one I'm talking about?" He moved again, a little forward, a little to the right, and willed Lucy silently to understand what he was doing.

"You remember?" Jackson said again. "That one where Mom was trying to get on the horse and Dad was trying to help her? He was three sheets to the wind and she kept sliding off before she could get into the saddle?"

Holden wiped sweat from his face with his bare arm, but

he didn't look away and he didn't loosen his grip on Angelina. "I remember. What about it?"

"I was just thinking about how hard the two of us laughed. It was great."

Holden looked at him uncertainly. "Yeah, it was. But that was a long time ago."

"Yeah. It was, wasn't it?" Jackson inched closer still. "I know we had some rough times, but we had some good times, too, didn't we?"

Holden sniffed and ran his free arm across his forehead. Cold steel glinted in the sunlight, and Jackson's blood ran cold. He didn't know whether to hope Lucy had seen the weapon or pray that she hadn't.

"Don't screw this up," he said evenly. "Please, Holden. Don't let things get ugly." Memories flashed through his mind like photographs and he prayed for the words that would keep them all safe. "Look at your daughter, man. She's scared to death. Is that really what you want?" He kept his voice low and even, his movements slow and steady. "Don't you remember what it was like when Dad went on one of his binges? Don't you remember how scared we used to be? Remember hiding under our beds so he wouldn't find us?"

Holden shifted uncertainly and Jackson knew he was getting through on some level. "Don't you remember how much we hated him for hurting us? For hurting Mom? Come on, man, do you really want to be like him? Do you want Angelina to feel that way about you? It doesn't have to be that way. You can put the knife away and let go of her. You don't have to be like him. It's your choice."

"You're just trying to take my kid away from me again," Holden argued. "Trying to make me look like a nobody in front of her. But she came looking for *me*. She wants me around, so don't try to make it sound like she doesn't."

A flash of movement behind Holden caught Jackson's eye. It disappeared before he could focus on it, but it appeared again a second later and he realized that Lucy must have slipped away and come up the other set of stairs.

Jackson's heart plummeted, knowing that she must have called for backup and they had only minutes left. Holden took advantage of Jackson's brief distraction and turned sharply, dragging Angel off balance, causing her to scream.

Jackson lunged at the same moment, aiming for the hand holding the knife and hoping he'd moved quickly enough to catch him unaware. If not, he might have just made the biggest mistake of his life.

HORRIFIED, LUCY WATCHED as Jackson dove at his brother. The flash of the blade as they tumbled over each other made her almost physically sick. But frightened as she was for Jackson, Angelina was her first responsibility.

Moving as quickly as she could, weapon drawn, she lunged from her hiding spot and went after the frightened girl who was falling in the tangled mess of arms and legs as the brothers went down. She tried to decipher where Jackson ended and Holden began, tried to find the blade in the scramble, but she was losing focus.

She pulled herself up sharply and slammed the impersonal walls into place. She couldn't let another child die on her watch. She couldn't even allow Angel to be injured. Somewhere in the distance, sirens began to wail, but they wouldn't arrive in time to help her. She was on her own.

Keeping one eye out for the knife, she grabbed Angel by the arm and jerked her upright forcefully enough to break Holden's grip. The girl staggered to her feet, wide-eyed and obviously terrified, but free and in one piece.

Battling tears of relief, Lucy shoved her toward the

stairs. "Go on. Try to get into the office and wait there until the other officers arrive."

But Angelina remained rooted to the spot, frozen, shaking, too frightened to move.

"It's going to be all right," Lucy assured her. "Now, go on. Get out of here so I can stop them from hurting each other."

Angel's eyes shot to hers, but she managed a nod and limped quickly toward the staircase. The poor kid. All she'd wanted was a father. That shouldn't be too much to ask.

The sirens drew closer and Lucy tried to get a bead on Holden, but they were thrashing around too much. Every time she thought she had him, she had Jackson in her sites instead. The only thing she could see clearly was Holden's hand still holding the knife and Jackson's trying to break his grip.

"Houston PD," she shouted. "Drop the knife. Drop it right now."

Obviously too high to think, Holden fought like a wild man. He bucked under Jackson's weight, tried to slam his knee into Jackson's groin, fastened his teeth around Jackson's hand and bit. With a roar of pain, Jackson rolled away, holding his bleeding hand against his chest.

Holden lunged after him with the knife. "You son of a bitch! You tricked me. You tricked me! You brought the cops here. What do you want? You want me dead?"

"Drop the knife!" Lucy shouted again. She couldn't let herself see the hurt in Jackson's eyes. She couldn't worry about his wounds. She couldn't let herself remember that this wild man with the knife was the brother he loved. If she thought about any of that, she'd weaken.

Writhing in pain, Jackson staggered to his knees and Lucy plunged forward, standing over his brother with her weapon ready. "Drop your knife, Holden. Don't make me do something we'll both regret."

Pure animal hatred flashed through his eyes, but he finally, reluctantly, loosened his grip on the knife and let it fall. Lucy kicked it out of his reach just as the first patrol car turned into the parking lot, then she reached down and hauled Holden to his feet. Close up, the resemblance to Jackson was stronger, and tears stung her eyes for his loss, for his disappointment.

"All you had to do was let her go," she whispered as the pounding of running feet sounded on the steps. "That's all."

She had no idea if Jackson would be angry or whether he'd forgive her if he was. But she'd done the only thing she could.

For Jackson. For Angel. And for herself.

CHAPTER EIGHTEEN

A BANDAGE ON HIS HAND, a couple of aspirin, and Jackson would be all right. That's what he kept telling everybody, but nobody wanted to listen.

Seething at the delay, he sat on the tailgate of some-body's truck while a paramedic frowned at his hand. But the bleeding had already stopped, and Jackson didn't see what all the fuss was about. It wasn't the first time he'd been bitten by his little brother.

Just minutes earlier, Holden had been driven away in a patrol car, still protesting the unfairness of his treatment, still shouting about the injustice that was his life. Jackson couldn't help wondering what might have happened if only Holden hadn't panicked. But he'd been too strung out to think clearly, and until that changed, he'd probably always wind up right back in the same place.

The paramedic dug into a kit at his feet. "We'll stabi-lize this with an antibiotic ointment and let the doctor check it once we transport you to the hospital. I want to get a look at that cut on your leg, too."

"It's a flesh wound," Jackson growled, craning to see inside the motel office where Lucy sat huddled with Angel. "I can take care of that with some peroxide and a Band-Aid. And I'm not going to the hospital, so do what-ever you need to do to make yourself happy and then let me get the hell out of here. I want to make sure my niece is all right."

"Look, buddy. Relax, okay? We don't want to take any chances, so it might be a little while. But the police are in there with her and I'm sure she's just fine."

Relax? After the past three weeks? After the confrontation he'd just had with his brother? After seeing Angelina for the first time in more than a dozen years? Impossible.

Scowling, the paramedic glanced over his shoulder, found his partner, and shouted, "Do me a favor, Boggs. Go inside and tell somebody that this guy wants to see his niece. I don't think he's going to hold still until he does."

Boggs sketched a small salute and disappeared inside the office. A few minutes later, the door opened again and Lucy emerged with Angel. She kept her arm around Angel's shoulders as they crossed the parking lot, and Angel walked slowly, as if she was reluctant to meet him.

His heart sank, but he'd already lost so many years. He didn't want to lose another minute. Of course she was nervous. Afraid, even, especially after what she'd just been through. Patience had never been one of Jackson's strengths, but he was learning. The past three weeks had taught him a whole lot about that.

As they walked toward him, he made a conscious effort to remove the frown from his lips and any residual anger in his eyes. Angel didn't need any of that.

Finally, they drew up in front of him and he got his first good look at the niece he'd never stopped loving. She was beautiful, as he'd known she would be, but he would have thought she was beautiful no matter what.

He could feel Lucy watching him, could even feel the gentle warmth of her smile, but he couldn't tear his eyes from Angelina.

Slowly, she lifted her gaze to meet his and he was overwhelmed by a feeling of familiarity equally as strong as the sense that he was looking at a stranger. He ached to jump down off the truck and grab her, but he didn't want to frighten her, so he settled for his best smile. "Hi, Angel."

"Hi."

"I don't suppose you remember me?"

She shook her head quickly. "No, but I know who you are. I found some pictures in my mom's room once."

"I guess we have some catching up to do, don't we?"

A quick smile flitted across her face. She ducked her head to hide it, but Jackson's heart soared at the sight. After only a moment, she lifted her gaze to his again. "I guess I made a pretty big mess, didn't I?"

He glanced at the three police cars still in the parking lot, lights flashing, at the paramedic truck and the jumble of officers still moving around the scene. "What? This? You call this a mess?"

Again, that smile darted across her face, but she seemed to relax a little. "I didn't know he was like that. I just wanted to meet him."

"He's not like that," Jackson said. "The drugs and the booze are. If you could have known him before they got hold of him, you would have liked him. Maybe he'll even take advantage of the help we're going to get him and you'll get a chance to know who he really is. If not now, then in a few years." Anything was possible. He'd learned that over the past three weeks, too. "How did you find him?"

"I just asked around online. There were these chat rooms, you know? Set up for different places? I found this one for people who live in Nacogdoches and hung out in there a while. I just kept asking people if they knew my dad. It took a little while, but I finally found this guy who

did and he told my dad to e-mail me. It's not that hard."
She darted a glance at Lucy. "Am I in trouble?"

Lucy rubbed her shoulder gently. "You've had a lot of
people very frightened. Hank has been worried sick about
you, and you could have been hurt. But I think that if you'll
promise never to do anything like this again, we can let this
one slide."

With a sigh of relief, Angel nodded eagerly. "I don't
think I'll be doing this again. I just wanted to meet him,
you know? I wanted to know what he was like and see if
I looked like him."

"You look more like my grandmother," Jackson said. "If
you'd like, I can show you a few pictures. And if it's okay
with your mom, I'll even introduce you to your great-
grandpa. He's been waiting to see you again for a long time."

"I think I'd like that."

"I know I'm not your dad, but I sure would like to be
part of your life from now on. If it's okay with you, I'll try
to work that out with your mom."

Angel looked him over, considering that. "How come
you never came to see me before?"

"It sure wasn't because I didn't want to." The paramedic swabbed ointment on his arm and Jackson winced
at the sting. "It's a long story, and I'll tell you the whole
thing later, I promise. But I always loved you, even when
I wasn't around." He had to stop for a minute while the
paramedic wound a bandage around his arm. "How did you
find out about the ranch, anyway?"

Angel's lips curved into a shy smile. "I'm a straight-A
student. I know how to look things up. Besides, Mom had
some stuff in this little lockbox in her room. It wasn't *that*
hard to open."

Jackson bit back a smile. A straight-A student. That

was good. That was very good. But he would have loved her even without the GPA. "How long have you known?"

"A couple of years."

"And you never came to us?"

"I didn't think you wanted me." The uncertainty in her eyes nearly killed him. "I talked to Hank about it and he said to call, but I was scared."

Jackson slid from the tailgate and gathered her into his arms. "I don't ever want you to be afraid of me, Angel. And I hope you've figured out that we do want you." He grinned a little and glanced around at the emergency vehicles parked helter-skelter in the parking lot. I wouldn't have gone to all this trouble for just anybody."

He didn't get a chance to say more. A car door slammed somewhere nearby, and Patrice came flying across the parking lot to scoop up her baby. Hank climbed slowly out of the driver's side and stayed near the car, giving Patrice and Angel their privacy. At the sight of her mother, Angel burst into tears and Jackson watched with a twinge of envy as Angel threw herself into her mother's arms. Three weeks ago, he'd been ready to take Angelina away from her mother if the chance arose. Now he realized that he could never do that. God willing— Patrice willing—he and Wiley would do whatever they could to make their lives easier. Having Angel around for two weeks out of every month while her mother traveled would be no hardship.

Reluctantly, he tore his gaze away and found Lucy, who was watching him with a mixture of sadness and jubilation. He grinned at her and motioned for her to come closer since he couldn't seem to get away from the paramedic. "We did it, Detective."

Watching Jackson and Angel together had been almost too much for Lucy, and the tearful reunion between mother and daughter cost Lucy her self-control. Knowing that this was the end of her time with Jackson made it impossible to stay dry-eyed. But he was so happy, she couldn't bear to ruin the moment for him, so she did her best to smile.

"Yes, we did. But you're not angry with me?"

"Why would I be angry?"

"For calling in backup. I know how much you wanted to handle Holden yourself."

Jackson shook his head and even managed to look a little sheepish. "I love him. He's my brother. But his problems are too big for me to handle. I'm going to talk to Wiley about getting him professional help. We've done it before, but he's never been interested. I guess we just have to keep trying."

"Maybe one of these days he'll be ready." She looked back at Angel and smiled. "She's really beautiful, Jackson. I hope everything works out for all of you."

"I do, too." He looked back at Patrice and Angel and his smile grew. "There's a chance, anyway. That's more than I had a few weeks ago." Turning back, he took her hand in his good one and pulled her closer still.

Greedily, she drew in his scent, his sound, his energy. She never wanted to let him go, but she couldn't hang on. Tears burned her eyes, but she refused to let them fall. There would be time enough for that later, when she was alone.

The paramedic finally finished what he was doing and moved away. When they were finally alone—as alone as they could be in the crowd—Jackson lifted her hand to his mouth and kissed her palm gently. "Don't you mean 'all of *us*'?"

"I'm going to be okay. I know that now. I may always need help decompressing when the cases are tough, but—"

He touched her lips lightly with his fingertips. "Lucy.

Honey. You still don't understand. I'm not going back to a life without you unless you force me to. I love you. I don't ever want to be without you."

Surely she hadn't heard right. "But what about…?"

"The ranch? We're selling it. Wiley? He's ready to move to Houston. My career?" He broke off with a laugh and kissed the tip of her nose. "I don't have that worked out yet, but you can rest assured I won't sit around doing nothing."

"But—"

"You don't want me?"

Joy bubbled up in her chest, but she still wasn't sure this was real. "Don't want you? Are you kidding? I never want to be without you again, but—"

"But nothing." He moved closer and slid both arms around her waist. "I love you, Lucy. I love you. It's as plain and simple as that. I know this isn't the most romantic location. I could do better if I had a chance to get some flowers, a little wine… But I can't wait. I don't have anything to offer you. I won't have a home for very much longer. Won't have a job, either. But there's a future out there for us somewhere, and you'd make me the happiest man on earth if you'd agree to be my wife and find it with me."

The tears she'd worked so hard to hold back filled her eyes and spilled onto her cheeks. For the first time in a long time, her life felt whole, and complete, filled with the people she loved and full of possibilities. She slid her arms around his neck and kissed him, drawing on his strength and giving him everything she had to give. "Oh, Jackson," she sighed when she finally pulled away. "There isn't anything I want more."

EPILOGUE

THREE WEEKS LATER, Lucy pushed open the patio door with one hip and carried a bowl filled with her mother's potato salad toward the table, already crowded with more food than they could eat in three days. Across the lawn, Wiley sat in the shade and told stories about the ranch from a folding lawn chair. Angelina, Hank and Lucy's dad all listened intently, to Wiley's delight. Even Jackson and Rush, who'd surely heard every story at least a hundred times before, seemed interested.

Wiley was a sweet old guy, exactly as Jackson had described him, and the affection between Jackson and his grandfather was obvious. In fact, they brought tears to her eyes almost as often as they made her laugh.

The gentle breeze cradled the mouthwatering scents of beef and her dad's homemade barbecue sauce across the lawn, and laughter sang out as Wiley reached the end of another story. She could hear soft voices coming through the kitchen window as her mother, Patrice and Annette put the finishing touches on the food, and contentment enfolded her.

She was here with the man she loved, surrounded by the people she loved and who loved her. Only Jackson's mother and Lloyd were missing, but they'd come from their honeymoon early and would be arriving soon.

Lucy's sessions with Cecily had officially come to an end, and though she was thrilled to be starting over with a clean slate, she had to admit the sessions had been good for her. She hoped she'd never again suffer a loss like she had with Tomas, but if she did, she wouldn't hesitate to phone Cecily. Without her help, Lucy might have struggled to move beyond the tragedy for years. Her parents might never completely understand her choice, but they'd gotten past their initial anger and they were trying hard to accept. And that was good enough.

As the laughter from Wiley's latest tale died away, Angel, who'd been sitting on the grass near Jackson's feet while Wiley entertained, noticed Lucy's full arms and hurried to help.

"Why didn't you tell me there was still more food to bring out?" she asked, nudging a bag of potato chips out of the way. "This is your engagement party. You're not supposed to be working."

Lucy settled the salad in the empty space and hugged Angel quickly. Being someone's aunt-to-be was a new experience for her, but one she could quickly get used to. She'd held back for the first few days, afraid of seeming overly familiar. But it had quickly become apparent to everyone that Angel craved affection, and now Lucy dispensed hugs as easily as Jackson and Wiley, Patrice and Hank. Even her parents had gotten into the act, treating Angel as if she'd always been a member of the family.

"I'm not such a great cook," Lucy said with a grin, "but I can carry things well. Besides, I'm too excited about being able to move back into my condo to sit still."

Angel plucked a carrot from the relish tray. "Do I still get to sleep over sometime?"

"Are you kidding? I'd love to have you stay with me."

"Can we have a girls' night where we do each other's hair and makeup and watch movies?'"

Lucy laughed. "Absolutely. But you'll have to tell me what we need. I've never had a girls' night before."

"We'll need everything," Angel said with a grin. "But don't worry. I can go with you to the store if you want."

Her eagerness touched Lucy. Angel's initial shyness around Jackson had disappeared within just a couple of days, and the exuberance for life that had been so much a part of her since then had infected everyone around her.

"I just might take you up on that offer," Lucy said.

Sobering, Angel squinted into the sun. "Did you go to my dad's hearing today?"

"Yes I did."

"Uncle Jackson says that my dad has to spend some time in jail. Is that because of me?"

Lucy sat on one of the picnic benches and patted the seat beside her. "Absolutely not, but it would have been better if you'd told your mom the truth about looking for him. Then she could have arranged some time for the two of you to become acquainted in a more structured way."

"If I'd told her the truth, she wouldn't have let me find him."

That was probably true, but Lucy didn't want to encourage an argument. "He's going to jail because of things he did," she said, "not because of you. We're all hoping that he'll take advantage of rehab this time so the two of you can get to know each other better."

Just then, she spotted her mother coming toward the door, arms loaded with a heavy tray. Behind her, Patrice carried a pitcher of iced tea and Annette brought up the rear, carrying a platter filled with low-carb snacks. The hearing forgotten, Angel dashed across the patio to open the door, basking in the smiles each of the women turned on her.

"She's really something, isn't she?" Jackson asked, straddling the seat behind Lucy and sliding his arms around her waist.

She leaned into him and nodded. "She's full of life, that's for sure. Were you able to get her room ready before you came over?"

"We put on the finishing touches just before we walked out the door. She seems happy with it, so I hope she'll be okay staying with us while Patrice is gone.

"I think she'll be more than fine," Lucy assured him. "She's lucky to have you and Wiley, and I think Hank will always be part of her life. It may not be what she was looking for when she started out, but I think she really is beginning to understand that she's surrounded by love."

"I hope so. I know just how she feels."

With her heart full, Lucy looked at her soon-to-be husband and their combined families. "So do I," she whispered. "So do I."

* * * * *

Watch for the next book in the
WOMEN IN BLUE series—
Linda Style's THE WITNESS,
coming December 2004.

HARLEQUIN *Super*ROMANCE®

Visit Dundee, Idaho, with bestselling author

brenda novak

A Home of Her Own

Her mother always said if you couldn't be rich, you'd better be Lucky!

When Lucky was ten, her mother, Red—the town hooker—married Morris Caldwell, a wealthy and much older man.

Mike Hill, his grandson, feels that Red and her kids alienated Morris from his family. Even the old man's Victorian mansion, on the property next to Mike's ranch, went to Lucky rather than his grandchildren.

Now Lucky's back, which means Mike has a new neighbor. One he doesn't want to like…

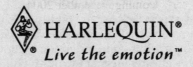

HARLEQUIN®
Live the emotion™

www.eHarlequin.com

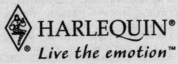

HARLEQUIN®

AMERICAN *Romance*®

A COWBOY AND A KISS

by Dianne Castell

Sunny Kelly wants to save the old saloon
that her aunt left her in a small Texas town.

But Sunny isn't really Sunny.
She's Sophie Addison, a Reno attorney,
and she's got amnesia.

That's not about to stop cowboy
Gray McBride, who's running hard for
mayor on a promise to clean up the town—
until he runs into some mighty strong
feelings for the gorgeous blonde.

On sale starting December 2004—
wherever Harlequin books are sold.

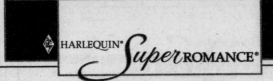

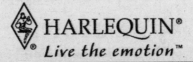

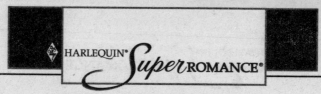

HARLEQUIN *Super*ROMANCE®

A six-book series from Harlequin Superromance.

WOMEN *in Blue*

Six female cops battling crime and corruption on the streets of Houston. Together they can fight the blue wall of silence. But divided, will they fall?

Coming in December 2004,
The Witness by Linda Style
(Harlequin Superromance #1243)

She had vowed never to return to Houston's crime-riddled east end. But Detective Crista Santiago's promotion to the Chicano Squad put her right back in the violence of the barrio. Overcoming demons from her past, and with somebody in the department who wants her gone, she must race the clock to find out who shot Alex Del Rio's daughter.

Coming in January 2005,
Her Little Secret by Anna Adams
(Harlequin Superromance #1248)

Abby Carlton was willing to give up her career for Thomas Riley, but then she realized she'd always come second to his duty to his country. She went home and rejoined the police force, aware that her pursuit of love had left a black mark on her file. Now Thomas is back, needing help only she can give.

Also in the series:
The Partner by Kay David (#1230, October 2004)
The Children's Cop by Sherry Lewis (#1237, November 2004)

And watch for:
She Walks the Line by Roz Denny Fox (#1254, February 2005)
A Mother's Vow by K.N. Casper (#1260, March 2005)

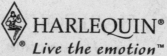

HARLEQUIN®
Live the emotion™